CAJUN PAYBACK

D1520732

KAREN YOCHIM

ISBN: 148230726X

ISBN 13: 9781482307269

Library of Congress Control Number: 2013915229
CreateSpace Independent Publishing Platform
North Charleston, South Carolina

Also by Karen Yochim

Mean Bayou

Swamp

Depression: Don't Take it Lying Down

Dedicated to the late Pappy Yochim and Buddy Yochim who first moved me to Louisiana and introduced me to the vast Atchafalaya Swamp. And to the Cajun people, the most self-reliant and resourceful group I've ever been fortunate enough to live among.

Thank you to Jeff Davis Taylor, Delia Taylor, Paul Marks of KBON, Lt. Moore of Louisiana Wildlife & Fisheries, the St. Landry Sheriff's Office, Police Chief Richard Mizza, Roland Rivette, Paul David, Dr. Neal Tishman, Twinkle Yochim, Tony LeClerc, Teresa Esther Chapoy, and Maria Muñoz.

1

WORST DAY

I'm one of those people who never forgets… either the good or the bad. I'm loyal beyond all belief if you ever did something for me, and the exact opposite if you ever did me wrong. And that's why I did the most outrageously boneheaded thing of my life that led to the worst situation of my life. This is how it all went down for me, Harris Viator.

Chief Ira told me to pick up a prisoner at our little two-cell jail in St. Beatrice City that is attached to the cement block police station, and drive him over to the Parish jail a block from the courthouse over in Eustis, forty-five minutes to the west. The Chief hates when he has to feed and look after any prisoners that are hauled in, and tries to get them out of his jail as soon as possible.

The Chief had been elected so many times that he'd gotten white-haired on the job. His reelection was such a done deal that nobody in town even bothered to take down their REELECT CHIEF IRA

BENOIT yard signs. One of the reasons the town kept him in office was he was so tight with the town's money, and unnecessary jail expense was just one more thing that didn't swell his budget. The Chief was so tight, it's a wonder he wasn't still using the 1800s decrepit handmade brick jail that still sat in back of town hall, now used for storage.

It was barely spring yet, but so hot and dry that the devil would have felt right at home in southwest Louisiana, and if you went outside you could smother in the thick dusty air. We'd been in a drought for weeks and counting. Louisiana is either a dust bowl or a mudhole, and we weren't expecting rainy season anytime soon. The drought was all the farmers that came into town to the feed store would talk about, and in the heat of the day St. Beatrice looked like a ghost town because everybody stayed inside racking up the electric bill with the A/C running full tilt.

Rocco Theriot, who drove a truck for his uncle's gravel pit, had been busted by a nosy meter reader for cultivating pot plants in a greenhouse on his property. My guess was he felt the need to supplement his steady paycheck. The meter reader had gotten suspicious of Rocco's four pit bulls that patrolled and slobbered in a fenced off area around the greenhouse in back of his tool shed, and ran his mouth to somebody to where it got back to the Chief. Consequently, Rocco had spent the night in lockup, and the Chief told me to get him out of there so he didn't have to be bothered to send for another plate lunch from Miss Josie's kitchen.

"He keeps bitching about our tiny cell. Let him see how he likes it over to Sheriff Quebedeaux's hotel-zoo. That'll straighten his sorry ass out in a hurry. He'll wish he was back here with us eating Miss Josie's jalopeño sausage cornbread."

So I picked Rocco up that morning and loaded him into the back seat of the patrol car. Now we had two Cajun hardheads in the car instead of just one. He didn't look too bad for somebody who was looking at months of jail time. Rocco was short like the rest of his family, but he was bulked up and revved up and usually hyper, so nobody cared to mess with him. He had short black hair and a full goatee, and that day his dark eyes glittered in the bright daylight.

"Damn! You got any shades?" he blinked when we got outside.

"No spares," I said, hustling him into the back seat of the patrol car.

It was hard to act official with Rocco because of our history. We had both played on the football team back in high school. And not only that, but he'd rescued my sister years before from a drunken moron date who was all over her at a rock concert in Baton Rouge when she was just sixteen. The boy had gotten so drunk that she didn't have a safe way home, and Rocco had kept an eye on the situation, then finally just knocked the kid out flat on the pavement outside the stadium. Then he'd driven her home along with his own date, the two hours back to St. Beatrice. Like I said I never forget, so I hated like hell to have to treat him like a prisoner and deliver him to the jailhouse in Eustis.

Although Rocco was never at a loss for words, that morning he sat slumped in the back seat, not saying much, so I left him alone to wallow in his miseries. It only takes about ten minutes to drive through St. Beatrice, but then as we were almost out of town, he sat up like he was coming alive once more, and started looking all around like he was onto something.

"Hey, man," he said. "How's about letting me have like five, ten minutes with my Theresa before they lock my ass up again? Who knows how long they're going to throw me in there for? All's I want is like a few minutes alone with her before I have to talk at her through the glass for who knows how long? I just want to, you know, like get with her for just a few minutes."

I looked in the rear view mirror and laughed. "You gotta be kidding!"

"No, man. She's my one and only. You know that. It's killing me that they're going to lock me away and I won't even be able to touch her for who knows how many months? Just over some *pot* plants. God Almighty, I'm going to lose my mind in there locked up with all those screaming crackheads."

I adjusted the mirror to see him better. He looked like he'd already lost it. His eyeballs were flickering back and forth like a pinball machine. "Rocco. I'm not going to lose my job I've had for ten years over your wanting to grab ahold of your woman. You must be already crazy in the head to even come up with such insanity."

"Come on, Harris. We go back a long ways. You know you won't get in no trouble over it. It'll only be just for a few minutes. I'm not going to do anything to yank your chain. I'm not going to do nothing but grab her, kiss her, and tell her I love her. I swear to sweet Jesus."

I just clammed up and kept driving, but then on the outskirts of town, we were getting close to the dirt road Theresa lived on. There was a cluster of roadside crosses at a nasty curve close to her road where two of our classmates had wrecked some twenty years before. The silk roses by the crosses were covered with road dust, so they were more gray than red. One of the metal crosses was tilting over, and part of an armadillo carcass was rotting away just a few feet from it. I felt a *frisson* like I always do when I pass that way, because I had almost been in the car with them that night, but had taken off from the party with another partner at the last minute. The guy I'd left with was Rocco's brother, who was dead now him too from a helicopter crash attempting to deliver some fresh crew offshore to the oil rigs. Like I said, we had some history that went way back.

"Come on, Harris. Just a few minutes. We're almost there. Who's going to know? I'm sure as hell not going to tell anybody. Are you?"

Now right here's where my life was hanging in the wind, right past Teardrop Curve. I've gone over this a thousand times since wondering what in the hell I was actually thinking at that moment. Maybe it was because I kept waking up the night before because it was so damn hot, and the coyotes were yipping and yapping all night from the woods in back of our house, so my brain wouldn't get into gear. Maybe it was because the A/C in the patrol car was doing such a sorry job that it was blowing lukewarm air, so my shirt was sticking to me, and my hands were sweating on the wheel. Who the hell knows? I've never been able to figure it out, and quit trying. Lately, I've just chalked it up to temporary insanity.

"Son of a bitch, Rocco, you better make it damn quick, you hear me?"

He started licking his chops when I abruptly swung off down Lassaigne Road. "You damn straight, Harris. You ain't never gonna regret this. I owe you, brother, big time!"

Theresa's trailer was set back a ways from the dusty road, and her car was parked by metal steps leading up to the front door. The trailer, once white, had gone dingy gray over the years, and her attempts to brighten the scene with pots of flowers by the sloping steps didn't help much. I knew way down the road beyond a row of trees was a sparkling new double wide, but Butch, the owner, was off shore, so there would be no witnesses to this ridiculous detour we had taken.

"Well?" I parked and swiveled, stretching my arm along the seat. "She gonna come out or what? You want I should beep the horn?"

"Come on, man. Give us a couple minutes inside alone."

I drummed my fingers on the upholstery, looking over my shoulder at him. He had his best hound dog look by then, his eyes pleading with me. Finally, groaning, I got out of the car and went around to let him out. He emerged from the car, hands cuffed behind him.

I jerked my head toward the trailer and tapped my watch. "Get going. You got five minutes. You're on the clock."

He jiggled his hands in back of him. "And what am I supposed to do with these?"

"Best you can, Rocco. Be creative."

"Come on, man." He was squinting in the fierce sunlight. "Take em off. What I'm gonna do? Run away? That what you think I'd do to you? After all we've been through? You know I'm not a piece of shit."

There's something about Rocco I can't explain. He's got a way about him. Always did have. My sister used to say he had charisma. She said you're either born with it or you're not. He got it from his daddy, she always said. The night that he rescued her from maybe a drunken car wreck or worse, my mother said he could charm the birds out of the trees. She kept trying to encourage Prissy to go out with him instead of her other knuckleheaded boy friends.

I stood there in the hot sun like a dummy for a minute, arguing with myself in my head while the classic rock station from inside the trailer blared. Finally, I clicked him loose, and barked at him. "Turn around, and run on in there. You're on the clock. Five minutes. If you make me come in there after you, I promise you, it won't be pretty cause I'm going to embarrass the shit out of you in front of your woman."

"Five minutes. I swear to sweet Jesus." And he bolted on toward the front steps of the trailer. Jesus didn't have anything to do with what happened next.

2

CATASTROPHE

Leaning against the patrol car, I watched two squirrels chattering and chasing each other up and down the swamp maples in the tree line between Theresa's property and Butch's. A crop duster was flying back and forth over the fields in back of the trailer either spraying herbicide, pesticide, fungicides, or fertilizer. It all sounded the same. Loud! The plane roared overhead to make its turns drowning out Journey's *More Than a Feeling* and I wondered how Theresa could stand the racket it made as it swept low over her trailer each time. Every now and then I'd glance at my watch to check on how fast Rocco's time was running out.

Then suddenly the front door of the trailer crashed open and Theresa comes stumbling out half naked and screaming like a bat out of hell, her long black hair all tousled and in her eyes. Her bare chichi's were heaving up and down, and the only clothing she wore was a ridiculously low cut pair of lacy underpants, if you could even call them underpants. I raced to the steps to catch her as she hurled herself into my arms, still screaming so loud I thought she'd blow out my eardrums.

"He's dead! He's dead!" she yelled and sobbed all at the same time. "Get in there! Go! Oh, my God!" She waved an arm toward the door.

Theresa's last name was Bigneaud, and with all the class and razor sharp wit of teenagers, we'd called her Theresa Big Boobs in high school. All I could think of at that moment, was that Rocco had had a seizure or a heart attack when he'd seen her half naked, knowing he was going to be locked up away from all that for months, maybe more. I sat her down on the steps and hurried across the threshold, expecting to have to revive him. The living room was so neat it looked unused, and I could tell at a glance nothing was going on in there. The narrow kitchen was separated from the living room by a breakfast bar, with nothing out of place there either, except for two empty coffee mugs with a casino logo on the counter. Ozzie singing *Paranoid* was coming from a radio somewhere towards the bedroom end of the trailer.

I passed down a cramped hallway, past the empty bathroom, and toward the first bedroom. That too was clean and tidy with a satiny, shiny spread on the twin bed that looked like something you'd find in a motel.

And then my skin began to crawl before I even entered the second bedroom that was the last room of the trailer. The first thing I saw when I stepped inside the room was the torn up double bed, sheets and pillows tossed every which way. A shattered ceramic lamp was lying on the floor, and on the wall some slivers of dagger like glass were still in the oval gilt framed mirror. Beyond the scattered mess, half in and half outside the wide open back door, was Leon deWitt, one of the locals, lying naked on the floor, mouth gaping, blood smeared across his face. His eyes were closed and his arms and legs were flung out at such crazy angles, it looked like he'd been dropped from a four-story building. There was a triangle shaped gash on his cheek, and the right side of his face was as red, swollen and shiny as boiled crawfish.

The crop duster, circling back around, flew over the trailer just then, and it sounded like he was coming in for a landing on our heads, but he was only making another pass over the bean fields. I kneeled on the back steps to take Leon's pulse, searching frantically outside with my eyes, but there was no sign of Rocco. As I fumbled for his pulse the Classic Rock program 'Ten in a Row' changed tunes and *Stranglehold* thundered on, which couldn't have come at a better time, because I don't think I could have controlled myself if I'd gotten my hands around Rocco's throat at that moment.

When my fingers found that blessed heartbeat in Leon's carotid, I couldn't have been more grateful, but even though Leon still had a pulse, I knew my life was over as I knew it, and it was anybody's guess where my future lay from there on out. As I phoned in for help, I knew the second thing I was going to lose right after my job, was my wife whose mother had for years been raging at her for marrying me in the first place. Livonia didn't think anybody was really good enough for Regina, and certainly not a small town cop like me, whose idea of fun was hauling the family over to Daddy's camp for some serious fishing and open pit cookouts.

Theresa came running back into the room as I gently lifted one of Leon's eyelids. His eyes were so rolled back, just bloodshot whites were visible.

"He's not dead? Thank God! I was so sure. Rocco kept kicking him all over and in the head too." Her tone changed rapidly from grateful to angry as she readjusted to the situation, and stepped closer to the back door, flailing her arms in frustration.

"What kind of a dumb ass cop would let a maniac like that loose when he's supposed to be on his way over to the lockup? What'd he do? Pay you off?" She was breathing so hard, I thought she was going to hyperventilate. Either that or kick me right down off the steps. I kept track of her from my peripheral vision, as I tried to assess the damage to Leon's head.

I kept my voice low and matter of fact as we're trained to do with hysterics. "Get something to cover him with and put some clothes on. And bring me a cold wash rag for his head."

As the crop duster continued to sweep over the fields, every few minutes roaring overhead, she laid Leon's shirt over his privates, and then slipped into shorts and a halter.

"So how did Rocco clear out of here so fast?" I asked when she brought me the cold wash rag.

"He stole Leon's ride which was parked right there." She bit off her words, pointing to a spot by the back steps where wide tires had made tracks in the mashed grass.

"What's Leon driving these days?"

"I don't even know. His GMC's over to Marvin's Garage, so he borrowed some friend's beater to run some errands."

"And you're one of the errands?" I pressed the cloth to Leon's forehead, and received a deep-toned moan as a reward.

She glared at me. "Do I look like an errand to you?"

"You sure you don't know what kind of truck he borrowed? I got to call it in. Think!" Leon moaned again.

"Who said it was a truck? I told you I didn't see what he drove up in. So *you* think! You're the one got us into this mess, *officer.*"

"I'm sorry, Theresa. He's so in love with you, I let him talk me into giving you all a few minutes alone before taking him over to the lockup in Eustis."

"In love? Rocco? That's a good one! The only thing Rocco's in love with is cold hard cash....*and* the man in the mirror. Some cop you are to not figure that out. I'm going to get a beer. I deserve it! Want one? Cause you're gonna need it when they get through with you for this insane, whacked out, retarded fuckup!"

Theresa flounced on toward the hallway, all righteous indignation. She kicked the broken lamp against the wall tearing a hole in the cheesy paneling.

And that rattled the wall enough to cause a dopey
picture of a horse's silhouette against an orange sun-
set to clatter to the floor. I knew her acting out was
just a preview of what I had in store for me at home
with my old lady once she found out what I'd done
to ruin our lives.

3

TAKING MY LICKS

Once the EMT's had carried Leon away in the ambulance to the Eustis hospital, and we'd put out a BOLO for Rocco, I headed back for the station to face the music with the Chief. My heart and the rest of my insides felt like someone had tipped a dump truck of cement in there. I'd have preferred to be in a dogfight arena with a pit bull than to face Chief Ira after what I'd done. I felt so ashamed and humiliated by my indefensible actions it was an effort to keep my back straight and my head up. Despite the intense heat, a cold trickle of sweat ran down the back of my uniform.

But stand up straight I did, and as I passed by the front desk and pushed open the swinging half gate toward the Chief's office, Rena tried to help by giving me an encouraging smile. I tried to smile but it was more like a grimace, as I pressed on past a row of file cabinets toward the partially open door to face the Chief.

His desk was piled with files and papers and reports, and he was writing something as I walked in. He gestured toward a chair by the desk but didn't look up until he finished. I sat, twirled my cap on my knee and waited, overflowing with remorse, so nervous it felt like bugs were crawling on me. Not that it would do any good, but I tried to look as normal as possible. The only sound in there was the Chief's pen scratching across the paper.

Finally, he put the pen down and sat back in his swivel chair. He lightly rubbed his eyes, then angled himself to face me and waited, his face weary, not angry.

"Chief, I....."

He put up a hand. "Hold it, son. I got to have some more coffee before I hear this. You want some?" I shook my head as he used the phone to ask Rena to bring him a coffee.

"Okay, now go ahead. Give it to me." He made a gimme gesture with his big fingers, leaned back, half closed his eyes, and clasped his hands over his oversized silver belt buckle.

Rena brought his coffee, avoiding my eyes, set the steaming mug gently in front of him, and left us closing the door quietly behind her. As the Chief's door stayed open most of the time, this tipped me off that she already knew this session was going to be a disaster. But I already knew that, and my insides still felt like cement.

So I told the Chief the story, almost choking on it. He kept his faded blue eyes on me through out, except for the couple of times he tilted his head back and surveyed the ceiling. When I'd finished, I focused on the trademark gray Stetson that he kept on an antique antler hat rack in the corner in back of his desk and waited to take my licks.

But the Chief surprised me when he finally spoke. He kept his voice low and talked real slow. "Son, look, you've always been a good cop. So good I really thought you'd one day take my place when I get ready to retire. But now you've gone and done something impossibly lame-brained here, and nobody's going to trust your judgment any more. I know this worthless P.O.S. Leon. I'm surprised he could spare the time from the racetrack to be slipping around through Theresa's back door. And what in the hell that flat out gorgeous Theresa sees in a sorry stray dog like that is a mystery. But fact is, his family is vindictive as hell, and they're sure to come after you for this. My wife's first cousin to his granddaddy, and I've seen enough of those people over the years to know how they operate. So, my advice to you is to stay low and keep your powder dry, and find you a good lawyer. Cause if those people think they can make money off of this, they'll take you for everything you've worked for all your life, and then some. You better pray Rocco didn't scramble Leon's brains, cause if there's anything broke in that worthless skull of his...." He let his voice trail off and slowly shook his head. "I hate like hell to do this, but you're going to have to turn in your badge and your gun," he said with resignation, slapping both palms onto the desk.

I stood, undid the badge and placed it in front of him. He dropped his eyes to my holster. "It's my pistol though."

He nodded. "Yeah, I forgot." He stood. "Go on home and tell Regina the bad news before she sees it on TV."

"And son," his voice was gruff as I turned toward the door, shoulders slumped like I'd just been kicked by a mule. "Everybody does at least one idiotic thing in their lifetime, and if they try to tell you different, they're either lying or too boring to even bother with. You'll get through this one way or another. Trust me. I'm a good judge of character."

4

GOODBYE REGINA

Regina and I lived in a two bedroom frame house built in 1940, on the opposite side of town from Theresa's trailer. We had bought it cheap from my old auntie when she went into the local nursing home. There was a deep back yard, actually rounding out to almost an acre and bordered by tall elderberries and scrub oaks. There was a half screened-in outdoor kitchen out back where I could go to when I wanted to cook something that would smell up or heat up Regina's kitchen like a crawfish boil or a fish fry for instance. The metal garage door was up and I could see Regina's black Honda inside, so I knew I could deliver the news and get it over with.

My two hounds, Willie and Merle, took time out from their snooze on the front porch to run and jump up to greet me. I spent a few minutes petting them and playing with them before heading up to my doomed discussion with Regina. They saw me to the front door and then promptly flopped back down on the deck of the porch where they took up sentry duty.

Regina was scrubbing down the bathroom with something so strong it bit at my nostrils and made me sneeze, but then she had always been a clean freak.

"How come you're home so early?" she asked without looking up, as she sprayed and scrubbed the pink tiles above the sink. "Dinner won't be ready for a while yet."

"Come on and sit with me on the couch and I'll tell you about it." I tried to keep my voice light, but it cracked, and she right away knew something was up.

She quit what she was doing and turned toward me. "What's the matter? Are you hurt?"

"Not so's you could notice," I said.

She pressed her lips together and put the spray bottle and scrubber away under the sink. "I'll be right there," she said, "just let me rinse my hands off."

Once we were seated in the living room, she sat like a school kid, hands folded, waiting for the day's lesson. Her hair was tied up in a red bandanna., and she wore denim cutoffs and a blue tee shirt with some white bleach stains on it. I remember exactly because I had a premonition this would be one of the last times I'd see her with us still together as a couple in our home. There was an icy sensation in my spine that hinted at what was coming next, but I chalked it up to nerves over the day's events and recklessly plunged ahead into the story.

After I'd recounted all of it, leaving nothing out, including my report to the Chief, she stared at me for a minute or two trying to take it all in. "Rocco? That guy from high school? Rocco did this to you? To *us*?" Then, jaw set, black eyebrows arched, but without a word, she leaped up and went into the kitchen to stir the meatball stew she had simmering on the stove.

Relieved that she hadn't exploded, or thrown one of the glass candy dishes on the coffee table at me, I followed her in there and sat at the kitchen table, waiting to hear her reaction. Tina, the rat terrier, pawed at her legs hoping for a taste of something. She ignored the dog, ignored me, and just kept slowly stirring as though in a trance. I became more hopeful with every second that she remained silent, telling myself she was thinking of how she was going to be standing by me, helping us get through this together. I even heard Tammy Wynette singing in the background of my mind, delirious as I was by that time.

"I'm sorry, baby. I really screwed up." I got up and moved toward her, arms reaching out, hands hovering near her shoulders. I wanted to stroke her and assure her that I'd make things right. We'd be all right. I'd find some other way to make a living. We'd make a new life. It would just be different. But as my hands rested on her back, she jerked them off with an abrupt shake of her shoulders.

"Don't!" she hissed.

So I didn't. I stood there for a moment, looking at my hands as though she'd burned them, then veered off to the right and opened the refrigerator to grab a beer. "You want one?"

There was no answer, and when I looked over at her and saw how dark and clouded her face had become, I knew that there was going to be no answer. Not then, maybe not for days. And nobody was going to be singing any country songs in our household. I saw at that moment that I was done for in all ways and from all directions. I'm a practical man. I know when I'm licked, so I took my cold one and slammed on out the back door to whistle up Willie and Merle, the only friends I was likely to find that day and for many days to come. Then I headed to the outdoor kitchen where I had more beers stowed in the camp refrigerator.

5

MY LIFE IN THE SHREDDER

Despite putting out the BOLO and his photograph on the local news for days, they never did find Rocco. The vehicle Leon had borrowed turned out to be a Jeep wagon. It was found in a mall parking lot almost to the Texas border, out of gas, low on oil because of a leak, but otherwise undamaged. Cajuns mostly need a really good reason to leave Cajunland, like a well paying oil field job in Port Arthur for instance. But under the circumstances, my guess was that Rocco was halfway across the country by then. Either that or he had circled back and was hiding out on somebody's abandoned houseboat somewhere deep in the Atchafalaya Swamp.

Either guess was plausible. Rural Cajuns can do just fine out in the swamp because most of them have all the skills needed to live as rough and bare to the bone as is required by circumstances. If he was hiding out in the swamp, some hunter or boater or a Fish & Wildlife officer would eventually notice him.

But if he'd left the state, there wasn't much chance of his being found, because Rocco was a wily s.o.b., and I knew he'd figure out how to cover his tracks like a pro.

Since the local news had loved the story, I was embarrassed to show my face around St. Beatrice, and looked for work elsewhere. Anywhere elsewhere. Regina still wasn't really speaking to me. Only when she absolutely had to, but she served our meals and took good care of the house, just like always. This cold war went on for days. I knew sex was out of the question, mad as she was at me, but she held so fast to her side of the bed that she even half slid off the edge of the mattress a couple of times. So even just the creature comfort of the closeness of her body was off limits to me.

We had some money saved, but that went fast. And then well into week two, I was coming up the back steps all thirsty from digging weeds around the garden, when she met me at the door wiping her hands on a dish towel. With a righteous look on her face, she announced that she wanted to get away for a while to her parents' house where they lived in Beauville, another small town thirty miles south of St. Beatrice. "I need to get away and think," she said.

"What's there to think about? Once I find a job things will get back to normal."

"You think that's why I'm leaving? Because you haven't found a job yet?" She looked at me in amazement.

"Well, yeah. You're tense because I screwed up and our money's almost gone. But it'll be all right. Just give me a chance to work something out."

She shook her head, jaw tight, and lips pressed together. Then she spoke very slowly as though she were talking to a mental defective. "It's not about you not having a job yet. It's about how I can't stand waiting for some little weasly, pot-bellied man to come driving up and slap a summons on you for civil court. So Leon can take everything away from us, cause you were so stupid and moronic and *retarded* as to take off a prisoner's handcuffs so he could run on into that *whore*'s trailer and kick him half to death."

She hadn't said more than three sentences for two weeks, and now the steam was coming out of her ears and fire was coming out of her mouth. I reared back in surprise at the venom.

"Theresa's not a whore," was all I could think of to say.

"Oh, and now you're sticking up for that *sleazy, in heat slut* who has ruined our life all because one man is not enough for her stuck-up narcissistic bitch self?" Now her face was red, and I could have taken her pulse because the vein in her temple rapidly throbbed against the skin.

"Take it easy. You're going to catch a stroke."

"No, *you* take it easy!" She spit the words at me. "Don't you get it? Leon's going to claim brain damage and take us for everything we've got. Say goodbye to this house. Your truck. My car, and anything else he can go after."

"Brain damage? With Leon, how could anybody tell?"

"Oh, yeah. Go ahead and joke, smartmouth. If there's money involved, he'll figure out a way to act crazy. Don't worry. We don't have a prayer of keeping anything we've got including the clothes on our backs. And I can't stay around any longer waiting for it all to come crashing down around us. I'm leaving. Mom said they'd make room for me in the house until they can get a new trailer delivered for me out in back by their tree line."

"Oh, so you've been making plans to leave right along? This is a done deal?"

"Somebody has to use the brains God gave them!" And she whirled and left me standing there on the back steps, breathing hard, my fists clenched on the shovel handle. I stared at the slammed back door, slapping mosquitoes, my brain stalled, the cold drink forgotten. My career was over. Now it looked like the marriage was over. What else could happen? It was only a matter of days before I found out.

6

THE MOTEL BY THE
SIDE OF THE ROAD

The house was as deafening quiet as a crypt
once Regina left, so I spent as much time as
I could anywhere but there. My parents had
long since retired to a small town two hours north so
they could be near to their camp on the Red River. I
didn't want to tell them what was going on because
my father has a tricky heart, and I knew my mother
would get so anxious and worried she would make
herself sick, so no good would come of telling them
anything. I had asked Regina to keep quiet about it if
they called her, but since Regina had never warmed
up to either one of them, it was doubtful they would
call her. All family conversations went through me
because Regina had made it plain to them over the
years that they were very low on her list of priorities.

Much of this had to do with the fact that Regina
and her mother saw themselves as way up the social
food chain. My parents live mostly following the

traditions of the old ways. They speak Cajun French with their friends and at home. They attend Mass each morning, and my mother belongs to a group that meets to say the Rosary five times a week at a nearby nursing home. My father still hunts and butchers his own meat. He even built a smokehouse. He makes his own *boudin* and *boulettes*. As a kid, it was my job to drag myself out of bed before dawn, roast the coffee beans slowly in a black iron skillet, then stretch my arms and grind the beans in the grinder that hung above my head on the kitchen wall. Like I said, we lived following the old ways.

My mother starts the day's cooking early in the morning, and everything that comes out of her kitchen is perfectly seasoned and fork tender. My father has kept his forty-year-old pickup going all these years by himself, and has never seen the need to buy a new one. They never understood Regina's ways, and if they were hurt by her blowing them off, they never said so.

When I went to visit, I was glad Regina usually had an excuse not to go along, because we all felt more relaxed and had a better time without her. My parents could speak French the whole time as they could not with Regina along because she didn't understand any of it except for *Comment ça va? Bien,* and *Merci.* She had never been even a little bit interested in picking up any of the language, and her eyes glassed over whenever my parents or I tried to teach her a phrase or two.

I knew I had to tell my parents what happened eventually, but I wanted to wait at least until I was settled into a good long-term job and had established a new life somehow. It was ironic, but I temporarily ended up taking Rocco's job driving the dump truck for his uncle's gravel pit. His uncle Grady felt sorry for me because of how Rocco had trashed my life, and called me to say the least he could do is provide me with a job until I figured out what I was going to do next.

So I made deliveries around St. Beatrice Parish of pea gravel and shell and limestone for people's driveways and roads. My paychecks weren't too shabby, and I was able to pay off some bills and put cash aside to help Regina each week until she could find a job. But even so, we still weren't communicating more than was absolutely necessary.

When I swung by their house to drop money off, my mother-in-law Livonia's mouth looked like it was chiseled in stone, and she looked down her nose at me like she smelled something bad. Joe, her father, standing apart back in the living room, tried to give me some moral support with a weak smile and a half-hearted wave, as though to say he knew what I was going through and to get used to it like he had had to do over decades of p-whipped marriage to Livonia.

In his youth after high school, Joe had been on the rodeo circuit, before he broke too many bones and had to quit. But over the years Livonia had broken him just as expertly as he had at one time broken wild horses. It wasn't long before I quit going over there altogether and when I had some money to help her until she found a job, I mailed a money order instead. Before too long, she did get a job answering the phone in a construction site trailer office and all interactions between Regina, her parents, and me ended abruptly. Truth is, I never gave her much thought after that. Maybe once or twice if I saw or heard something that reminded me of her, but she was easy to forget after the way she'd dumped me just when I needed her most.

I learned that summer that no matter how carefully you took care of your life, no matter how safe and secure what you'd built up seemed to be, out of nowhere as fast as a snap of Fate's fingers, everything can be turned upside down and inside out. What you thought you had can dissolve just like morning field fog is burned off by the rising sun. And before you know what hit you, it's like you swapped places with somebody else, and you're in another life and another country altogether.

But I was able to plod along as I tried to adjust to my new life, and I kept telling myself things would get better if I just kept on keeping on day after day. But then, just like Regina had predicted, a summons was delivered. The man wasn't pot-bellied or even weazly, but she got the rest of it right. There was a civil action against me, and Leon had figured out a way to claim he had brain damage. The way I heard it he claimed he could no longer tell the difference between a Trifecta or an Exacta at the track, and he couldn't even study the racing form anymore, because the beating had left him so squirrely and fuzzy in the head.

The bottom line was, that by the end of that winter, a jury trial had left us with just what Regina had feared. Nothing. Zero. Zip. Since they had never been able to catch up with Rocco Theriot, they came after me with everything they had. Leon had hired an out of town lawyer whose reputation was so bad that three Sheriffs around the state of Louisiana had been on the prowl for years for any evidence at all to haul him in on. It was whispered around the three parishes that he was involved in cocaine smuggling from Mexico, real estate kickbacks and scams, misuse of trust funds, and of course ethics violations up the ying/yang. If you had seen the shuffling, jerking, mumbling show that Leon put on in the courtroom, it would have been hard to keep a straight face.

Rodney Clayton, the scumbag attorney had coached him well. And Rodney wasn't shuffling, jerking, or mumbling. He was smug, self assured, and whenever he mentioned my name and pointed a pudgy manicured finger to where I sat, the hounds of hell couldn't have snarled better than he did. The jury bought the whole overblown, jerry-rigged show. All I was able to rescue from my old life was my hounds, my rifle, shotgun, two pistols, my fishing tackle and some cash I'd stashed in a tin box under the bed that nobody but me knew about. The only reason I still had those essentials of living is because Rodney Clayton didn't know about them.

The week after the trial, Rocco still hadn't been tracked down, and Grady felt so bad for me he gave me an '82 Chevy pickup he had been saving in the barn until the day he had the time to restore it.

"I love this old truck, but you surely need it more than I do. Anyhow, I asked the Good Lord what to do for you, and He said to give you the truck even though it hurts my soul to part with it." He laughed then. "Hell, it would probably just sit there in the barn til I croak anyhow, cause I'm always too busy to fool with it."

We put a new battery in it, changed the plugs and the oil, put new tires on it, and got the truck going by the next day. I was very grateful to Grady for all he'd done for me, but it was time to move on. I couldn't stand staying around town anymore. Just the thought of passing by what used to be our house– the same house that would soon have Leon's truck parked in the front yard made me queasy.

They say when you've lost everything, you're free, and that's true. I *was* free. Letting my imagination run away with me, I considered all sorts of possibilities I could go for: Stunt man in Hollywood... cowhand in Texas...the pipeline in Alaska... roadie for a rock band...but it was all fantasy and daydreams and I couldn't settle on just one of those ideas. Meanwhile, I had to find a place to live that was out of town. It was embarrassing to run into people who knew the stupid thing I'd done. They were mostly kind-hearted and no one laughed in my face, but I could see the sympathy in their eyes, and it hurt to be reminded constantly of how Rocco had made a chump out of me.

The best ideas sometimes come out of nowhere when you're least expecting it, and I suddenly had an idea that wasn't adventurous or even interesting on any level, but it did have one strong factor going for it...practicality.

Within half an hour of having this great idea, I took off for an old widow lady's cheap motel in the tiny town of Ida on a two-lane northeast of Eustis that I'd passed a few times while making deliveries for Grady. It was such a relic from the past, the blinking sign called it a motor court: *The Magnolia Motor Court* to be exact. The rooms were all lined up in a row along a cracked cement driveway next to a rectangular patch of grass. Shingles were missing from the roof, and the stucco had thriving patches of grimy gray mildew.

The old lady's frame house was set toward the rear of the property with a small sign: *Office* over a corny black and white drawing of a hand pointing to the house. The only people who stayed in the motel were some Mexican roofers who took up three rooms on a weekly basis, and an occasional traveler too tired to drive any further to find one of the modern motels off the exits of the main highway cutting through Eustis.

Celeste, the owner, was so happy to get another weekly customer, she even let me keep Willie and Merle out in her fenced backyard. What she said with her cigarette raspy voice was, "I'll be glad for them to be there. I need watch dogs. You never know these days who's going to come creeping around in the middle of the night to rob you or slit your throat." (She had no idea at the time how prophetic those words would turn out to be.)

She gave me the key with a red diamond shaped six-inch plastic plaque attached to it by a metal ring, and pointed out the closest room toward her house.

"That way you can hear if your dogs start barking and there's somebody sneaking around the property up to no good."

Celeste was one of those people you immediately know you're going to have no trouble getting along with. Just meeting her raised my dragging spirits, and I got the feeling that maybe I was going to come out of all this without going on a three day bender after all. I had promised myself I was going to get lost in a bottle of Black Jack soon as I found somewhere to land. I told myself I deserved to get lost in a quart or two of whiskey after the wringer I'd been through.

But once I had the dogs situated inside the chain-linked yard, filled their water bowls, and unloaded my things into the room, I started thinking instead about how I could maybe pressure-wash the dingy stucco of the motel for her. Then maybe I'd even climb up on a ladder and see about replacing some shingles up there on the weathered, ramshackle roof. In spite of her dyed red hair, I figured Celeste was somewhere in her late seventies, and even though she came across as all lively and independent, I sensed that she could use all the help she could get and then some.

Soon as I stowed my gear, I studied the room to find the best place to hide my guns and cashbox. The small room smelled musty and had no closet. The space under the double bed was boxed in by varnished boards. I could pry one side open, hide my guns, then nail it back, but a thief would be likely to look there. The only thing I could think of to do was to stash what I could above some of the square ceiling tiles. What I couldn't hide there, I'd have to carry around with me in the Chevy.

I'd brought in the cooler from the truck, so I popped a soda and flopped down on the bed to take a break. There was a clock radio on the bed stand, and I clicked it on. It was already tuned to a country station, and wouldn't you know it, they were playing *Hello, Walls*. I laid back on the bed, pressed the cold can to my forehead, and sang my new theme song right along with Faron Young.

7

HANDY MAN

What my grandfather and father had stressed to me over and over throughout my childhood and teenage years had stayed in the back of my mind throughout this dismal mess: *No matter how many times they knock you down, you gotta keep getting right back up!* By afternoon of the next day, I'd rented a pressure washer and cleaned up the exterior of the motel and Celeste's house as well. She was so happy about how fresh her property looked, she invited me over for a steak dinner and a work conference so we could make a list of what else needed doing around there, and how we could deduct it from the rent.

After we'd eaten steaks, gravy and real mashed potatoes, homemade yeast rolls, field peas, and salad, we made up a list over coffee and her specialty: Pecan cake with cream cheese frosting. I had not only found a new home, but stumbled upon a great cook, and that's saying something in

Louisiana where great cooks are as commonplace as mosquitoes.

I figured the list she wanted doing would take me a while. She wanted each of the motel rooms painted, except for the ones that were currently in use. There were some plumbing fixture replacements needed, and some rotten boards that had to be replaced here and there. There were sagging rain gutters and fascia boards to repair, and a new lock that a drunk had broken trying to get in the wrong room. This was good news for me because I'd be able to look for a job in the morning, then work at the motel in the afternoons and evening.

After our business talk was over, she invited me into the living room so she could play some songs on the piano. Her living room was spacious and an upright piano against one wall held many framed family photographs, including a few really old ones in oval frames covered with antique bubble glass. There were photos of Celeste and her late husband, Marvin LaFleur, who had been the cook on a tugboat for years before retirement. There were photos of the two of them on horseback, in an outboard, and one with Celeste playing piano in a saloon with Marvin and a group of people around her. There were also a few signed and framed photographs of the great Johnnie Allen with Celeste standing next to him in one of them.

"You played piano in a club somewhere?" I asked taking up a framed photo of her and examining it. Celeste was all made up, and wore a sequined dress with her long red hair worn loose. "Wow! You used to be glamorous, huh?"

"What do you mean, used to be?" She laughed, sat down and began to play some songs in Cajun French, which I knew well because my parents and grandparents keep the radio tuned to a Cajun French radio station that plays nothing but traditional Cajun music. She played *Grand Mamou, Allons a Lafayette, La Letter Qu'elle Ma Laissée, J'ai Passant Devant la Porte,* and *La Bague qui Brille.* Her gravelly voice just added to the performance, and it was easy to see that she loved an audience because she really put on a good show. She finished up with *Crazy Arms* and *Waltz Across Texas,* then stood up and took a mock bow.

"You should still get out and play somewhere once a week. You're great!" I told her, clapping.

She laughed. "I do play once a week. Right after we finish our card game. Over at Acey's Lounge. I've played two nights a week there for years. Acey sits in with his fiddle when he isn't too busy. And he's damn good too."

"Did you ever make a CD?"

She rolled her eyes. "No, but my fans keep nagging me to do it."

"Do it. I'll sure buy one."

"Oh, one of these days I'll get around to it."

"Make a song list of the songs you play the most….the ones your fans like best. Then go into a recording studio in Lafayette. It'll be great!"

"I'd have to get Acey to come in on it with me. We're so used to working together…for years now."

"All the better."

"You need to come by some night and listen."

"I will."

"You know where Acey's is?"

"Sure. It's over there on the highway on the left going out of Ida as you're headed toward Eustis. I've stopped off there to play *bourrée* once or twice. You weren't playing though."

"I play Friday and Saturday. Their regular *bourrée* game is on Wednesdays. That's how come you missed me."

She closed the keyboard cover on the piano, then served us some homemade *Soco* in gold-rimmed brandy glasses, and we moved to a couch covered in a worn midnight blue brocade and a half dozen gold fringed silk throw pillows. A black enamel box held a deck of cards on the coffee table that Celeste took out and began to shuffle.

"Come on. Let's have a quick game or two. We'll keep the betting low since you're out of a job right now. How's about a quarter a game?"

The couch was so comfortable and the *Soco* so good that I right away agreed with enthusiasm. We ended up playing for almost an hour before we called it a night, and I went back to my room, feeling no pain after all the brandy. I hadn't played much since getting married, so I had gotten rusty, which is my excuse as to why Celeste *bourréed* me over and over. Besides beating me at cards, she made me laugh a lot, and by the time I was back in my room, it didn't seem quite as lonely, and the walls weren't closing in on me near as much as they had before.

8

LOLLIPOPS

During the next two weeks, I'd painted the five interiors of all the rooms that weren't occupied by the Mexican roofers and me. Besides the painting, the carpentry and some plumbing fixture replacements, I fixed any faucets that were leaking, changed out the washers in all the faucets that were dripping, and even put in some landscaping to dress the place up some. A few flowering bushes and some crepe myrtles around the front and in that boring stretch of median grass made a big difference in the look of the motel from the road.

The *Magnolia Motor Court* sign should have been in a museum of American artifacts, but for the time being, I touched up the letters and angled three spotlights on it from the ground. By the end of that second week, Celeste actually had rented out a few units to out of state overnight guests.

"This keeps up, and I'll have to hire a housekeeper again," she said as she pulled the sheets off one of the double beds and threw them into her laundry cart.

"I hope I come up with a job soon so it doesn't have to be me," I said from the walkway where I was painting one of the ornamental iron uprights supporting the overhang.

"I heard of a job that just came open," she huffed as she shook pillowcases off the pillows and tossed them into the cart.

"Yeah, where?"

"You gotta love this one," she laughed as she rolled the cart out the door of the room.

"I'm listening."

"Look down the highway that way." She squinted and pointed north.

I turned my head and looked, but didn't see anything but a stretch of road with a gas station/grocery store combination, a few scattered houses, and a welding parts outlet.

"What? Where?"

"Right past that welding place. See it?" She laughed again so hard it made her cough.

"I can't see that far."

"It's a strip joint, sonny. It's Nick Soileau's dump, LolliPops, and it's the only strip club for miles around. His security guard, bouncer, whatever, tried to break up a fight Wednesday. One of the men held a knife to his throat, so he quit the job. Marvin and I knew Nick from way back. The job's yours if you want it."

"Security guard, huh?" I went back to painting scrollwork on the ornamental iron. "Sounds interesting. I'll run by there and apply when I'm done here."

"You don't have to apply. I already called Nick about it. Like I said, the job's yours if you want it. All you have to do is go meet him in his office and fill out some necessary forms."

I just stared at her.

"What's the matter? You got something against naked ladies?" She kept laughing all the way down the walkway as she wheeled her cart toward the laundry room.

I watched her walk away, then looked back up the road, trying to compute what she'd just told me. During the short time I'd been staying there, we'd become friends and spent most of our evenings together. She always cooked great food and served it up in the dining room that was separated from her kitchen by an archway. Then we'd make plans for the next day's work over coffee and dessert. After we cleared away the dishes, she'd play half a dozen songs at the piano. She knew so many, I don't remember hearing any of them more than once.

After the music, we'd sit on the couch and play *bourrée* or low-ball while we drank the *Soco* she always had plenty of. Her cousin in Ville Platte made the brandy and kept her pantry closet supplied with glass gallon jugs and quart Mason jars full of it. On one of those evenings I drank enough brandy to confide in her what had happened to cause me to lose everything so that I had to live hand to mouth in her low rent motel. Turned out she already knew most of the story from the Eustis newspaper and TV news, but had been too polite to bring it up.

"One day she'll regret running out on you," Celeste solemnly predicted about Regina as she shuffled and reshuffled a new deck so fast the cards were a blur. She wore gold rings set with rubies, diamonds, and sapphires and her nails were long and a shimmering deep red. "But she's young yet. Give her enough time and like the song says, she'll come running back."

"Oh no," I said. "That's it for me. She walks out on me at the worst time of my life." I shook my head. "No way I'm taking her back."

"You say that now, but you don't know how you're going to feel down the road." She pushed the deck forward for me to cut the cards. I knocked on the deck with my knuckles, then held out my hand.

"You want to put a little money on that?" I asked.

"I don't bet on people's love life. That's a good way to lose your tee shirt," she laughed and dealt us another hand.

I heard the washing machine start up as I put the last brushstrokes on the scrollwork and decided to quit for the day and drive to Eustis to get a haircut so I'd look good when I met Nick Soileau. I smiled to myself as I washed the paintbrush at an outdoor faucet. A security guard at a strip joint. Me a bouncer? Having to look at naked ladies for hours each night? A picture of Regina's disapproving face flashed before my eyes. I flicked some water off the paintbrush at her frowning face. I was beginning to really like the idea of this new job already.

9

LA COMIDA

That night the Mexicans fired up the grill outside on the grass beyond the walkway. They threw some steaks on the rack and Cornelio called me over to join them for dinner. I thanked them and jumped into the pickup for a beer run to the gas station a few miles up the road. I bought two six packs of Corona and a bag of fried pork rinds because I knew that's what they liked, and headed back, looking forward to those steaks.

Ismael was flipping the steaks when I drove up and parked. I hailed him and handed over the beers to Jorge who smiled and carried them off to a metal ice chest by the doorway to one of their rooms. Ice crackled as he snugged each bottle into the cooler.

"Come, come," he waved me inside a room. There on the double bureau were plates of guacamole, chips, chopped red onion, bean dip and sliced cayenne peppers.

One of the men was fiddling with the tuner on a worn, duct taped radio and adjusting the antenna, trying to clear up some static on a radio station playing Ranchera music. He succeeded and Jenni Rivera singing *Asi Fue* came in crystal clear, then Vicente Fernandez followed with *La Ley des Monte*. Living almost next door to the men, I'd learned to like their favorite singers and the lively music was good background for a party mood and added spice to our neighborhood dinner.

I took an ice cold beer from Jorge and scooped up just enough guacamole on some chips to take outside on a paper plate without making a pig of myself. Ismael wiped his face with a white motel towel he kept slung over his shoulder and signaled that the steaks were getting close to ready.

We all congregated around him and raised our beers to each other in a toast.

"I'm going to see about a job in a strip joint," I told them.

They shook their heads to show they didn't understand so I tried my broken Spanish.

"*Senoritas. Chi-chi's. Trabajo.*"

"¡Aaah! ¡*Si*! ¡*Si*! ¡*Si*!" they laughed pointing at me. Jorge formed the outline of a woman's body with his hands.

"Guard." I patted my side like I had a pistol.

"¿*A donde*?"

I pointed down the road. "LolliPops."

"¡LolliPops!" They all laughed, and Manuel mimed a woman dancing to the music on the radio. Jorge clapped me on the back, motioning around at the four of them. "¡*Sabemos*! ¡*Sabemos* LolliPops!"

"*¿Quando?*" Jorge pointed at me again.

I shook my head and shrugged.

The steaks were ready by then and Ismael forked them onto double paper plates, handing one to each of us in turn. Manuel gave us each a fork and we sat on folding chairs here and there around the sidewalk and the grass bordering the driveway. Each of the men fished in their jeans for pocket knives to cut their steaks and flicked them open with a click and a flip of the wrist.

I keep a sheathed fishing knife under the seat of the pickup that I retrieved, and then we all got busy at the steaks. *La Iguana* played in the background, and once in a while the men would look over at me and laugh, shaking their heads in delight at what might be my new job.

When we'd finished eating, I helped them clean up and carried the black trash bag to the dumpster. They let me have the steak bones for the dogs, and I carried them back to Merle and Willie in the fenced yard in back of Celeste's house. Returning, I thanked the men for the dinner and the company. They had already doused the coals in the grill and were going to their respective rooms winding down for the night by turning the music off and getting ready to watch Mexican Westerns from a stockpile of DVDs they'd brought back from Texas.

"*¡Buenos noches y muchas gracias, muchachos!*" I was quite the linguist. They wished me the same, and I turned in for the night, full of anticipation for the next day's meeting with Nick Soileau at LolliPops.

10

NICK

The next day, I had scrubbed up, shined my boots, wore a new shirt Celeste had surprised me with, and arrived at LolliPops ten minutes early. Nick Soileau turned out to be rather short, with a carefully trimmed goatee and squinty eyes. We sat in his long narrow office that doubled as a storeroom. Metal shelving held bottles of liquor and wine. Cases of beer were stacked up along a cement block wall. A sagging, frayed couch held a few racing forms from the casino an hour away, and some ad tear outs for LolliPops from the local weekly paper. The room smelled like Pine Sol.

I sat in a wooden chair, while he rocked back and forth in an upholstered office chair in back of his black metal desk. On the desk were the wrappings and a few crumbs from two hamburgers, and a paper boat with some shreds of ketchup drenched fries. A zipped blue bank pouch and piles of papers, memos, and a coffee mug holding an assortment of pens and pencils had been shoved aside to make room for the take-out.

We had talked briefly about my work experience, and after I'd filled out some paperwork, I explained in as few words as possible what I'd been through and why I was no longer with the Police Department.

"That's the deal. I lost it all for being dumb enough to trust a guy I knew all my life."

He shook his head in disbelief at the story. "Man, I bet you'd like to strangle that bastard. You don't know where he's at? Me, I'd be on his trail like stink on shit. And once I found his ass, I'd drag him back wrapped up in chains like a mummy so he couldn't get away again, and then I'd Special Delivery him to Sheriff Quebedeaux so he could clear my name. No need for homicide…just clear my name, you sorry sack of shit."

"My day will come," I nodded.

A side door to the building slammed, and he looked toward the office door. He called to the young woman walking down the hall wearing a striped tee shirt dress with an oversized leather bag slung over her shoulder. "Lenny. Ask Jesse to bring us each a Coke, will ya, please?"

She ducked her head inside the door. "Sure, Nick."

"Wait a minute, Lenny." He pointed to me. "You want something else instead?" He raised his eyebrows and held out his hands.

"Coke's good."

"Lenny. Come meet this guy first. He's here for the security job."

She took a few steps forward, nodding to me. "Hello. I'm Lenny. Nice to meet you." She ran fingers through her long dark hair, smoothing it.

"This here is Harris Viator." He rubbed his hands together. "He look like he can handle the drunks?"

She squinted one eye and looked me up and down. "Looks like he can hand out a little whoop ass. Sure he can." She met my eyes. "Wish you'd been in here last night. One of them was playing snatch and grab it. Two of the regulars handled it for me and threw him out on the street." Then she wheeled around and sauntered back down the hallway as though she knew my eyes were following her.

Nick jerked a thumb after her. "One of our dancers. She's a good kid. Now some of them…look out!" He shook his head. "I'll let you find that out for yourself. I stay away from all of them, me."

Lenny reappeared a few minutes later with two frosted dripping cans of Coke on a tray. "Jesse is taking a delivery. He asked me to play fetch."

"Thanks, Lenny. That's great." She placed a purple napkin with the gold Lollipops logo down on my side of the desk before setting down the can, then did the same for Nick.

"Jesse says to tell you he's getting low on pretzel nuggets," she called over her shoulder as she made for the door, flipping the round tray sideways and tucking it under her arm.

"Yeah, yeah, okay. Thanks." Ignoring the Coke, he leaned back in his chair and laced his fingers behind his neck. "So, since you're out of a job right now. How about starting as soon as I can get the paper work done? What the hell? You look like you can handle what we get in here. I'll see if I can speed things up. It don't feel right not having somebody on the job. You never know who's going to get messed up and cause a problem at one-thirty in the a.m. when I'm looking forward to going home and catching some zzz's."

"That's great. Just call me at the motel and I'm good to go whenever you say."

"Dress casual. I'm not looking to intimidate anybody here. And like I said…stay away from the girls. That's how I lost a guy last year. Franny. Her ex is a maniac who drives non-stop showing up all the way from El Paso wanting to take her back with him, and now Jerry's arm is broke in two places. Anyhow, only a dickwad wants to watch drunks yelling and stuffing bills in his girl friend's cootch. Before you know it, somebody's lying on the floor with a broke jaw. Just stay away from the talent. Even if they come on to you. Tell em you're married or some damn thing. Just don't piss em off. Then they sulk. One thing I can't stand is a sulking woman. And a sulking stripper is even worse. Very bad for business." He tore off the tab from his Coke and held it up in a toast. "Thanks for coming by. I'll be in touch."

11

DEBUT AT LOLLIPOPS

My first night was brutal. A wife came busting in the front door, stormed past the beefy guy taking the money, shook him off when he grabbed at her, and like a flash, was at the bar pounding at her husband's back and screaming at him because he was in a strip joint and they had twin babies at home. *Welcome to the Jungle* was blaring from the loudspeakers as the husband, red with anger and embarrassment, swiveled on his barstool and sliding off it, laid a bill on the counter and followed her out the front door. The wife was a beauty with long black shining hair and a great figure. It was understandable why the guy sheepishly followed her out back to his roost. Some of his buddies from the construction job looked after them dumbstruck, then one of them laughed, breaking up the silence, and bought them all another round.

A few minutes later, one of the strippers tripped on her stiletto heels on stage and twisted her ankle, so she was out of the game for a while. Amber, a woman so stacked she made me blink a few times stormed out on stage in a few minutes to take her place. *Round and Round* played as she paraded back and forth in front of the men, then began her routine, arching her back, bending over backwards like a contortionist, and twisting and lunging like a circus performer all to the pounding beat of the music. The men close to the stage stared stupified, as two stuffed bills into her thong. One of them stood and reached toward her as though he would hug her legs, but I sat him back down and warned him he was on his way out.

The same man lunged at another man at the next table within the hour. In doing so he knocked over the small round table where he'd been seated so that I had to yank him by the arm and lead him out of the club. He struggled and slurred curse words all the way out to the bright lights of the parking lot. "Asshole!" he yelled as I slammed the door after him.

Then Lenny, the young woman that I'd met in Nick Soileau's office came on stage as I came back from evicting the drunk. She wore a long purple robe with gold buttons and collar and purple satin stiletto heels. She strutted around the stage and head held high, began to dance and slowly slide the velvet robe from her shoulders. Beneath it she wore a gold bra and flimsy purple tiny skirt. She danced to *Rock Candy* and unclipped the wraparound skirt letting it fall to the floor as the men stared.

One of them started blowing kisses at her and another made come on gestures with his outstretched hands. She smiled a million dollar smile and stuck her thumbs into the glittery golden thong she wore pulling it away from her body as though she would take it off. But instead, she unfastened the golden bra and let it fall to the floor, making at least one man lose his mind. He started some drunken howling like he was baying at the moon until his buddies all laughed at him and ordered him to chill.

Lenny leaned over and with mock seriousness placed her hands under her breasts and offered them to him just a foot from their table. He leaned forward and mock kissed her, making smacking noises with his mouth, then stuffed bills into her garter along with his friends. She danced and then began a complicated slowly twisting set of moves that mesmerized me. I was dumbfounded, to be honest, and didn't hear Nick approaching from behind my right shoulder.

"Don't get any ideas, buddy. That one's for me, not for you." He sidled away, and I tore my eyes away as she bent over, peering through her legs, long hair fanned out on the floor, and smiling as the men stared, hypnotized. Nick went back through his office door and I turned my eyes back toward Lenny's act.

She had so many bills sticking out like green leaves from the gold velvet garter by that time that she only hustled the men for a few more minutes at the edge of the stage before suddenly whirling around and flouncing away to disappear behind the burgundy backdrop curtain. The men at the front tables looked after her in silence for a moment in a stupor, blinking their way back to reality. Then picking up their beers, they came out of their trance and resumed drinking while signaling the waitress for more.

My mouth was dry after watching Lenny, and when the next dancer came out, I returned to the front of the club on the other side of the bar and asked Jesse for a drink. He quickly handed me a can of soda and I stood at the side of the bar to drain it, watching the men as they talked and drank all along the bar. I felt like a chump because a stripper had gotten to me. It had been a long time since I'd seen a woman naked or even half naked, but I'd never seen a woman naked who looked like Lenny, and it took me a good ten minutes to recover enough to get my mind back on the job.

* * *

When the last lingering customer had been prodded to shuffle reluctantly on out the door, and it was time for me to shut it all down, I checked the parking lot to make sure no drunks were loitering around the premises. I strolled the perimeter and checked around in the back to make sure all the stragglers had gone. The parking lot and the rear of the building were lighted with high metal cone lamps throwing beams of bright light over the entire deep lot, and even onto the plumbing supply outlet next door. Nick believed in high visibility and I was glad of it. Made my job easier. As I passed back toward the front parking lot, Lenny came out an exit door right in front of me with three other young women,

Amber, and the twins Renée and Lucy, all four women hauling oversized purses on their shoulder, handbags so heavy that they had to lean sideways for balance.

They were laughing at a joke Amber had told and Lenny laughed so hard she stopped walking for a few seconds. "Amber! Stop it! You're killing me!"

The twins and Amber waved goodbye to her and made for their cars, briskly walking with long strides at a matched pace, arms swinging, with the same energy they'd all shown on stage.

Lenny, walking slower, started for her car, a red Charger. She slid into the front seat still laughing at the joke and rummaging for her keys.

"Damn!" she said, peering into the purse as she rooted around in there, flinging a hairbrush, lipsticks, mints, and a scarf onto the car seat. I stepped closer to her while she hunted through the leather bag.

"You should always have your keys out and firmly hold them in your hand before you come out here. Something happens and you can use them for a weapon," I lectured.

"I know, I know. I forgot." She tossed a few more things from the purse over her shoulder as she continued to hunt.

I waited patiently as she searched, and then triumphantly, she finally held up a key chain with the key dangling from it. "Thank God! You might have had to take me home," she winked at me.

"So, how was your first night on the job?" She raised an eyebrow and gave me a cynical look.

"Not bad."

"Did you enjoy staring a hole through me?" She laughed, wagging a finger. "Nick doesn't like that, you know. The help staring at the dancers."

"I know. He let me know you and him were...."

She threw her head back laughing. "Nick said that? He wishes! Don't worry, he wouldn't have a clue what to do with me if I did go out with him." She inserted the key into the ignition, but before turning it, she looked up at me as she blew a strand of hair from her face. "Really. Don't believe anything he says. He lies like a rug."

I wanted to ask her why she was working in a dump like this for a boss that lied like a rug, but she gave me a sideways smile and said, "Hey, we're all headed for the casino. Do you want to join us there later when you're done locking up?"

"The casino?" I looked at her like a dummy. "But I'm not allowed to socialize with you Nick said."

She threw her head back and laughed out loud. "Nick! What did I tell you about him? You coming or not?" She had already started the engine, and waited for my answer as the engine purred.

I shook my head. "Not this time. I have to get up early. I have another job."

"Chicken," she murmured, and twisted her head to look over her shoulder before throwing the car into reverse. I stepped quickly back and watched as she drove on out of the parking lot, just minutes after the twins took off in a Honda with the left rear brake light out, and Amber followed them in a red Camaro.

12

BODYGUARD

It didn't take but a couple of weeks on the job to recognize the established patterns at LolliPops. The nights were similar in that there was the obligatory fistfight every night, usually after midnight. There was the usual assortment of regulars who remained civilized and abided by the rules, so as not to poison the well of their favorite watering hole and I got to know most of them by name. These regulars tended to sit at the horseshoe shaped bar that was situated halfway between the tables fronting the stage and the row of pinball machines off to the side by the front doors.

Consequently the bar split the huge room into two sections: one half for the men hungry for the sight of top heavy naked women, and the other half into a more laid back bunch of regulars who had seen it all before too many times to care enough to look up from their beers and conversations and give more than an occasional glance toward the performers.

Continuous rock music blared with such volume that the word 'conversation' is misleading. What they really had to do is lean in and yell over the music if they had something to say. I have always been a big rock fan, but LolliPops delivered a blasting overdose of *You Shook Me All Night Long, Cherry Pie, Ax to Grind, Closer, Nasty Girls, Sex in an Elevator, Gonna Raise Hell, Back in Black,* and others that were tattooed on my brain during the weeks I worked there.

The regulars were mostly the construction crews that stopped by on their way home for a few beers, some lone forlorn stragglers; and the half dozen office types that looked like they sold insurance or real estate. Then there was the crowd that started sauntering in after eight for an after dinner hour or two, and later the rowdy bunch that became loud and feeling no pain toward midnight along with a smattering of professional men who didn't want to be recognized and who sat alone quietly at a corner of the bar or a back table safely in the shadows.

Quite a few of the regulars were there to drink with their buddies and seldom bothered to glance up from the bar or the pinball machines while the strippers danced. I didn't pay much attention to them, but played offense and kept my eye on the men who sat at tables near the stage, and nightly had to keep a few dim bulbs from grabbing at the girls when they strutted by the front of the stage, or sneaking an 'accidental' feel when shoving bills into their garters. On average, I had to throw out two per shift, something Nick didn't like and that he chided me about nightly.

"Don't be so quick to eighty-six my customers. Make them sit farther back if they get too worked up. They're harmless." He frowned at me and bit off his words.

"As in sit them in the corner? You didn't hire me to teach kindergarten."

"Just chill a little. You're not Wyatt Earp." He started to point a finger at me, then changed his mind and dropped his hand.

"Do you want the girls protected or not?"

"News flash, Harris. They're strippers. Not nuns." He made a chopping motion with his hand.

"They're also paid performers. They didn't sign on for getting felt up."

"Yeah, but I notice you get extra jumpy if one of them gets too close to Lenny."

"I look after all of them." Nick was really getting on my nerves, and it was a struggle to keep my voice level.

"Just remember what I told you about Lenny. I do the looking after Lenny. That's private stock. Nobody touches that but me. Nobody!" He narrowed his eyes and jutted out his chin, then started again to poke a finger at my chest, thought better of it, turned instead, and swaggered back to his office. Nick had a hard time controlling his natural pit bull nature.

I knew right then that I'd better start looking for another job or I'd end up in jail one day for losing it and sucker punching Nick. One of the main things in life is to recognize your limitations and try to work your life around those short comings. And I knew that flying off the handle at jerk-offs was one of my weaknesses.

That same night, my Mexican neighbors from Magnolia Court came in to say hello, sat at a table, and had a great time glancing over at me standing there near the wall keeping watch over the crowd, as they pointed and laughed good naturedly. They would watch the dancers, then look at me, watch the dancers, then look at me all the while tipping their chairs back and drinking from their Coronas. They didn't stay long as roofers have to get up in the dark in order to show up on the job at dawn so as to work in the early cooler hours as much as possible. When they left they made a point of filing out past me, telling me good night, and shaking my hand, congratulating me on my new job.

"*Felicidades, Jefe*," said Ismael, patting me on the shoulder.

"*¡Felicidades! ¡Que bueno trabajo!*" crowed Manuel, pride in me showing in his dark brown eyes.

"*Vamos a casa, pero felicidades*, man," said Jorge.

If I knew enough Spanish, I'd have told them to save the congratulations as I was pretty sure I wouldn't be on the job much longer. I was going to hate to have to let those guys down…they were so happy for me.

But by the second month on the job, Nick spread the word that he had been cited by the Health Department and he had to close down until he could have some work done on the bathrooms. Leaky plumbing inside the building was just one of the problems, and there was major trouble somewhere along the old sewer line to the street. The club would be closed during the week and wouldn't reopen until the weekend. He would pay us all so we could pay our bills, but it would count as vacation pay. This brought on groans and a lot of private bitching from the help, but there was nothing anybody could do about it.

Lenny caught up with me outside that night when she was leaving by the side door with the twins and Amber. She slowed down, dropping back to let her friends go on ahead to their cars, and keeping her voice low, asked me what I was planning on doing while we were off.

"Haven't even thought about it. Why?" I asked, surprised by the question.

"Because I want to go up to my family's camp a few hours north of here and I hate to go there by myself, that's why. It's in the woods and I could use the company."

"What about the club rules?"

"I'm not going to tell anybody. Are you?" She flashed me a wicked smile. "Don't worry. It's not like I'm trying to come on to you. I just think you're a stand up guy and I like you. I like how you keep an eye on me in there, and I would feel safer if you were with me up at the camp. You've seen those slasher movies where beautiful young women go stay in a cabin in the woods? Well, that's not all fiction. That stuff really happens out in the boonies. I'd be real happy to pay you if you need the money. Call it bodyguard detail. Except this is more like two friends going on a camping trip."

"Call me and we'll talk about it. But forget about putting me on the payroll. I already have a job."

"Tell me your number and I'll remember it."

I gave her my number and she sailed off toward her car. I waited in the parking lot until all the women had gotten safely to their cars and driven off, then went back inside to finish closing up, wondering what in the hell I was getting into now.

13

THE PINEY WOODS

Two mornings later, and Lenny was picking me up for the drive north to her family's camp. She angle parked in front of my room, while I was sweeping the motel walkway. She wore boot cut jeans and a black tee shirt, black roper boots and a forest green visor cap advertising the Wallace Feed Store.

"You own horses?" I asked.

She tapped the cap. "No, but that's where we're headed. The big town of Wallace, Louisiana."

"Let me put this broom up, and I'll introduce you to Celeste. She's my landlady. You'll like her."

I stowed the broom in the utility room next to the ice machine in the breezeway between the rooms and Celeste's house. She strolled after me. "You always do the sweeping up around here?"

"I'm the handy man here for Celeste. Keep everything running for her. Come on." I led her down the brick lined path to the house, crossed the porch, and used the heavy brass knocker to rap on the front door.

Lenny glanced at her watch. "It's so early. You sure she's up?"

As if in answer, Celeste opened the door, wearing a long white chenille robe, tied tightly at the waist and embroidered slippers. Her face looked freshly scrubbed and she wore no makeup. Fiddle music played in the background from the local Cajun radio station, KOUI.

With a bright, welcoming smile she chirped, "Good morning," and nodded at both of us in turn. "Come in, come in. Want some coffee?" She stepped back and beckoned us inside. The house smelled of cinnamon rolls. She baked biscuits or cinnamon rolls each morning and brought me a plate of them when I was doing the morning chores around the motel.

"No, no, Celeste. We better get going. We've got a long way to go today. I just wanted you to meet Lenny...Leonée Badon."

"How do you do." Lenny offered her hand.

"Pleased to meet you," Celeste said, shaking her hand. "I hope you all have a safe trip."

"Thanks. And if there's any kind of trouble here, be sure to call me right away."

"Oh, don't worry. I'll be fine. I put together some snacks in a sack for you to take along in the car for the long drive." She picked up a plastic container from the hall table and handed it to me. "Just some chips and dip and a couple of sandwiches. Nothing fancy."

"Thank you so much. How kind you are to think of that," Lenny said.

"Why, sure, *chère.* You all have a good time, and we'll see you when you get back."

She waved us goodbye, and I introduced Lenny to Willie and Merle. She made a fuss over them, reaching over the fence to pat their heads and scratch their ears, and then we headed back to the room so I could pick up my battered suitcase with a few changes of clothes, and we loaded up. Lenny's brown and white rat terrier, Bijou, jumped up and down as we got into the car. Dogs always worry you're never coming back, so when you do they trip all over themselves with excitement. Bijou was no exception, and to calm him, Lenny let him lie half on her lap with his other half on the seat between us.

As she slowly drove from the motel, Lenny asked, "How did you luck into this arrangement with such a nice landlady?"

"Sheer good luck. Was looking for a place to hole up for a while until I could get my life back on track. It all worked out great because of her. You should hear her sing and play piano. She's been performing all her life. Still plays over at Acey's Lounge couple days a week."

"I'd like to go hear her some time. Will you take me?"

"Well, yeah, sure." I was mystified. What did a gorgeous woman like Lenny want to keep company with a washed up broke cop for? And what about Nick? There had to be something to all that, even though she denied it. He didn't strike me as the delusional kind. I couldn't figure any of it out, but didn't worry about it too much as just being near her felt so great.

I watched her as she headed north on the highway. Seeing her dressed down, her hair tied back in a ponytail and minus all the stage makeup, she was no longer the flashy showgirl I was accustomed to seeing. She was actually quite plain looking, but she would still stand out in any crowd because of that outstanding figure.

"It's not polite to stare," she said with a small smile.

"I'm not used to seeing you without all that stage makeup. I like the way you look today… all natural."

"Me too. All that glam stuff gets old. I hate it. And to think we have to pay Nick to work there cause he's so cheap, or the guys that he fronts for are so cheap. New Orleans scumbags. Sleazeballs. Us dancers have to make it on tips. The cash is pretty damn good though, I have to admit." As if to change the subject, she turned on the radio and a pre-set country station came on with *Angel Flying Too Close to the Ground.*

"You like Country? Might as well get in the mood for north Louisiana. It's redneck. Ever been up there?" she asked, "or don't you ever leave Cajun country?"

"I had to go pick up a prisoner in Monroe one time. My parents live on the Red River over near Natchitoches."

"We're going further up, almost to the Arkansas border. Might as well be in Arkansas, really."

"You want me to drive?"

"Maybe later if I start getting drowsy."

I hadn't been driven around by a woman since I was a kid. But she seemed to know what she was doing, so I tilted the seat back to relax and enjoy the ride and tilted my visor cap down to block the sun.

The drive north took almost four hours. At one point, we pulled off at a rest stop, sat at a picnic table, and ate the snacks Celeste had provided. Lenny had brought a small cooler with sodas on ice, and we clicked the cans together in a toast to our trip. She'd also brought a food packet for Bijou. When we'd finished, we walked around with Bijou on a leash for a few minutes on the designated dog walk and stretched our legs before getting back on the road.

By the time the foliage started changing to mostly piney woods lining the highway, Lenny had begun pressing me for details of my past. I danced around the questioning because I didn't want to relive any of it. I was trying to forget, but didn't want to tell her it was none of her business either. So, I told her as little as possible to get the idea across that I had messed up badly and lost my job and everything else because of a screw-up. I trusted the wrong guy, and I let her wonder about the details.

It wasn't long after that she announced we were almost there and slowed for Wallace, a town so tiny it was barely more than a crossroad. We passed a gas station, the feed store, and one of those old-time frame buildings with a grocery store on the ground floor and living quarters on the second floor. Thick woods surrounded the town and a few scattered trailers and houses were set well back in the privacy of pine trees, scrub oaks, and bushes with packed dirt or pea gravel driveways leading to them.

"This is why we always load up with whatever we need whenever any of my family comes up here. But there's always enough food and drink in the freezers and the pantry at the camp to last for weeks." She waved at a police car half hidden in the pines a quarter mile past the town limits. "That's Roderick. He's always hoping to catch a speeder. Just about the only income Wallace has. He has to get his salary from somewhere. Remember that if you come into town. It's really a speed trap. Go one mile over the limit and here come the blue flashers."

A few miles further, and she turned off to the west onto a gravel road leading deep into the piney woods. She drove slowly a mile down this road and signaled where her family's property started. "Okay. This is it. Our land starts right about here." She took a deep breath. "Smell that clean air? I always forget how great it is to breathe that fresh pine air." She smiled over at me, her eyes sparkling.

"Now the caretaker, Quintus, is sort of eccentric, but he's very reliable. He looks after this place like you wouldn't believe. Has for years and years. Since I was a little kid. All one hundred acres of it. Almost all woods, but over there… a bass pond's back in there." She gestured toward the woods as we drove slowly by. We had turned off onto a gravel road about a quarter mile back, and both sides of the road were hardwoods and loblolly pines.

A giant sized black mailbox and a *No Trespassing* sign were positioned a few feet from the entrance to the circular shell driveway of the main house. Lenny turned the wheel and the Charger crunched over the gravel as she slowly drove at least a hundred feet toward the main house.

"Place looks great." That hardly needed saying. The grounds were clipped and mowed. The bushes lining the circular gravel driveway were trimmed so flat on top you could lay your plate on them and eat your lunch. But I wasn't prepared for that house. It was a long, long glass and log structure...couldn't say cabin. Two stories with redwood balconies running along the front, and a porch so wide you could ride horseback from one side to the other.

"This is a camp?"

She laughed. "That's what they call it. Come on. Let's get our stuff and I'll show you around."

I followed her inside with the suitcases through the thick carved front door. The house had the strong clean smell of sage. "Smells great in here."

"Quintus always smudges the house before we come up. Like the Indians do. Burns sage in a skillet and walks the smoke all through the house. Never a musty smell in here. He always makes it smell fresh for us. He's got some Comanche in him way back."

"Where's Quintus now?"

"Probably down in his trailer back there in the woods. He'll come by later to make sure we have everything we need. He always stocks the refrigerator when one of us is coming up. Want a beer after that long drive?"

"Sure. Where do you want me to park the luggage?"

She pointed toward the stairs. "Up there. My room is next to the master bedroom. To the right. You can tell. It's the one with the old quilt on the bed."

I took the luggage up, found her spacious room and placed the suitcases on luggage racks, then took a minute to look in on the enormous high-ceilinged wood paneled master bedroom. I blinked at the size of it, then went back downstairs and found her busy thawing steaks and vegetables in the immense kitchen.

It was crazy to call this a camp when the kitchen alone was big enough for a restaurant. A huge stainless refrigerator and a granite topped island took up the center space. Copper skillets and saucepans hung from a black wrought iron rack over the island and several chrome and black-cushioned bar stools bordered it. A nest of chef's knives was housed in a wooden rack over the butcher's block table close to the stove, and there were enough cabinets for three normal kitchens.

Terra cotta Mexican tiles covered the floor, and small decorative Mexican tiles covered the back wall of the stainless double sink. An open louvered door led to a pantry closet off the kitchen large enough for three or four homeless people to live. Inside the pantry, floor to ceiling shelves were fully stocked with cans and jars of food and condiments. Another louvered door led to a laundry room with industrial sized washer and dryer. More ceiling to floor shelves held stacks of towels, sheets, blankets and some neatly folded clothes.

"You're kidding, right? This is your family's *camp*?"

She laughed and took two beers out of the refrigerator. "Did I tell you my father is a show-off? He's always working to impress people. He throws big weekend parties here for political friends. He's got his eye on the governor's mansion."

"I don't think the governor's mansion will be big enough to suit him."

"My father is a piece of work…and did I mention that I hate his guts? He stole this camp for a fourth of what it's worth cause of a bank V.P. buddy who called him an hour after the bank board made their decision to foreclose. So he worked a sweetheart deal. The best places never come on the market you know, thanks to what goes on behind the scenes. *Never* underestimate what damage a twisted weasel banker and a crooked lawyer can get away with. If the public only knew the shit that goes on behind closed doors, there'd be blood in the streets. Why do you think I work in a nudie bar? I do it to embarrass him, that's why. He's a con man, and all his worthless scheming friends are also."

"You really get angry about it, huh?"

"Oh, yeah. I used to idolize my father as a kid. Then I started piecing together all the crap he and his so called professional friends get away with… the ways they slice and dice their way to slick profits. Makes me sick. At least with the street thugs you know what you're getting up front cause they dress the part. These so called respectable thieves hide behind their suits and ties. Creeps me out."

She nodded toward the back door. "Enough of all that. Come on. Let's take these outside onto the deck. We can relax from our trip." She whistled for Bijou as we were going outside.

We took our beers out onto the back deck and relaxed back against soft green mats covering the redwood chaises. The deck overlooked thick piney woods surrounding a broad sloping expanse of at least an acre of lush mowed grass. Fifty foot long raised flower beds were densely packed with red, orange and gold flowers. I recognized some of them: petunias, roses, and red, purple, and white salvia. The air was fresh and laced with the scent of pine. The sky was beginning to fade from the bright blue it had been earlier, and was subtly slipping into twilight.

The chaises were close enough together so she could take my hand, and this surprised me enough that I quickly glanced over at her, but she just kept staring straight ahead as though nothing out of the ordinary had occurred. We sat like that for a long while sipping our beers and quietly holding hands, as I kept trying to keep up with what was going on.

My suitcase was upstairs next to her suitcase in the bedroom of a house luxurious enough to be featured in an elite slick magazine. I was holding hands with a woman who has the figure for, and could easily be the centerfold in Playboy, and this whole trip was *her* idea. She was thawing sirloins for our supper, and it looked very much like we were about to spend the night in the same bed together. Even more remarkable, I barely knew this woman, no pun intended. What the hell did all this add up to? *Don't ask!* I told myself. *Thinking will only get you in trouble. Don't be a schmuck. Enjoy it while it lasts.*

When we'd finished our beers, we went back inside for some snacks and then took bowls of chips and dip on trays back outside onto the deck along with more beers. By then, we needed porch lights and they all came on at once with a timer, and a few floods dramatically lighted the expanse of lawn. Once we finished eating, we carried the trays back into the kitchen, put Bijou back into the house and then returned to the deck.

Quintus came strolling across the lawn from his trailer back in the woods a few minutes later. He walked with a slight limp, wore baggy, creaseless trousers and a wrinkled khaki shirt. Two black shepherds trotted by his side. As he came closer, with the shaggy eyebrows and long gray hair, he could have easily been mistaken for a homeless man living on the streets. He appeared aged with a network of wrinkles on his cheeks and a sagging chin line. His lower lip was swollen with a plug of tobacco, and his hair was held back by a strip of rawhide tied at the nape of his neck. He wore a faded gray fedora adorned with a black grosgrain ribbon with a bright orange feather stuck into it. He kept himself in shape though; his stomach was flat and his shoulders broad. His sleeves were rolled up and his arm muscles well defined.

"Good evening, Miss Lenny. Glad to see you made it up here safe."

"Thank you, Quintus. Same back at you. This is my friend, Harris Viator. We'll be staying over a day or two."

I stood up and shook hands with him. His hands were callused and much rougher than mine. His grip was strong. "Good to meet you."

"Same here. You all going to need anything? You found the food to your liking?"

"It's all great, Quintus. Thank you so much. And the grounds look wonderful. Makes me want to roll around in the grass."

"You used to do that when you were little."

Lenny scratched the dogs' ears. "I see Shooter isn't missing any meals."

"He's been steadily putting on weight."

"Shooter was dropped off by unknown parties last year. Dumped here," Lenny explained to me. "His ribs were showing, and he acted scared."

"Shooter's still jumpy. Startles easy. I think they beat him."

Lenny massaged the dog down his back. "Shooter and Jet sleep by Quintus' bed. Right, Quintus?"

"Every night. They each have their own rug by the bed. Wake me up to go out if there's anything going on outside. But I don't let them out. Coyotes. Coyotes got the Doberman up the road and the Campbells' pit bull also. All in the same night. Pieces of them scattered around the man's yard."

"That's awful, Quintus. Make sure you keep Jet and Shooter inside."

"We make our rounds each night and then again before dawn. I never sleep more than four or five hours, so we patrol the grounds. Sentry duty."

"Makes me feel safe, Quintus."

"Right. That's the idea." He wiped his mouth with the back of his hand. "Well, I'm going back down if you don't need anything more. Just ring the bell if I can do anything for you." Quintus nodded at me and tipped his hat to Lenny.

Lenny pointed to the large iron dinner bell hanging from a pole to the side of the terrace. "I ring that if there's something wrong. It's loud enough to wake the dead."

We said our good nights, and watched silently as Quintus made his way back down the rise toward the woods and his trailer, with Jet and Shooter close to his side.

As he stepped onto the narrow path through the woods to his clearing, I took Lenny's hand.

"Quintus. Odd name. What's his last name?" I asked.

"I don't even know," she laughed. "Isn't that something? After all these years? We just call him Quintus. It could be Ferguson maybe. Or wait. Maybe it's Donaldson." She shook her head. "Just can't remember for sure."

"His accent's not Louisiana."

"Not really. Who knows where Quintus started out? He's okay though. He's been there for me for years. And he's gotten me out of some nasty situations with snakes and once a skunk. I feel safe around him." She slid her legs around on the chaise. "You about ready to go in?"

She unfolded herself from the low chaise and stood, looking down at me. "I need a bath after that long drive and before I start cooking. You mind?"

I tried to act nonchalant, but the woman took my breath away. *Be cool,* I told myself as I followed her into the house. "Come on up with me. You can talk to me through the bathroom door."

We took drinks upstairs, and she slipped out of her shoes as we entered the bedroom. "I won't be long," she said as she disappeared into the bathroom, closing the door after herself, but leaving it open a crack. "Don't go away," she said, and in a moment, I heard water gushing into the tub and pictured her peeling off her clothes. That wasn't hard to do as I'd already watched her peeling off her clothes many times already.

It had been years since I'd slept with anyone but my wife. Over ten years in fact, and I felt nervous as I stood waiting at the window of the bedroom looking out at the woods. In a few minutes the scent of jasmine spilled out from the half open bathroom door. I breathed deeply of it and although I was looking out at the mixture of hardwoods and pine, I was picturing Lenny's beautiful body slipping into the sudsy bathwater.

She splashed around in there for a while, and after what seemed like half an hour but was probably only around ten minutes, she called out, "Hey, aren't you going to come scrub my back for me?" I peeled off my shirt, tossed it over a chair and entered the steamy bathroom. She was submerged in iridescent bubbles almost up to her breasts, and even though they were covered with bubbles, it was as though she was doing one of her teasing routines on stage. Her hair was clipped up on top of her head in a twist, and damp curls trailed onto her forehead. She laughed at me as I stared at her, and she slapped the water with the palms of her hands like a little kid playing in the bathwater.

"Well, come on. What the hell are you waiting for? Yesterday?"

It was right about that time that the old, reliable lizard brain woke up, and its message was clear and direct: *Outta the way, chump! I'm taking over now.*

14

RENARD'S DISAPPEARANCE

We lay naked on her bed together recovering from that first sexual experience, still breathing hard and glistening with sweat. That smell of jasmine from the bathtub still filtered through the steamy scent of sex like we were in a mist. "Whew!" she finally said. "You're something else." She kissed me on the shoulder, the throat and the mouth then rolled to the side of the bed. "Hungry? It feels like supper time."

She padded to the walk-in closet, pulled a terry robe off a hanger, and slipped into it. I pulled on my jeans and a fresh tee shirt, and followed her downstairs to grill the steaks. I tended to the beef, while she put together a salad. After pulling up the barstools to the kitchen island, we ate as greedily as we'd gone at the lovemaking upstairs for the past hour. We also drank most of one of her father's prize bottles of wine that he kept in a hidden case in the walk in closet of the master bedroom.

"He'll never miss it," she assured me when she brought it out of hiding, "but even if he did, so what? He just keeps it around to impress certain people when they come down from Baton Rouge. He could care less about fine wine. He's just as happy with a Bud. But everything is about image with him."

"You're a hard woman."

"Like I said, there's no love lost there. He lost it a long time ago. I used to think the sun rose and set in him until I woke up to the fact that he's a selfish pig who will do anything to get ahead. My mother still doesn't see it, but she loves him and love is blind as they say."

"Maybe he'd rather have a beer, but I'm loving it," I said as I poured us each another glassful. "No wonder people fork over fifty bucks for a bottle of wine."

"Fifty bucks? More like a hundred and fifty. But he gets cases of it gratis as thanks from one of the nastier clients that he does shady legal favors for."

"And how do you know his secrets if you stay away from him?"

"I'm not above eavesdropping when he's in his study with one of his pals back at the house. I've had a hidey place since I was a little girl. He doesn't even remember there's a back door to the closet in his office where he stores old file boxes. I've picked up enough bits and pieces over the years to figure out some of his schemes. Real estate scams and kickbacks from realtor buddies he recommends to clients. Then a piece of the action under the table after the realtor flips a property they low-balled up front to the victim. There's money laundering in the mix as well, but I couldn't prove any of it, or trust me, I would. His favorite saying when some friend tries to brag about how he pulled some dirty deal off is, 'Don't tell me. I don't want to know.' He's a piece of work my father is." She grimaced in disgust. "But let's not talk any more about Lucien. Why spoil a blissful few days together, huh?"

"Agreed."

"Cheers," she toasted. "I'm so glad you came up here with me." She looked wistful there for a moment, and then looked fully into my eyes. "Really, really glad.

"To think when I met you in Nick's office that day that we'd end up like this together in just a couple of months. Life's crazy, huh? You never know what's going to happen next…and that's the way I like it."

She took a prim sip of the wine and set the stem glass down carefully on the gleaming granite. "Did you…you know…feel anything when you first met me?"

"How do you mean?"

"Like did you want to get to know me better? Were you attracted to me?" She sounded almost shy.

"What? Who wouldn't be?"

"Just asking," she said. "Cause I felt something right away. Just curious if it was mutual." She passed a hand slowly over my chest and let it rest lightly on my thigh. "Why don't we clean this up and go back upstairs? Or would you rather watch a movie? We've got plenty of movies here in the den. Whatever you want. There must be a hundred DVDs in there at least."

"I don't think I could keep my mind on a movie right now."

"Me either. So let's clean the kitchen up and go back upstairs then." She leaned over and kissed me with the taste of wine on her lips, her robe falling open enough to show me again what I was in for. The wine we'd drunk and the sight of her nakedness made me lightheaded. The woman was driving me crazy. The kitchen had plenty of windows and I hoped Quintus wasn't walking the dogs anywhere near the house and able to see her. I tucked her back into the terry cloth and wrapped the robe tighter around her.

"Prude," she smiled.

"I don't want anyone wandering around outside to see those," I said.

"No one's around for miles except Quintus. And right now, he's watching the nightly news. You can set your watch by him."

I kept it together enough to help her load the dishwasher, put things away, and wipe off the counters. You know how it is when you are suddenly immersed in the heat of a new found passion. Nothing is the same, and you feel like that other person must have a magnet hidden in there somewhere because you can't stay away from them. This kind of delirium causes many people to behave in irrational ways. Territorial. I'd seen it too many times as a cop, and now I was feeling it too. But no man would blame me. Not if they ever laid eyes on Lenny.

And so it was that within an hour of going downstairs, we were back upstairs again falling onto the already rumpled king-sized bed. The quilt was lying on the floor, the pillows scattered all over, and the blue sheets were still damp, but we didn't even bother to straighten anything out or fluff the pillows. There was no time; we were in too much of a rush. But then as things settled down and we became more familiar with each other, the frantic part was over, and we could take it easy and slow and make it last until we were ready to take a break and get some sleep.

It was somewhere around midnight when we were lying in each other's arms, cooling off and resting that I casually asked her why she hated her father so much that she would take a job stripping. I was already thinking up ways I could get her off that stage and out of the club. Not being judgmental about other strippers, but I didn't like the idea of other men staring at Lenny's naked body. All right for me, not for them. Even though things were steamy and intense between us, I knew I didn't have any right. And I felt uneasy because I felt myself getting in deeper each hour that we were together.

The cynic in me stepped in then, *Hey, asshole. Back off. How do you know you're not one of many she's brought up here for a few days? Your ego is running away with you. Calm down.* But the way she looked at me and the way she held onto me so tightly made me believe this was as important to her as it was to me.

"How is it that a gorgeous woman like you is not spoken for?" I asked, still in disbelief that she was lying next to me.

"I'll tell you why. Because my father made the love of my life disappear almost a year ago. Poof!"

She blew out a puff of air. "Gone. Just like that. He's the devil incarnate." She frowned and turned her head away.

"What do you mean disappeared? What happened?"

"Disappear! Just what I said. My father didn't like Renard…at all. The feeling was mutual by the way. And my father is not above clearing any obstacles away whatever they are. That's what I believe, but I won't get anybody to listen to me. They would just think I'm crazy." She bit off the words and slowly formed her hands into tight fists.

"Disappear? What do you mean?"

"What do you think I mean?" She rubbed the back of her hand across her mouth.

"You mean like run him off?"

"That's a nice way of putting it."

"Surely you don't think…"

"What else? He didn't like Ren. Renard. A swamp Cajun living on a houseboat in the Basin? Please! He hoped I'd marry someone who could do him some good. A rung up. Somebody who could help him in a run for the state legislature. Remember what I told you…his evil eye is on the Governor's mansion, believe it or not. Some fantasy, huh?" She squeezed her eyes shut. "Ha. Governor Badon. Only a narcissistic ego maniac like my father could come up with that."

"Why didn't he like Renard?"

"Cause Ren is….was, a trapper. A fisherman. One of those dark-skinned swamp Cajuns…had some Chitimacha Indian in his bloodline. That just wouldn't fit into any of Lucien's plans for the future."

"What makes you think Renard is dead?'

"I *know*. There are just things you know. But I can't prove it. And if I can't find his body somewhere to even prove he's dead, I sure can't prove that evil bastard had him killed." She grasped a handful of the sheet and twisted it like she was wringing it out.

Moths batted against the porch light just outside the window.

"Tell me more about this." I leaned on one elbow and watched her carefully, but didn't touch her, not wanting to interrupt. The heat of her anger was causing her perfume to rise, and I could see the pulse beating at her temple as her heart rate picked up.

"Maybe I've said enough for now. I don't know you well enough...yet."

"We just had all this…" I motioned toward the twisted sheets, "…. but you don't know me well enough?"

"That's different. Sex is one thing. Secrets are another."

I waited, still not touching her, but didn't take my eyes off her. An owl hooted from the woods not far from the bedroom windows, then another answered from deep in the woods to the rear of the house, back near Quintus' trailer.

"So, you have these theories…but zero evidence. That right?"

"I'm going to get some evidence though. Some day, somehow. That's where I hope you're going to help me."

"Me? Is that what this is all about?" I felt something hit me like a cold draft in the room.

"You mean like I brought you up here to seduce you and then use you? You mean like that?" She smoothed a hand over my chest. "You think I faked all this?"

I didn't answer.

She kissed my neck and then raised up and kissed me lightly on the mouth. "I wasn't faking anything. I'm not that good of an actress. But I admit to liking that whole policeman thing. Made me hope you might have a way of looking at this that I haven't thought of."

The owls kept hooting back and forth as I remained silent thinking about what she said, and wondering if I was being played.

"Anyhow," she said absently. "Sounds like you have your own story to tell."

"Don't know you well enough," I countered.

She smiled. "Fair enough. You keep your secrets to yourself, and I'll keep mine to myself then." She rolled her body sideways so she was facing the wall.

I put a tentative hand on her shoulder. "Come on. Tell me more about this. You've got me interested."

There was a long silence. The moths kept fluttering and batting at the light at the head of the outside balcony and stairs. The owls' hooting grew muffled as they flew further from the house. Some coyotes yipped in the distance, the sound growing steadily louder as their nightly run came closer to the camp.

"I'll tell you more if you vow you'll never repeat any of this. I want my father to think he got away with it. Then one of these days, I'll trap him somehow. Just haven't figured it out yet."

"You can tell me."

"Renard and I were in this bed. It was like two in the morning when he woke up hearing something outside. He was pulling on his jeans when I woke up. 'What are you doing?' I asked. 'I heard something out there. Just going to check it out. Go back to sleep,' he says. He went right out through those French doors and down the outside stairs there." She pointed toward the closed balcony doors.

"He said to go back to sleep, so that's what I did… to my shame. We'd been up late watching movies and talking and I was groggy with sleep. If you knew Ren, you'd know how it was with him. He took care of things. As long as I was with him, I didn't worry about anything. So I felt altogether safe and went back to sleep. I slept until morning and when I woke up, he was still gone." She spoke toward the wall, not meeting my eyes as though she was still bearing the burden of guilt for going back to sleep that night.

"And then what?"

"Then I went outside looking for him. Calling for him. Went for Quintus down at his trailer. We hiked all around for an hour or so, then I came back and started calling people. His brother. His sisters. His friends. Nobody had heard from him. Then I called the law. Put on a pot of coffee, ate some breakfast and went out there again calling, searching, and hiking around. Quintus and I wandered the property all that day with the dogs looking for Ren.

"By the next day, the local police, Chief Roderick and two others came out and helped us search. Then some of the other residents out here, from other camps joined us. Hunters, their wives and girl friends. Even their kids helped us on the hunt. Ren's brother Jo-Jo came up. We stayed at it all day thinking he'd broken a leg or something.

"My father made a big show of hiring a helicopter pilot to scout the area. He brought in a cook to grill chicken, burgers and sausages for everybody. Brought cases of bottled water. A restaurant sized urn to make continuous coffee. He wasn't fooling me. I knew he had done something, but I kept it to myself. Biding my time."

"Where was your mother all this time?"

"My mother is a wuss. She stayed home like he told her to."

"So the search covered the property and then everybody gave up?"

"They finally decided he must have taken off and left me, and that I'd eventually hear from him. Jo-Jo and I knew differently. Jo-Jo knew he'd never take off without telling me and his brother. Roderick called it off, and everybody drifted away. It was already dark out anyhow. My father told me to go back to town, but Jo-Jo stayed here with me, and we stayed another week just in case something turned up. Some clue. Anything at all that might give us a lead. Finally, we gave up and went home. Me to pack my things and leave my father's house to get away from him and rent an apartment. Jo-Jo rented his own house out and took over Ren's houseboat out in the Basin. He keeps hoping somehow Ren will show up there. I talk to Jo-Jo every week on the phone. Sometimes he comes by the apartment."

"And you say this happened how long ago?"

"Just a little over six months ago."

"And this is when you got the idea to work at the club?"

She nodded. "I wanted to embarrass my father. I was filled with rage, and this was the best way I could think of to express it. How's it look for a man who wants to run for office to have a daughter working at a low-life strip joint? Oh, and don't worry, he *was* furious when he found out what I was doing. I thought he'd pop a blood vessel and croak on the spot. A lawyer friend of his came in there one night, saw me, and tripped all over himself running out of there to go rat me out to him." She laughed with delight. "The bastard. Hire somebody to get rid of the love of my life and see what happens, you scum!"

"Did he go to the club and try to haul you out of there?"

"Oh, no. He would never make a scene like that. He wouldn't even give me the satisfaction of seeing him all red in the face and throwing a fit. I heard about it from little sister. She's a Momma's girl and does everything she's told to. Sissy's the total opposite of me, but she's a good kid in spite of it all. A goody-goody. Wouldn't say shit if she had a mouthful of it as they say." Lenny paused to yawn and stretch, then curled up against me.

"One of my father's closest buddies, this sleaze realtor, Moe, comes in there to stare at me often enough. He's tried for years to get me to go out with him. You've seen him in there. He's always alone and sits apart from everybody at the bar hoping nobody recognizes him. I know damn well he had one of his office buildings torched one night for the insurance money. I wouldn't go out with that dirt bagger if he was the last man on earth."

"That's a serious accusation. Arson for insurance fraud earns hard time in Angola."

"You think maybe I'm making this up? That hiding place in my father's study at home that he never knew about? I heard Moe boasting about the fat check he got from the insurance company for the building fire. My father said, 'Stop! Don't want to hear anything about it.' What does that tell you?"

"A childhood memory? I wouldn't bet on it."

"I would. You don't know my father and you don't know Moe. Two textbook sociopaths."

"So you went around eavesdropping on people when you were little?"

"The only way I could get near to my father. He was always too busy for any of us. When I was little, I used to like to be near him any way I could, even if it meant sneaking into that closet."

"Little spy tactics, huh?" I smoothed her hair and caressed her shoulder.

"Comes in handy." She took my hand and passed the back of it against her face. "Hell, that's enough of that story. More in the next installment. Revenge is a dish best served cold as they say."

She slipped her arms around me, tucking her head against my chest. "Sorry for the sordid story, but you asked for it."

"Yes, I did. But you've said nothing to convince me your father had anything to do with it."

"Renard would never have run out on me. We were headed for the altar. I know my man. We were as tight as two people can be. We were like this." She crossed her index and middle fingers. "He never would have left me all alone like this willingly."

"Now of that you don't have to convince me. A man would have to be an idiot to leave you. But you have no evidence whatsoever. I get it that you think your father is dishonest, but that doesn't prove he got rid of your boy friend. Not at all."

"That's because you don't know my father. He's capable of anything, has no scruples and thinks he's entirely above the law. The only thing wrong with breaking the law is getting caught at it. That's how he does business. And how all his close friends do business."

"Doesn't matter. You still have no evidence."

"I will one of these days, and I won't give up looking for it."

We kissed goodnight and she closed her eyes with her head tucked against my shoulder and my arms around her. She had flung one leg over mine and when her breathing deepened and slowed, I knew she was asleep. But her story kept me awake for another half hour as I thought back over all the things she'd told me and tried to make sense of the puzzle.

Finally, the warmth of her body and the gentle hooting of the owls far away and the faint yips of the vanishing coyotes lulled me to sleep, and we slept like that, wrapped closely together until dawn.

15

PICKING UP A SCENT

The next day we took a walk with Bijou through the woods to the west of the house to the pond. The ground was covered with a carpet of pine needles and the fresh smell of pine filled the warm air as birds sang above us and flitted back and forth over our heads like a Disney movie. The pond lay roughly a quarter mile from the house and was in the middle of a clearing covered with small golden daisies, goldenrod and other wildflowers along with high grasses gone to seed. Quintus kept a path cleared through the high grass, and we followed it down to the water's edge.

"I can't stay here long. It upsets me. They dragged the pond with heavy chains and hooks to make sure Renard hadn't somehow fallen in and drowned. I keep backflashing on them doing that whenever I see this place."

"Let's leave then."

"It's okay. I have to get over it sometime."

I surveyed the wide pond and asked if they had any rods back at the house. "We could be eating fresh bass for supper."

"I'll look in the storeroom for you if you want. But I'm thawing some deer steaks for tonight."

We sat on a rough plank bench as Bijou sniffed around in the grass and snapped at shimmering green dragonflies. Bees were buzzing around and visiting some purple flowered bull thistles scattered in the high native grasses that stretched from the edge of the piney woods to the pond and far beyond to the trees lining the road. We sat quietly enjoying the warmth of the sun and the drowsy sounds all around us, so relaxing that my eyelids felt heavy.

Lenny tilted her head toward mine and lightly stroked my leg, so that I was going even deeper into a trance with the peacefulness of the scene. But then she suddenly interrupted this blissful state and sat up straight.

"You know, I was thinking about that story you told me," she said, "and I was wondering why that name Rocco sounded familiar. I remember now one of the girls at the club saying something about a Rocco."

My eyes snapped wide open, and I turned my head to give her my full attention.

"I think she...Amber...said something about her ex having a friend named Rocco."

"When was this?" I tried not to sound too eager, but I wasn't successful and my tone was sharp.

She looked up and to the right, then shifted her eyes to the left, searching for the answer. "Maybe, I don't know… a couple of months ago."

"You ever meet Amber's ex?" Again I tried to sound casual, but the words came out like I was interrogating her.

"No."

"So you don't know where he is now?"

"Not really. But I do know he raises pot somewhere. That's the reason they broke up. Amber didn't want to have anything to do with that. He bought land out of the area when they split. Maybe even out of state. I can't remember exactly."

I was on full alert by then. "When we get back, can you find out where he is now from her?"

"Sure. I'll think of some reason to ask her."

"Don't let on that I'm interested."

"Do I look that dumb to you, Mister?" she laughed. Bijou jumped halfway into the air and snapped at an iridescent dragonfly, missing it by an inch. The sun grew brighter, and I pulled the visor of my cap down to block it. A bass jumped in the center of the pond and splashed down. Bijou got excited then, put his nose to the ground and snuffled off through the grass. He had just caught an intriguing scent, and was off and running like a horse out of the gate.

"I hope he doesn't run into any of those fire ant mounds. Insects love Bijou. If he gets any bites, I'll have to give him Benadryl and rub Cortisone ointment on him for two weeks."

As we continued to bask in the sun holding hands and watching Bijou racing around chasing butterflies and chameleons, I felt as excited as he was by this lead Lenny had just given me. And just like the little hard headed terrier, I had picked up a scent and would keep my nose to the ground until I'd followed the trail to anywhere it took me. Anything to get my hands once more on Rocco.

Lenny wanted me to somehow figure out how to find her missing boyfriend, dead or alive, but I was much more interested in finding Rocco, and I wanted him to be very much alive. I had plans for him. Dead wouldn't work. He had to be alive otherwise he couldn't clear my name. And he was going to have to pay me back somehow for at least some of my losses. Lenny had her agenda, and I had mine.

I looked calm that day in the sun by the pond, but my thoughts were racing, and the blood was humming through my veins just as lively as the bees so hard at work in the field around us.

16

CLUELESS

We stayed over one more night. Lenny and I were so into each other that I almost forgot why she chose me in the first place, and how she was using me to help her find her missing boy friend. So use me. Just being near her felt so good, I didn't really care if she was using me or not. I would have volunteered to be used from the get go if I'd only known that was the plan. Our attraction was strong. If we took a walk, we'd stop after half a mile and head back to the house. If we started to watch a movie, we'd start up all over again on the couch in the den and let the movie play on while we ignored it and started yanking off our clothes.

Lenny was playful and goofed around a lot. Once we were fixing snacks in the kitchen when Quintus walked up to the back door, saw us messing around through the window and backed off without knocking, his eyes not on me, but on Lenny's pulled up skirt while she was flashing me. She didn't see him, so I quick stepped in front of her to shield her from view. I hadn't liked the expression on his face when he saw her bare skin. He'd backed up too slowly, and his gaze had lingered too long.

"We just had some company," I said.

"Huh, what?" She looked out the window and saw Quintus walking back down the sloping lawn toward the woods. "Oh, just Quintus? What's the matter?"

"He got an eyeful."

She made a dismissive gesture with her hand. "Oh, so what? Hope he doesn't catch a stroke over it."

"You need to be more careful though."

"Don't worry about Quintus. Anyhow, that's not the first time. He's caught me nude sun bathing on the balcony and on the deck. He's harmless."

"So it doesn't bother you if men see you naked?" I realized what I'd just said and quickly corrected it. "I mean off the job."

"So you got something against the human body?" There was an edge to her voice.

"No, it's not that. It's a matter of drawing attention where it might get you into trouble one day."

She put a hand on her hip. "Oh, so you're one of those who likes to say, 'She asked for it,' if a woman gets raped?"

"Lenny! Take it easy. What I'm saying is, bare naked women get to men. Some of the men aren't so stable they can handle it. You know that." I spoke slowly as if talking to a child.

"So we have to be penalized and cover up and hide our natural skin from the freaks of nature? Is that it? Be ashamed of our bodies cause of a few idiots?" She pursed her lips.

"Well, yeah. If you want to put it that way. It's not to protect them…it's to protect you!"

She clicked her fingers a few times. "Hear this, Harris. You sound like Renard. He had similar things to say on this subject. And I'll tell you exactly what I told him…I'll dress as I please when I please. And I don't like being told what to do…especially in my own house." She turned and opened the refrigerator to close down the conversation. "Enough of this arguing. Let's have another beer."

I'd seen too many bad things happen around women who let their guard down, but I dropped it, and didn't push any further regarding boundaries and how she could better look after herself. I didn't want to come off as an overbearing jerk and spoil the idyllic time we were having that was already coming to a close much too quickly.

So I changed the subject and suggested we take a ride around the property in one of the camp's 4-wheelers. There were two black Kawasaki ATVs in one of the metal storage buildings, and we had toured the place once before with one of them. We'd had a good time, so much so that it cried out for a repeat. We rode around the property, saw a few deer, counted ten hawks, and some rabbits, and then rode up and down the gravel road for an hour, where we saw six vultures picking at roadkill…a smashed possum.

There was an old cypress farmhouse from the twenties toward the back of the property and we followed a dusty tree lined dirt lane back to see it. It had a rusty tin roof and even a leaning old style cypress plank outhouse.

"That's a nice old house. How come Quintus doesn't live in it?"

"Oh, I don't know. He used to, but he wanted to be closer to the main house. So my father had that trailer brought in for him about five years ago."

"I grew up in a house like that."

"It's just used for storage now."

"You know that outhouses are good places to look for antique bottles and such. Ever check it out?"

"No. Why would I want old bottles anyhow?"

"Not just bottles. Things get dropped down into outhouses over time. Loose change. You name it."

She tilted her head and gave it a second look. "I know one thing. It's a three holer." She laughed. "Want to see?"

"I believe you. They had to make room for all the kids in the family in the old days."

"I actually used it a few times when I was exploring out here and had to go really bad. There's wasp nests and mud daubers in there, I know that much." She squirmed in the seat. "Don't get me started on wasps. Probably hornets too. Ever get stung by a hornet?"

"Too many times."

"Once is enough."

We circled the house a few times. The yard needed mowing and glossy buttercups and dandelions flashed bright yellow throughout the high grass. There was a rain barrel under the eaves and an upside down wheelbarrow by the front steps. Besides the outhouse there were two cypress tool sheds and a rusted pickup stored in a pole barn.

A faded orange cat took off running from a pile of tires at the back of the barn when we passed by.

"Did you know you had a barn cat?" I asked.

"Oh, they come and go. Keeps the rats down."

After checking out the old homestead, we got thirsty and decided to head back to the main house. By then, the dirt lane was dappled with sunlight through overhanging branches as the afternoon was fast getting away from us.

I'd promised Quintus I'd stop by the trailer and help him move a couch, so after we'd put away the 4-wheeler, I headed over there, and Lenny went upstairs to take a bath. We weren't looking forward to having to leave our hideaway and go back to our separate living quarters in Ida, and to the club where we had to pretend we hardly knew each other. "The day is slipping away. We only have one more night together," she'd said with a glum expression as she started up the stairs.

When I reached the trailer, he opened the door, greeted me, and asked me to help him carry an old couch out of his trailer that he was replacing with a newer one that one of the neighbors had given him. Since the dogs had helped break down the old one, it was only a matter of time before the newer model was lumpy and worn also. We set it outside under a metal overhang next to the trailer that formed an outdoor room of sorts. Quintus laid a blue tarp over it to keep it dry. "What the hell. I can take a nap out here now if I want."

Also under the overhang was a cylindrical three-foot high wood-burning stove with a black tea kettle resting on its cast iron lid. I pictured Quintus in wintertime holding out his hands and warming them as he waited for his dinner to cook over the coals. Beyond the overhang, a muddy golf cart with a striped awning was parked next to a tan Ford 150. The bed of the pickup held a few hay bales and a galvanized tool box.

He kept the inside of the trailer as clean as he could with two big dogs sharing his space. We set the newer couch against the wall across from a small TV set on a dated stereo cabinet. He had a few copper bowls filled with a variety of smooth black and grey stones on the table next to a thick family Bible opened to Isaiah 53. Above the table, a long black feather was tucked into the frame of a faded print of a dying Indian on horseback. A silver St. Christopher medal on a chain dangled from a handmade varnished wooden cross that hung near the door, above a four pegged board holding several camo visor caps and a few leather leashes. A shotgun leaned against the wall by the door.

"You Catholic?" I asked, pointing to the St. Christopher medal.

"No. Somebody lost that in town. I found it in a gutter and cleaned it up. When I go, I go to a Pentecostal Church on the far side of town, but I hardly ever make it over there."

"You must be like me. Once in a while I get to Mass. Something always seems to get in the way of me going every week."

"Yep. Same here. Always something." He held up a finger. "Wait just a minute. Be right back." He walked down a narrow dark hallway to the rear of the trailer.

"Before I do anything else, I'm going to cover this couch," he said returning in a moment, and unfurling a green striped sheet. I took two corners of it and we lowered it over the couch so he could carefully tuck it into the cushions. "This way they won't mess the couch up quite as fast. Maybe I can keep it nice for a while." The sheet didn't go with the black and red Indian rug that was nailed on the wall above the couch, but Quintus wasn't much of a decorator, and I was sure the dogs wouldn't mind.

"You want a beer?" he offered as he stood back and eyed the way the couch looked with the covering sheet. One of the shepherds sniffed the couch, then stepped up on it and after going around in circles a few times, curled into a ball. The other one lapping at a water bowl on the floor of the kitchen finished drinking and trotted into the living room to check out the couch. He also carefully sniffed around, then slowly eased up on the cushions and leaned comfortably against the first dog as he settled in for a nap.

"No thanks. Just finished one up at the house. I better be getting back to see what Lenny is up to."

"Well, thanks a lot for coming by to help then."

"Any time." He shook hands with an energy that expressed his appreciation and gave me a crooked smile. Right after that I left, slowly walking back toward the main house as a brown field rabbit ducked back into the cover of a two-cord wood pile, a stump for splitting wood beside it. Quintus had an enviable job and a comfortable setting with plenty of privacy. It was a job I envied.

We had planned to cook deer sausage and potatoes for supper, and I was beginning to feel hungry, but when I got to the house Lenny was upstairs calling to me from the balcony. I went up the outside steps to the bedroom, and once I passed through the French doors, she greeted me with a kiss and a cold one. "Drink up, and then lie down. You've been lifting couches and helping Quintus, and now I'm going to give you a massage as your reward."

She was barefoot and wearing a short little see-through gauzy dress, her hair all loose and freshly washed. I forgot all about the deer sausage and did what she said. I drank up and then lay down. I can be very cooperative when I want to be.

17

BIJOU

The next morning we got up early, scrambled eggs, heated some rolls, and ate breakfast out on the deck so we could have a last look at the piney woods and the clear blue open sky. Then after straightening the place up, we walked down to Quintus' trailer to say goodbye. Lenny handed him a rolled up bill for a tip, and I reached in my pocket for a bill, but she signaled not to do that. We thanked him for taking care of everything, and then we started back up the sloping lawn to the house.

"How come you stopped me from giving the guy a tip?" I asked.

"I gave him a fifty. That's enough. Don't worry, he gets a healthy paycheck plus a free place to live. Quintus isn't hurting."

"He's got it made," I said. When we got back, we packed the car, collected Bijou and reluctantly left the camp for the trip back to Ida.

As we passed through Wallace, we stopped at the general store to pick up a few snacks and drinks for the long drive home. The old frame building was roughly forty by sixty feet and sat on property that took up most of the block. It had a rusted tin roof and an overhang in the front that covered the sidewalk like a walkway. Rakes, shovels and hoes were upside down in a barrel by the front door. A push lawnmower sat beside the barrel along with a galvanized wheelbarrow and several galvanized washtubs.

Two old men sat on a wooden bench beside the for sale items and nodded to us as we walked inside the front door. It was shadowy inside, the flickering fluorescent lights set in the high ceiling above the beams did not throw enough light for the expansive store. Free standing wooden shelves held a great variety of hardware items, even a wooden barrel full of nails, along with canned goods, mops and brooms, cleaning supplies, pet supplies, auto supplies, and various miscellaneous items.

Longleaf pine boards were used in the construction of the ceiling, and straw hats and visor caps hung from long hooks attached to the rafters. High shelves ran along all the walls holding a great variety of large items, such as galvanized buckets, tubs, and even an infant sized gray coffin.

One wall in back of the counter held six shelves of various brands of liquor in quart and pint sized bottles, dozens of bottles of wine and cartons of cigarettes. There were live worms for sale, along with fishing gear, such as nets, bait buckets, hooks, sinkers, etc. While Lenny walked around picking out what she wanted for the trip, I wandered around enjoying this old store that Lenny told me had been in town for four generations.

While all this was going on, suddenly a man started yelling in front of the store Through the glass panes of the front door we could see a man holding his hand and cursing at Lenny's car. I ran outside to see what was going on with Lenny close behind me.

A man by the car was swearing at Bijou who with paws on the partially open glass of the back seat window was snarling at him, teeth exposed.

"Back off!" I ordered him, stepping between him and the car.

"That dog bit me!" he yelled, face red and breathing hard. "He needs to be put down."

"What the hell are you doing by my car, Junior?" Lenny got into the mix on the other side of the man.

"I went to pet your dog and he bit me! I'm calling my dad. He needs to be put down."

"Over my dead body, Junior. Got any more ideas?" Lenny pushed past him and stood, chin out and arms crossed, between him and the rear window.

"What's going on here?" Roderick, the Police Chief pulled up in his cruiser next to the Charger and cut the engine with his flasher on.

"Her damn dog bit me!" Junior raised his arm to show the Chief the slight puncture on the heel of his hand.

"Where's the dog? I don't see a dog."

Outraged, Junior pointed to the rear seat. He's right there!" He was so exasperated, his voice squeaked on the word 'there.'

"Why were you in Lenny's car?"

"I wasn't *in* the car. I just went to pet the dog.... and he bit me! Take him to the pound. He might have rabies."

"Idiot! You never go to pet a dog in a vehicle. The hell's the matter with you? Get outta here before she arrests you for trying to break into her car."

"What about the rabies?"

"Your dog has his shots?"

"Always."

"Go home, Junior. Help your mother hang out the wash. The dryer broke."

The young man stood jaw gaping, holding his wrist. "You're joking, right?"

"I'll show you who's joking. Go back to the house. You're disturbing the peace."

Junior glared at Lenny and at me. "We're not finished with this."

"Oh, yes, we are finished with this unless you want me to lock you up for a few nights to cool you off," the Chief assured him. "Now get moving!"

Junior finally obeyed, and shaking his head all the while passed on down the sidewalk toward the outskirts of town. The clerk at the store stood at the threshold of the front door watching the incident.

"Sorry about that, Miss Lenny. Don't know what's the matter with him. You know how Junior is. Goes off his nut once in a while. His mama spoiled him. Not my doing."

"Real glad you showed up, Chief. He wanted to kill my dog."

"Not on my watch. I'll keep an eye on him. You picking up some supplies?"

"Just some snacks for the road. We're leaving town in a few minutes."

"Meant to come out to see you but got side-tracked. Everything okay out there at the camp?"

"Everything's fine, Chief."

"You got a good man with Quintus over there looking out for you."

"That's for sure, Chief. By the way, didn't mean to be rude. This is Harris Viator, a friend from home."

The Chief touched the shiny black visor of his cap. "Nice to meet you."

"Same here, Chief." I nodded to him.

"Okay then, have a safe trip. Hurry back, Lenny." He started the patrol car and eased away from the scene at a crawl.

"Let's get out of here," Lenny said. "I picked out pretty much everything we're going to need for the trip back." She glanced over her shoulder at the store.

"Stay here with Bijou and I'll go pay for what you got so far."

She was patting Bijou and scratching behind his ears. "Poor baby. I hope you don't get rabies from biting that man."

When I returned with the paper sacks of chips and sodas, I stowed the cans on ice in the cooler on the floor in the back and slid onto the front seat. "The clerk in there wanted to know what was going on with Junior. I tell him, and he says Junior's elevator doesn't always go to the top floor."

"Sometimes it doesn't even make it off the first floor," she smiled. "Don't mind that freak. He's always been a little off. Still lives at home and he's almost thirty. Roderick keeps him on a short leash."

"Maybe that's what wrong with him."

"Could be. Open those chips, and I'll give a couple to Bijou, and I wouldn't mind popping one of those sodas either, please."

All the way home, Bijou lay halfway over Lenny's lap as she drove. We didn't talk much as neither of us was looking forward to splitting up when we got back to town. We'd gotten so used to being together the past three days and now we would have to pretend we barely knew each other at work, and have to go home to our lonely beds when we weren't working. After the last three days that would be a very unwelcome change.

When she dropped me off at the motel, I kissed her for what would be the last time for I didn't know how long.

"Hate to leave you." she said, making a face.

"Yeah. Thanks for everything. See you at the club. And please see if you can slyly find out anything about that ex of Amber's."

"I'm on it," she said, and then she gave me the keys to the trunk and I retrieved my suitcase, returned the keys to her and leaning over, kissed her one more time. I kept thinking of her after she drove off as I opened the motel room and put my gear away. The room smelled musty, so I left the door open and put the fan on in the window unit to clear the air.

After a few minutes Celeste showed up at the doorway. "Welcome home," she said all smiles. The dogs
started howling then and I followed her up the walkway to go play with them in the back yard for a while.

"I have a roast in the oven. You hungry?" she
asked as she opened the gate to the backyard for
me. The hounds were so excited they were bouncing
up and down and feverishly yelping for attention. I
kneeled down and hugged them both at once which
wasn't easy given all the commotion.

"I'm always hungry," I replied as Merle licked my
face.

"Great! Dinner will be ready in about half an
hour." She went on into the house through the back
kitchen door while I wrestled with Merle and Willie
and let them slobber and jump all over me.

18

HOT TIP

Later that evening as I was feeling drowsy and lying semi-slumped against the pillows on the bed in my room watching an old Lee Van Cleef Western, Lenny called to say goodnight.

"Everything okay at your place?" I asked.

"All's good. Bijou's curled up asleep in his bed. And I'm almost ready for bed too. So worn out."

"Long drive will do that to you."

"Already got something for you though. Told you I was on the case."

I sat up. "What? What you got?"

"That guy? That friend of Rocco's I told you about? Last Amber heard, he was growing weed up in Arkansas. Has a still too. Luther Willis."

"Where in Arkansas?"

"Somewhere up there in the woods. Near as she can remember it's somewhere not too far from Falling Waters, Arkansas. They're in the Ozarks close to the Oklahoma border."

"I've hunted with friends in north central Arkansas, near the Missouri border, but don't know the northwest part much. I'll check my road maps for it."

"He's not *in* Falling Waters. Somewhere near there though, out in Back of Beyond. That's all she knows."

"How'd you get her to tell you?"

"Just called to chat and warmed her up by asking how she'd been doing at the casino. She plays the slots there every day. Gambling addict. She's even been through Rehab up in Shreveport, but it didn't last. So anyway, I got her talking about her favorite subject...the casino. Then when she'd talked herself out, I told her I'd been up in north Louisiana at the camp, and this and that until I got to a place where I could casually ask her about her ex. Girl talk. You don't want to know."

"You're something else."

"I know it. You owe me."

"How can I pay you back?"

"Just give me some of that Cajun payback," she whispered, then laughing, she hung up on me.

I kept watching the Western, but didn't really see it. My mind was whirling. I instinctively knew this was an opening, a break, and somehow I'd have to get a few days off again from the club to go hunting in the Ozarks, and it wasn't even anywhere near hunting season yet.

19

RATTED OUT

I needn't have worried about getting some time off to go searching for Rocco in Arkansas. Five minutes after I showed up at LolliPops for work the next day, Jesse, the bartender told me Nick wanted to see me in his office. Jesse had a glum expression when he told me so I knew he knew something not good was coming my way. There was no usual greeting, no "How's it going, man?" Just a jerk of his thumb toward the office and "Nick wants to see you."

"What about?"

Jesse shrugged and kept his eyes on the dishwater as he plunged some glasses up and down on the vertical bristle scrubber in the bar sink.

My antenna went up and my stomach tightened. It felt like I was maybe getting the ax. I crossed to the halfway open office door and gave a couple of knocks before opening the door further and ducking my head in.

"You want to see me?"

"Come on in," Nick called from his desk. "Have a seat." He made a gesture toward a chair across from where he was seated. Fumbling through a stack of papers, he kept his eyes averted, then tossed a few pieces of paper into the air in disgust and leaned back in his chair.

I sat and waited expectantly as he stared at me for a moment, then smacked his hands onto the arms of his chair. "What the hell did you have to go and get hooked up with her for, you dumb fuck?"

I put on what I hoped was my most baffled expression. "What?"

"Don't pretend you don't know what the hell I'm talking about. You can't bullshit a bullshitter. You oughta know that from being a cop, for Chrissake!"

I kept my mouth shut and just looked back at him with a poker face.

He raised a hand in the air sideways and brought it down on the desk like a knife. "I told you! From the git go, I told you! Keep your clappy paws off the girls. And I *told* you not to even so much as look at Lenny. Lenny's off limits! Did I not say that? Did I not make that clear? Are you so stupid you don't get it?" He stabbed a forefinger to his temple repeatedly like I must be retarded or crazy. His face was getting red, and he brought his hand down again and again in a slicing motion to the desk. Then, some of his anger out, he took a deep breath and leaned back in the chair again. "Go on, get the fuck out of here! You're fired. Sayonara. G.F.Y."

"Who said what to you?" I sat very still, making no move to leave.

He looked at me, a puzzled expression on his face, forehead furrowed. "What the hell is it to you how I know what goes on around here? You think I'm going to tell you who ratted you out? Get outta here before I have you thrown out of here. And don't ever let me see you so much as step onto the parking lot. You're barred from LolliPops."

"You're nuts. Get some therapy," I said as I got up and walked to the door. It was mystifying, but I knew there was no point in pushing Nick to reveal his source, and if I hung around much longer it was going to get physical. I already knew how lousy jail food is and it wasn't in my plans to ever eat any of it.

When I got out into the hallway, I turned toward the Exit door. No point in saying goodbye to Jesse. He already knew what was going down. I wasn't supposed to interact with the girls anyway, so no point in saying goodbye to any of them. I just rammed the bar of the Exit door and trudged on out of there, letting the heavy steel door slam shut in back of me. And there I was, out on the street again.

So I did what any other security guard at a strip joint who was fired would do. On the way home I stopped at a gas station slash convenience store and picked up a six-pack. I planned to go home, nurse a few and work off steam doing some chores around the motel.

Once back at the motel room, I was pulling on my jeans and a tee shirt when Lenny called on my cell phone. "I just heard!" was how she began.

"Where are you?"

"In the dressing room. I'm gathering up my things and getting ready to go cuss Nick out and then I'm out the door, me too!"

"Nothing wrong with that. That place is a dead-end for you, and I hate to see you in there."

She lowered her voice. "I have an idea who snitched."

"Tell me later. I'm going to finish my beer and go mow the grass. Don't get into it with Nick. He's liable to stroke out if he knows you're leaving."

"Ha, ha. I can only wish."

She clicked off and I went on outside to start up the mower. I learned a long time ago that anger is a great source of energy to get things done, and I was feeling more than enough of it to fuel the rest of the day doing some ever needed maintenance work around the place. The grass needed edging all up and down the driveway, and along the walkways, and I'd do it after mowing. If I worked hard enough and long enough, I'd wear myself out and maybe forget about wanting to sucker punch Nick. There's always another better way to look at a situation, and if my getting fired was all it took for Lenny to quit dancing in a strip club, and treating a bunch of drunks to her gorgeous body, it was all well worth it. She'd just have to find another way to work out the anger toward her father. And knowing Lenny as much as I already did, I was quite sure she'd think of something.

You know how it is with a shakeup event...the pieces fall in all sorts of haphazard ways, and you never know just what it all is going to lead to. I was looking forward to finding out what was going to come out of this particular set of circumstances. One thing for sure, anything to do with Lenny was bound to be interesting and worth hanging around for.

20

TO THE RESCUE

I finished mowing and had just started working with the edger when Lenny rang again on the cell phone. "It never rains but it pours."

"What happened? You all right?" I was hot from mowing and just holding the cell phone against my ear made it slick with sweat.

"Quintus!" she said out of breath. "He's been arrested. I have to drive up there and get him out of jail."

"What'd he do?"

"He shot some warning shots at an intruder last night at the camp. It was Junior skulking around the premises, peering in the windows of the main house with a flashlight. Now Junior's saying he tried to kill him. Roderick arrested him about three in the morning."

"Pick me up. I'll go with you."

"My father's driving up there too. I don't think you want to meet him."

"So? Come on. I'm no rookie, Lenny."

"Haven't you had enough trouble for one day?"

"No. I love trouble. Keeps me awake."

"Are you sure you want to go all the way back up there? I can take care of this by myself."

"Pick me up. We'll drive up and take care of Quintus and come right back so I can get back to work here at the motel."

"I don't know. Doesn't seem fair to drag you into this."

"I'll go tell Celeste. How long will it take you to get ready?"

"I'm already ready. I was heading for the car right now. But I'm not taking Bijou back up there. Junior might do something to him."

"Not around me he won't."

"I know. But I feel safer leaving him behind for now."

"All right." I clicked off, wiped my face with the hand towel I'd draped around my neck, wiped off the damp cell phone, put away the tools and went in to talk to Celeste not surprised at all that chaos had set in. It's always that way when things start shaking loose. Something I'd had occasion to notice in my life so far…trouble usually comes in a one-two-three jab.

21

LUCIEN BADON

We didn't make it to Wallace until noon, but by the time we got to the police station on a side street a block from the general store, Quintus had already been released to Lenny's father, and all charges dropped. A pleasant middle-aged woman informed us of this from behind a glassed-in counter in the middle of the small, low cement block building.

Once out on the street again, Lenny threw up her hands as we walked to the car.

"See, what'd I tell you? With my father...I call him Lucien by the way...it's always his way or the highway. He probably paid Roderick off to make it all go away."

"Not much of a case there anyway. Junior's word against Quintus, and since you say Junior's a few cards short of a deck, who's going to believe him?"

"Wouldn't matter one way or the other. Like I said, things always work out to go Lucien's way."

"You complaining cause he got Quintus out of jail?"

"No," she said as we cruised past the town limits sign. "Quintus is like a father to me. I'm just giving you the big picture is all."

We passed Roderick's patrol car parked in the usual spot by the same grove of trees and bushes as last time. "He's back on track working the town's speed trap hustle."

"Of course he is. And now you're about to have the great honor of meeting the treacherous Lucien Badon. Make sure you believe nothing, absolutely nothing he tells you. He's sure to run a bunch of crap by you. And he usually pitches his b.s. with plenty of charm, so don't be taken in by it."

"I usually have a highly functioning bullshit meter."

"Not to be unkind, but it wasn't working at all when you got your life ruined by that Rocco guy."

"Like I said, usually it's working. There have been a few exceptions."

We were passing over the gravel road leading to the camp and I kept my eyes on the woods on my side of the road. Wildflowers lined the ditch between the road and the trees. Joe Pye weed, dandelions, swamp mallow bloomed, and an armadillo disappeared into a clump of goldenrod. A gray coating of dust raised by passing vehicles partially covered some of the growth. The bright red of a cardinal flashed between two flowering privet bushes.

"Yep. Dear old dad is here. Remind me not to bitch slap him, will you?" She pulled in the circular drive, and pulled up in back of a black Impala.

"From what you've told me, I expected a Mercedes or a BMW," I said.

"Don't worry. He's got a Cadillac back at the house. He brought Mother's car today for some reason."

As we walked up the path to the house, I was almost looking forward to meeting the man and watching the two of them together. Through my work as a cop I had learned not to take someone else's opinion of someone as my own until I'd met and talked to the person myself. Even though I felt a strong bond with Lenny already, I was not willing to take her word for a person I'd never met and was determined to make up my own mind about her father.

Lenny didn't bother knocking on the front door, just opened it and led me on inside. We found Lucien out on the back deck drinking a beer with his driver.

Lenny swished on through the back door, all confidence, shoulders back and head held high. She motioned me to follow. "Hey, Lucien. Got someone for you to meet," she said, her tone energetic and deceptively sociable.

Her father turned around in the padded chaise and stared through dark glasses, his expression flat. "Hello. Come on and join us then." He nodded to the driver who stood and began to walk away. Lucien was a solidly built man, stocky, with dark hair combed straight back and a smooth skinned face. His eyes were dark like Lenny's, and I could see a similarity in the strong chin and wide cheekbones.

"Don't leave on our account, Tucker," Lenny said. "Sit."

"No thanks, Miss Leonée. I have some things to do on the car before we get back on the road."

"You're not even staying over?" Lenny turned to her father. "After all that drive up here?"

"Can't. I have a meeting first thing in the morning. We just drove up to take care of this idiotic mess Junior, the wannabe burglar, got Quintus into. The only mistake Quintus made was firing off a shot that missed." He turned his body, lowered his dark glasses an inch, and stretched out his right hand to me. "Lucien Badon."

I reached him in time to shake his hand. "Harris Viator."

"I know who you are." He gave me a sideways smile that said he also knew all the details of the mess with Rocco.

"What?" Lenny placed her hands on her hips and her face darkened. "What do you mean? You two don't know each other."

Lucien smirked and adjusted his dark glasses back into place. "I read the papers." He reclined back on the chaise. "Come on. Sit down with me and have a beer.

He called to Tucker who was just crossing the threshold of the French doors. "Tucker, please bring us each a Heinekin's before you tend to the car, will you?"

"Right," Tucker said and vanished into the house.

"So," Lucien said, as we settled on two other lounge chairs. "You came up to help Quintus get out of jail, but I beat you to it, right?"

"Came soon as I heard. You know I'm not going to let him sit in jail overnight." Lenny took off her scarf and fluffed her hair.

"That's a loyal friend. But then, you've always been that way." He smiled at me.

"She really always has been like that. Always taking up for the down and out. I don't know who she gets it from. Always taking in strays. When she was a child, it was abandoned dogs and kittens. Then she graduated to people."

"Why do you have to always make helping people sound creepy?" Lenny asked him.

"What?" Fake surprise registered on his face. "Helping people? That's my middle name. After all, little girl, that's what I do best."

Lenny rolled her eyes.

Tucker returned with bottles of beer on a tray and set one on the wrought iron side tables by each lounge chair. "That be all, Mr. Lucien?"

"That's fine. Thank you. I'll see you at the car in about half an hour. Just want to catch up a bit with my daughter." He looked at his watch, then back to Lenny.

"Still dancing at that high-toned club?" He looked at me shaking his head. "Sent her to private Catholic schools all her life. And this is what comes of it. A career at LolliPops stripping for a bunch of lowlife drunks."

"I see you keep up with my career....*and* friends," she said pointing a finger at him. "What've you got? A tail on me now? By the way, some of your sleazy attorney friends stop in there more than you'd like to know. You'd be surprised at how many of those *low-life drunks* are friends of yours, including Moe who never misses a chance to try to get me to go out with him. I'd rather get a whiplash."

"I have my sources," he said smiling as he glanced over at her, "and don't have to hire any P.I.'s to find out what I need to know."

He looked out over the sloping lawn as he said, "My daughter may be going through a bit of wild child rebellion, but I'm damn sure going to make sure she's safe." He drained the last of the first beer and picked up the second, looking thoughtfully at it for a minute. "Of course," he added, looking directly at me, "it's at least good to know she's currently being looked after by a former cop."

Lenny set her mouth in a firm line and glared at him.

"Oh, Lenny," he changed his tone. "Don't get all worked up. Would you rather I didn't give a damn about what you do with your life?"

"Don't give me that. You don't give a damn about anything but your career. Never have, never will. I don't expect anything from you except distance."

He laughed. "Come on. Let's not fight in front of our guest. Here we are looking out at that beautiful rolling lawn and those woods. The sun is shining and the sky is blue. Enjoy yourself."

He looked at me. "Sorry, Harris. Our family...always so outspoken." He shook his head again. "Didn't mean to be rude. How do you like the camp here?"

"It's great," I said, and left it at that, not wanting to sound chummy and further aggravate Lenny who looked like she just might do a little of that bitch slapping she asked me to help her avoid. Her arms were crossed and she tried to hide the anger with a poker face, but it wasn't working. Her brow was furrowed and eyes narrowed.

"If you want to get in a little fishing while you're here, there's all the equipment you need in the house. Has she shown you the pond out there yet?" He pointed toward the trees that hid the pond from view.

"Oh, so you already know we were here before," she accused, "Quintus has a big mouth."

"Don't be harsh. It's Quintus' job to tell me what goes on up here. Besides, what do you care? Is your relationship a big secret?"

"We're friends, that's all."

"Yes indeed. Friends. I'm sure you make a lot of them." He finished his beer, turned in the chaise and sat up straight.

"Well, it's getting late. Tucker and I better hit the road. Stay on and enjoy yourselves as long as you like."

He nodded to both of us in turn and stood, picking up both his empties by the neck and taking them with him back toward the house. "Call me if you need anything, Lenny. Come see your mother. You've stayed away much too long. She's worried about you. Of course she doesn't know what you've been doing. I tell her you're working in a dance studio. Not *too* much of a lie." He gave her a mock salute and turned to me.

"Nice to meet you, Harris. Keep her safe for me, will you? She likes to get into adventures, and this worries me because she's so unpredictable." He disappeared into the house and quietly slid the door closed, still watching us from behind the glass.

"Creepy bastard!" she said, still fuming and then sank into silence and nursed her beer. She didn't speak again until we heard the Impala start up and drive away, gravel crunching as it slowly passed over the driveway.

I waited a few beats before risking a comment. "You two are like oil and water."

"That's not even close. It's more like contempt and hate all rolled into one."

"He does seem to worry about your safety though."

"That's all a front. Can't you see that? Just a front to make people like you think he's a concerned father. Nothing could be further from the truth. All he cares about is what comes back on him. If the people around him add to his image....or his net worth. Me being a stripper infuriates him....not because I'm dancing naked in public, but because it embarrasses him politically...makes him look bad. Other than that, he could care less what I do. Don't let him get over on you."

"Why don't you forget about him and let's take a walk down to check on Quintus and say hello before we start back? I want to hear the details of the way it all went down last night."

"I have a better idea...let's see Quintus later." She quickly changed her tone and softened up. "Instead, why don't you and I go upstairs and distract ourselves for a while? Maybe that will shake my mind loose from these evil thoughts I'm having. Cause right about now I'm hoping Lucien catches a stroke on the drive home." She sat up in the lounge chair and ran her fingers through her hair, then raised an eyebrow at me.

"Come on," I stood and held out my hand. "Maybe we don't have to get back today after all."

"Oh, but Bijou's alone in the apartment," she said. "Ahh, wait a minute. He's got plenty of food and water and I did put newspapers down for him." She rose from the chair and took my hand. "Bijou will be all right until tomorrow. We can stay over and start back in the morning. Come on."

22

QUINTUS

After we'd been together, 'distracting' ourselves over an hour upstairs, we were feeling hungry and Lenny decided she'd not only make us some supper, but she'd also bake some brownies to cheer up Quintus after his ordeal. She found a box of brownie mix on the pantry shelf and got to work making a batch of those along with a shrimp jambalaya she put together for us in a twelve-inch, stainless lined copper skillet.

After we'd eaten, she did up the brownies in a cookie tin, tied a ribbon around it, and we headed down the sloping lawn to Quintus' place with a flash-light for the path through the woods. We hadn't gone down the pine needle strewn path far when the shepherds started barking as soon as we came within a hundred feet of the trailer. The outside pole light came on right away and Quintus came to the door to see why they were barking.

"Hey, Quintus, it's us!" Lenny called.

"Hello, come on in," he called back as he hushed the dogs. "Go, sit!" he ordered as he waited by the door until we reached the front steps. Standing aside by the door to let us pass, he motioned for us to sit on the new couch. The dogs sat obediently by the entrance to the kitchen as Lenny and I sat together and Quintus pulled a rocking chair close to us. A spicy pot of chili simmered on the stove, and the television was tuned to a news show.

"Sorry to barge in on you, but I baked you some brownies. We're so sorry about what happened to you." Lenny handed him the gift box.

"Brownies!" He untied the ribbon, lifted the lid and sniffed. "I love brownies! Thank you."

"You're welcome. Least I can do for what you went through. Do you mind telling us the details of what happened?" she asked.

"No, not at all." He put the lid back on the box and leaning over, set it on an end table under a black ceramic lamp. "I woke up after midnight like I often do. You know how I roam around at night with the dogs cause I have trouble sleeping. So I pulled on some clothes, took my shotgun," he motioned toward the door where the shotgun leaned against the wall, "and went out for a walk with the dogs like always."

"This is last night, right?"

"Yeah, and when we get down the path to the edge of the woods, from that far away I can see a man in shadow moving up at the house by the French doors on the balcony. The floods are on as usual around the perimeter, but up at those doors, it's not well lighted. I yell, 'Hold it or I'll shoot your ass!' and then he starts racing, pounding fast down the stairs and around to the front of the house. The dogs take off, and I shoot toward the ground to warn him. 'Hold up!' I yell again, and start running. But by the time I get up to the house, the dogs are snarling and raising hell out front and carrying on at the guy's car and he's inside trying to crank up the engine. By the time I get there, he's scratching off, spinning gravel, and the dogs are chasing the car down the driveway.

"They chase him a ways down the road, then come back, and I climb the stairs to see what the man was doing at the window. He had been trying to jimmy it open and when I started yelling and he took off, he left his knife stuck between the glass and the latch. I leave it where it is and go back to the trailer to call the police. I get Roderick on the phone…he's only half awake and groggy. I tell him about the attempted break-in, and he says he'll come out at first light to see about it and look around. So I put on some coffee cause I know I won't be getting back to sleep, and the next thing I know Roderick's calling me back and telling me to meet him at the house cause he changed his mind and decided not to wait til morning."

Lenny looked at me and then back at Quintus. "Thank God you're a light sleeper! So how did Roderick end up blaming you for anything?"

"It's crazy. I go back up, this time without the dogs, and meet with him at the driveway. I walk him back and we climb the stairs. He yanks the knife out with a handkerchief and slides it into an evidence bag, then we go back down and he tells me how Junior says I was trying to shoot him, and how all he was doing was coming to leave a note for you about the dog bite. How he was still angry about that and how he wanted you to apologize."

"What a liar! What was he planning? To break in and leave a note on my pillow?"

"Roderick said the knife must have already been there for some other reason. That Junior would never break in somebody's house. He looked at me accusingly like I was making the whole thing up to cover my tracks for trying to shoot Junior."

"Unbelievable!"

"Yeah, it really is. I told him to check it for fingerprints, and he said running fingerprints costs too much money, and he would only do it if a break-in had occurred. But, he tells me I can't go around shooting at people outside of a house. Only if you're inside and they break into the house, or if your life is in danger. 'You could have killed Junior!' he keeps saying." Quintus glanced over at the dogs who were by then lying down, side by side, heads resting on crossed front paws.

"So, I tell him how I was just shooting a warning shot toward the ground. I told him we'd go find the shell back near the woodline if he didn't believe me. But it didn't make a dent. No, Junior ought to know if somebody was trying to shoot him or not."

"Time the town of Wallace hires a new Chief of Police. Roderick's incompetent," Lenny said.

"Yeah, well, what's new? Trouble is nobody's around here to replace him. And to make it all even more crazy, Junior wants to be reimbursed for the dogs scratching and gouging the paint on his car door. That old orange beater he's been driving around for the past fifteen years, dented up and burning oil, blowing black exhaust."

"Don't pay it. The hell with him," she said.

"Mr. Lucien already took care of everything. He paid off Roderick to make this all go away."

"He should have sued him instead for attempted burglary," Lenny huffed.

"I know, but he doesn't want bad blood with Roderick. He's not here that much to look after the camp, and he doesn't want to bring down any local trouble on me."

"Okay, so now what? What happens to Junior now that my father got the whole thing dropped?"

"Nothing. Nothing's going to happen to Junior."

"Figures. The criminals are the ones that get all the protection, right, Harris?" She looked over at me.

"Better get some security cameras put up," I advised. "They catch a lot of people. Even just deer cameras work great."

"That's a good idea," Lenny said, looking back and forth at Quintus and me. "I like that because Junior's so weird, he'll probably come back again. I'd like to see Roderick deny he's trying to break in if we've got it on film."

"Cameras would be good," Quintus said. "I'll suggest it to your father."

"Thank you for interrupting the burglary," Lenny said. "I'm so glad you did. Who knows what that derelict would have done if he'd gotten inside? Probably vandalize the place to get even for Bijou nipping him. He barely broke the skin. A tiny red spot is all." She shook her head. "What a weenie he is. But, look, we interrupted your program. I'm sorry. We'll leave you alone so you can get back to it. We've got to leave early in the morning, so we'd better try to get some sleep now." She stood and took a look around the room. "You sure have made this place comfortable, Quintus." We started moving toward the door.

"Oh, look," she said. "A St. Christopher medal. I never saw that here before." She stepped forward and cradled it in her hand where it dangled from the cross.

"I found that actually," Quintus said. "Somebody must have lost it in town. It was lying all coated with mud in the gutter."

"Glad you saved it before it was washed away down the storm drain." She dropped her hand and we said goodnight. I shook Quintus' hand and then we left.

"Renard had one like that," she said as I clicked on the flashlight, and we crossed the clearing toward the path through the woods.

"Like what?"

"A St. Christopher medal. Only his was gold. I gave it to him, and he always wore it on a gold chain around his neck. He would never wear jewelry, but he wore the medal because I gave it to him. I wanted him to wear it for protection cause he was out in the swamp trapping and fishing at night all the time."

"Did you tell that to the police when they were searching for him?" I took her hand as we made our way back up to the house.

"I don't know. Maybe. I don't remember."

"Did they use metal detectors at all?"

"No. Why would they? They were looking for him lying somewhere above ground. Unconscious or wounded from some accident or an attack of some kind. Coyotes maybe. Nobody was trying to find him buried somewhere."

"And like you said, some people thought maybe he just took off and left you stranded…so they didn't look hard enough or long enough." We'd reached the sliding glass door to the kitchen.

"Exactly. And also if Lucien wanted him to disappear, his body will never see the light of day, of that you can be certain."

"Never say never, *chère,*" I said as we locked up and went upstairs to bed.

23

JO-JO

After returning home, I had a lot of catching up to do around the motel. I worked in the yard, edging and mowing and weeding. I helped Celeste with some minor repairs at her house, changed the filters on all the air-conditioning units in the rooms, and hosed out the Dumpster. Celeste brought me a bowl of Cowboy stew and a plate of homemade rolls on a tray when I was finished, so I took the food into my room to relax.

Each room has a small round table and I set the tray down and drew a chair up to eat and relax. Halfway through Celeste's delicious piping hot stew, the phone rang. It was Lenny.

"You have a few minutes to spare? Can you come by my place? There's someone here I want you to meet."

"And who would that be?'

"It's Jerome…Jo-Jo. The brother I told you about? That lives on Renard's houseboat in the Basin?"

"Sure. I'll come by if you want. Give me an hour. I've been working and I need to clean up."

"We'll be here."

I cleaned up, washed the dishes in the bathroom sink and returned them to Celeste with gratitude for all she did for me and her fine cooking, then drove over to Lenny's apartment about eight miles away. I turned off the highway onto her street and followed the paved road past a few blocks of residential neighborhood, then a pet boarding business and a beauty parlor to a row of flowering pear trees that partially hid her apartment building from view.

The two-story building was constructed of cement block with an iron balcony running the entire width and stairs at each end. In the middle of the building was a breezeway so you could pass through to the back parking lot without having to walk around the building. The manager was sweeping the cement in the breezeway with a push broom.

I parked in front, and hurried up the nearest stairs to her apartment at a corner of the building, and knocked. As though she was waiting by the door, she opened it right away and took my hand. "Come in. Come in. Jo-Jo's waiting on you. He wants to meet you." Her perfume blended with the smell of roasting chicken coming from the rear of the apartment. She wore short denim cutoffs with some of the threads hanging down from the unhemmed edges, and a low cut turquoise tee shirt cut low enough to make me wince. "You're going to fall out of that shirt," I warned.

"See, there you go again." She wagged a finger at me. "What'd I tell you about that?"

I followed her down a short hallway lined with framed photographs of her in a variety of locations with friends, always smiling and waving at the camera. One photograph was of a man I figured was Renard. He stood arms held slightly out at his sides, dressed in jeans and a black tee shirt, cypress trees in the background. His skin was dark and his eyes brown. He wore a cap with the visor bent in the middle, and his expression was grave, as though he didn't want his picture taken.

Jo-Jo sat on the white leather couch drinking a beer. I could see the resemblance to his brother except he was smiling as he stretched out a hand. Half rising from the couch, he shook my hand vigorously and his palm was hard and dry, the skin so tough it felt like turtle shell.

"And this is Jerome Bergeron, Harris," Lenny said. "Harris Viator, meet Jerome. Just so you know, he looks almost exactly like his younger brother. You look at Jo-Jo, you're looking at Renard."

Jo-Jo laughed. "Not quite. I have a few gray hairs already and a few pounds on him."

"Close enough," Lenny said. "Look, how about I just go get us each a beer? Harris, have a seat over there in that chair. It's the most comfortable in the room."

"Call me Jo-Jo," he said as he sat back down and stretched out his long legs. "How you doing?"

"I'm good. Thanks." I nodded and sat in an up-holstered armchair on the other side of the glass coffee table from him. There was a pause as I kept my eyes on the magazines and some photos that were spread out on the table.

"You like that?" He pointed to the coffee table. The base was a two-foot wide cedar stump.

"I do like it." I turned my head sideways to examine it better. "You make it?"

"My brother did. I have one like it at home he made for me."

Lenny returned then with the beers on a tray along with some chips and salsa. She set the tray down on the glass and then flopped onto the other end of the couch from Jo-Jo.

"You all help yourself," she said. "We can all eat here if you want. I put a chicken and a casserole in the oven not too long ago."

"Sounds good, but I can't stay too long. There are some things I still have to take care of back at the motel. I've been running all weekend."

"Keeping you busy, huh?" Jo-Jo said amiably, stretching out his long legs and crossing his ankles. He wore scuffed black biker boots and his jeans were worn thin at the knees.

"Jo-Jo came by to tell me a few things I thought might interest you," Lenny said.

"I'm listening," I said, as I held the glass sideways and poured the beer slowly.

"Tell him, Jo-Jo," she said, leaning over and scooping up salsa with a chip.

Jo-Jo looked at me. "I guess Lenny told you about my brother going missing and all a while back."

"Yes, she told me." I leaned back in the chair and waited.

"I've been staying on his houseboat hoping I'd hear something…anything that might give me a clue as to what happened to him. Hoping he'd somehow come back in the middle of the night and wake me up. I don't sleep good anymore cause I've always got one eye open waiting on him."

"I can understand that."

"And I can't figure it. Can't come up with any ideas at all as to what happened. But one thing I didn't know before…well, his woman from way the hell back…Germaine Stelly…She's like his girl friend from far back as high school. She lives back in the swamp with her parents and brothers. The Stellys are old-time. Hunting, trapping, fishing, whatever it takes to survive out there. Her father kept a still back there for years…probably still does. They have their camp out beyond Stump Pass on a ridge where they can see who's coming and going. It's almost completely hidden by cypress and willow trees. You have to know where to look to ever find them, and if you did find them, you better hope they don't mind you coming around their set up." Jo-Jo looked over at Lenny and she nodded at him to go on.

"I ran into one of her brothers at a bar in Leveetown the other day. We got to talking and it slips out that Germaine knew about Lenny here…. before Renard disappeared. I figured she knew about Lenny when it came out that he had come up missing from the camp up in Wallace where he and

Lenny were holed up, but I don't know how she'd of found out before Renard disappeared. No way. Renard never told anybody about Lenny, except for me. He didn't want it to get back to Germaine. He had left her but he didn't want to rub it in by letting her find out he had a new woman."

He paused then, and I frowned as I sat quietly thinking about this.

"You see?" Lenny said, leaning forward for a handful of chips. "She couldn't have known, Jo-Jo says. So what does that tell you?" She popped a chip into her mouth and looked directly at me as she crunched down on it. I raised my eyebrows and drank some beer as I pondered it, but had no answer for her.

"Well, Harris, what do you think?" she urged, popping another chip into her mouth and leaning back against the cushions waiting for something, anything that I might come up with.

"How the hell should I know?" I finally said. "What do *you* think?" I turned it back on both of them, looking first at Lenny and then at Jo-Jo.

"I think it's very weird that she found out about me when only Jo-Jo knew," she said, narrowing her eyes.

"It really is. See, she and Ren have so much history together. That's the thing. They've been through a lot. They even had a baby that died in childbirth. Germaine was bit by a moccasin when she was close to delivering. Those people don't use doctors. They do their own thing. Her foot and ankle swelled up like a balloon. They took her by boat to land and got her to an Emergency Room, but it was too late. They delivered the baby, but it was stillborn."

"That's got to be hard to recover from," I said.

"She was always into old time healing plants and then she got into it even more after that. She started bottling a tonic that they sell to a lot of customers. Germaine never goes anywhere. She stays out there in the swamp. The brothers come in from their place and deliver bottles of it to their regular customers. It's good stuff. They say it cures anything you got."

"What's in it?"

"She keeps it a secret. I know damn well there's alligator oil in it though. I'll never forget that smell. Ma used to chase us around the house and make us take a spoonful of it every day. Works too. We never got sick." He wrinkled his nose. "It's nasty though."

"You too?" I laughed. "I got the same treatment as a kid. My parents are old time too. And I ran away from plenty of alligator oil in my time. Never got away with it either. They always caught up with me." Remembering the taste of it I took a swig of beer before speaking again. "So, Germaine's a hermit and stays out in the swamp all the time. Right?"

"Always has," Jo-Jo took a long drink from his beer, then wiped his mouth with the back of his sleeve. "She doesn't like it in town. Doesn't like people much either."

"Then how could she have found out? You must have some ideas?"

Lenny pointed a finger at me. "Can't you see? It all comes back around to my father. I think he must have found out about her and made sure Germaine found out about me. Somehow got word to her about me so he could agitate and stir the pot. Hoping she'd do something to break us up.... so she could get him back out to her swamp lair. Spider lady." She shuddered and squinched up her eyes. "Woo-wooo," she moaned, wriggling her fingers.

"You don't know that," I told her. "Maybe one of her brothers saw you all together somewhere and told her."

"It's possible, but unlikely. Renard and I never went anywhere near Leveetown. We stayed miles away from anywhere near there and if we went anywhere it was up to the camp in Wallace. Renard loved it up there. If we stayed around here at the apartment, he would get stir crazy. Renard had to be outdoors to be happy."

Or in bed with you, I thought, but didn't say it out loud. I emptied the beer and placed the empty back on the tray.

"I'll get you another one. You ready?" she asked Jo-Jo. He nodded and finished his off. Lenny left with the empties and Jo-Jo slid an arm along the back of the couch, relaxing back into the thick cushions.

"What's she like? This Germaine?" I asked him. "She the jealous type?"

Jo-Jo laughed. "She'll rip your liver out and slap you with it. She's a lean, mean machine and her brothers are ten times worse."

"So why did Renard get mixed up with her?"

"High school. She didn't used to be like that, but as she got older, she turned out more and more like her father. Alcide is one nasty son of a bitch, let me tell you. Even a moccasin would take one look at him and turn and race away he's that bad. Evil is more like it. I wouldn't call Germaine evil, but she's working on it. Renard got sick of her temper and her demands, so he left. Took him long enough, but he'd put up with her tantrums for seven or eight years and that was enough for him. She told him she'd put a curse on him if he left, and he said, 'Go right ahead. Do what you have to do. Staying with you is a curse anyhow. Damned if I do, damned if I don't.' And that was the end of it. He met Lenny just a week or two later." Jo-Jo jerked a thumb toward the kitchen just as Lenny came out with more beers.

"You been talking about me behind my back?" She smiled as she sat down and placed the tray of beers on the coffee table.

"I was just telling Harris about how you met Renard."

"I wish I'd never met him now," she said her mouth downturned. "He'd still be alive."

"You don't know he's dead," I said, reaching for a beer.

"Well what else could he be?" she asked, then looked over at Jo-Jo. "Another one who thinks he ran out on me."

"I never said that," I cautioned. "What I did say is you have no proof of anything as yet."

"Not yet. That's true," Jo-Jo said. "One thing though…if Renard was alive he'd be in touch with me. No doubt about it. He'd get word to me somehow of where he was. He'd never leave me hanging like this….or her." He gestured toward Lenny with his thumb, but didn't look over at her as he reached for another beer.

Lenny pulled her legs up on the couch and carefully arranged herself into a crosslegged sitting position, rocking back and forth until she got comfortable. She sighed when she was settled, closed her eyes and leaned her head back to a resting place against a velvet throw along the back of the couch. "That's right, Jo-Jo. He never would let either one of us be hanging out here in the breeze like this. I heard what you said about Germaine putting a curse on him. Looks like it worked, and he's gone for good. I just have to get used to it, and so do you. But somebody's going to have to pay for it."

"And somebody will," Jo-Jo promised, stretching out a hand to pat her knee.

"Rest easy, *chère*. It's all going to get taken care of. Just as soon as I figure it out."

"I already told you what happened," she said, eyes still closed.

"And I heard you," Jo-Jo said, "But I'm not as sure about it as you are." He turned his head and looked out the sliding glass windows that offered a view of the narrow iron railed balcony. A row of potted ferns lined the space, so there was room for only one small wicker chair out there.

The smell of the baked chicken grew stronger and Lenny sniffed the air, then opened her eyes and straightened her head. "You know what? I'm going to check on our dinner. Smells like it's almost ready. What do you think?" She unfolded her legs and stood. "You all getting hungry?"

"Thanks, but I can't stay. I have to get back to the motel. I'm in the middle of some things I have to do."

"Aw, come on and eat with us. You have to eat dinner somewhere. Might as well be here with us."

"No, thanks. Really. I have to get back." I finished off the second beer and stood. "Good meeting you, Jo-Jo," I said and offered him my hand.

He stood and we shook again. "You want to burn one before you go?" he asked and pulled a rumpled joint out of his shirt pocket.

"Thanks. I'd better get back." Lenny came around the coffee table and took my hand.

"Come on," she said. "I'll walk you to the door." She pulled me along after her back down the short hall and opened the door for me. "Sorry to lay all that on you," she said in a low voice. "You have to understand…it's been tough on Jo-Jo and me."

"I'm sure." She stood on tiptoe and gave me a quick kiss on the mouth. "You're not running off cause of Jo-Jo, are you?" She had a worried look on her face. "He won't stay long. He'll probably leave right after dinner," she whispered. "Then…well…." She placed a hand on my chest.

"It's not Jo-Jo. I've got a lot of things to do." I gave her a quick reassuring kiss. "Put a shirt on over that, will you? You're half naked and you've got company."

"Damn it, Harris. You've got to stop this. It's really getting on my nerves. I already told you I don't like people giving me orders. I'll dress the way I damn well want to in my own apartment. If you don't like it, you don't have to come around."

Her lips got tight and small spots of color showed in her cheeks.

I started to say something along the lines of : *Sorry, got no right to tell you what to do,* but thought better of it. Our eyes held for a few beats, then I turned toward the door.

"The hell with it! Do whatever the hell you want!" I blurted out, then crossed the threshold and wasted no time getting out of there.

She stood in the doorway and watched me as I hurried down the stairs. Once on the ground floor walkway, I glanced back in anger and she was still standing there, a sad look on her face like she was thinking of other times, other places.

Go ahead. Walk around bare-assed if that's what you want. I'm out of here! I felt the heat of anger all the way to the truck and all the way back down the highway to the motel.

24

FALLING WATERS, ARKANSAS

After that spat with Lenny, I was glad to have something to do to get my mind off my frustration with her. Still aggravated the next morning and angry at myself for feeling so down about it, I whipped myself into shape and made arrangements with Celeste to leave for Arkansas and get on with my hunting trip for Rocco. I took the roll of wrinkled bills I'd been able to save during my weeks at LolliPops from its hiding place taped under a bureau drawer and thought…hoped…I had enough in that stash for gas and food needed for the round trip. I picked up a few plastic jugs of water at the grocery store and placed them in the bed of the truck along with a loaf of bread and some salami so I wouldn't have to stop at any restaurants on the way up. Running out of money and having to wash dishes in some strange town would not help me find Rocco.

The drive to Falling Waters took over seven hours because I couldn't drive fast on all those curving roads through the endless small towns and villages of the foothills. It had been a long time since I'd been in the Ozarks hunting wild turkey with an army pal from Forsythe, Missouri, and an even longer time since I'd been in the wedding party of an Army friend who lives in Leslie, Arkansas. Like many other Cajuns, I seldom left the state of Louisiana because there is always so much going on in the state to do. Also like many other Cajuns, I take my own spices with me when I do leave Acadiana, because the thought of bland food scares us. Some even take their own rice with them. I don't go that far, but I do keep a bottle of hot sauce and a container of Cajun seasoning in the truck when I leave home, just in case.

I stayed well below the posted speed limit in all the little towns I passed through, as I had to watch every dollar, and it would break me to get a speeding ticket. The further I drove, the sweeter was the mountain air laced with the smell of pine. Whenever I stopped for gas, I'd fill a jug from the spigot and it was always spring fresh and crystal clear with the magical taste of mountain water.

When I finally reached the tiny, tree shaded village of Falling Waters, I stopped for supplies at a two-story frame building with an old fashioned faded *General Store* sign out front hanging from two chains. The building looked as though it had been built in the early 1900s, and the metal roof was rusted with a few shiny silver replacement panels patched here and there. A few boards of the building were slipping and uneven, but overall the store looked well maintained. There were window boxes at some of the second story windows with blooming geraniums, so I gathered that the owners lived over their store.

A few pickups were angle parked in front of the store, so I pulled in beside a vintage Chevy and got out to stretch and take a measure of the town before going inside.

Across the street was a café in a narrow frame building with a stucco front. "DINAH'S CAFE" was painted in bright red colors across one of the windows and a man and woman sitting at the window watched me as I stretched. I was thirsty so got on with it and went on inside the General Store. No one was there except for a woman at the counter who was breaking open coin wrappers and filling the cash drawer with change.

"Hello," she said without smiling.

"Hello back at you," I said. "I'm looking for the sodas."

"Right over there," she said matter of factly, pointing at a cooler to the right of the counter.

I walked over, grabbed a few cold drinks and carried them to the counter. "And the motor oil?"

"Back wall," she said without looking up.

I found the auto supplies three aisles back and brought two cans of motor oil to the front, but only after pulling down a *Falling Waters, Arkansas* visor cap from a rack on the way.

"That'll be it?" she asked, finally closing the drawer and looking at me for the first time.

"Yes, and please direct me to the police station."

"At the caution light….there's only one. That-a-way…then hang a right. Can't miss it."

She rang up my purchases on the old-fashioned register and announced the total in a flat voice.

I fished out the necessary bills and slid them to her over the scarred wooden counter top. She packaged my goods in two brown paper bags and ran a tongue over her teeth as she gently pushed them forward.

I picked up the bags and turned to leave.

"You from Louisiana?" she asked.

"Yes…how'd you know?"

She smiled for the first time. "All's you had to do was open your mouth."

"Sure," I smiled back at her and made my way outside.

As I placed the bags inside the truck, I glanced across the street at the café. This time the window was empty. I planned on eating in there later, but first wanted to introduce myself to the police chief.

The police station was a small brick building, probably built in the fifties. The United States flag ruffled from a metal pole out front and a patrol car was backing out of a paved driveway as I waited to pull in. The policeman in the cruiser gave me a look over and a nod as he drove slowly away, watching me in the rear view window.

I parked the pickup and took a drink from one of the sodas as I rehearsed what I wanted to say to the chief. Finishing the soda, I crunched the can, dropped it into the trash bag I keep in the truck, got out and crossed to the main entrance.

Still deciding how much I'd say and how much I'd leave out, I entered and immediately caught a whiff of floor wax. The wood floor of the station house was so shiny it gleamed, and I followed a long black rubber mat that led to the receptionist who was reading something on her computer and listening to someone talking on the phone, all at the same time.

The woman wore a blouse buttoned up to the throat which made me smile as I thought of how Lenny would look all buttoned up like that, and her hair was plaited in a tight French braid down her back. She glanced at me and held up a forefinger to let me know she'd be right with me.

"Right. All right. I got it. I've got someone here now. Talk to you later." She hung up the phone, shaking her head. "Some people!" she complained, then smiled at me. "Sorry about that. Complaint about a tomcat! How can I help you?"

"Just drove up from Louisiana. I'd like to speak to the Chief, please."

"Your name?"

"Harris Viator."

She wrote it down. "What's your business?" she asked, holding the pen poised over the notebook.

"Involves a wanted man."

"Well okay!" she said cheerfully, as though glad this wasn't about a lost dog or cat. She patted her hair and buzzed the Chief, leaning over to speak softly into the speaker. "Somebody's here to see you all the way from Louisiana, Chief. Something about a man who's wanted for something."

"Send him on back," was the muffled reply.

"Right down the hall there," she said, twisting her arm to point behind her as the phone rang again and she picked up the receiver.

I walked down the hall along a long mat runner. Somebody was taking extra care to protect those oak floors. The Chief's door was open and he sat behind a gray metal desk. He was a wiry thin man, gray hair combed straight back with a crease in it from the visor cap that was hanging from a hat rack in back of him. He had a prominent Adam's apple, a sharp chin and bony shoulders. When he saw me, he leaned back in his chair and waved me inside. A small sign on the front of his desk identified him as Chief Greg Wooten. I caught a whiff of a familiar citrus aftershave.

"Afternoon. Welcome to Falling Waters. What you got?" He gestured toward a metal chair in front of the desk. "Have a seat."

"Thanks, Chief. I just drove up from Louisiana.... St. Beatrice Parish. My name is Harris Viator, and I used to be a cop down there, but no longer. There's an escaped prisoner from St. Beatrice that I've traced to your area. Without boring you with all the details, suffice to say that the reason I'm no longer a police officer is because he escaped on my watch. I had a sterling record until this incident and it's in my best interest to find him so I can at least try and set the record straight."

"What's the man's name?" The Chief sat up and rested his hands on the desk, one folded over the other.

"His name is Rocco Theriot and I've brought a picture of him to show you." I placed a copy of one of the newspaper clippings on his desk. The photo was a clear close up of Rocco's face.

The Chief stared at the picture for a few beats, then handed it back. "Haven't seen anybody looking like this around here, son. Sorry I can't help you. What makes you think he's around here anyhow?"

"I heard he's joined up with a friend of his who allegedly grows pot near here."

The Chief raised an eyebrow. "And what's his name?"

"Luther Willis."

He slowly shook his head. "Never heard of him either. Looks like you're getting the run around maybe."

"Maybe. But I trust the source."

"You planning on staying on a few days?"

"I thought I would take a room somewhere around here and see what I can turn up. If I find out anything of interest, you'll be the first to know."

Wooten gave a brief nod. "See that you do. Don't go taking this on yourself if you do find your man. That don't go over around here."

"I know the rules, Chief. And I'll abide by them."

"Make sure you do....don't go off half-cocked. You'll only make it worse for yourself. I'm guessing you've got plenty of steam saved up in there that wouldn't take much to blow the lid off."

"I can handle it, Chief. And I will turn it over to you if I pick up his trail."

"That's good. Long as we understand each other. Let Rhonda out there make a copy of his picture to leave with us." He gave me a semi salute to let me know we were finished and as I stepped toward the threshold he asked, "Where you planning on staying at?"

"Don't know yet."

"Let me know when you do. There's a motel up the road a few miles or you could stay at Miss Irena's place. She rents rooms out of an old two-story down the street, a few buildings past the café."

"Thanks, Chief. I'll look into it, and I'll let you know where I check in."

"Don't forget what I said. Take it easy."

"Yessir." I went on back down the hallway, glancing at some framed faded black and white photos of the town on my way through. Rhonda was writing on a memo pad when I returned, a half empty Branson, Missouri coffee mug beside her.

"Hey," she said, twirling the pen. "How'd it go? The Chief could help you?"

"No, but he asked me to have you make a copy of this picture." I handed her the clipping.

She looked at it. "He doesn't look like a crook. But then they don't always. Hang on just a minute and I'll go copy it for you." She got up and eased her way out of the tight space between her desk and the wall. The copy machine was across the room and I watched her as she walked toward it. She wore boot cut jeans and red leather western boots with gold tips. She quickly made the copy and returned to her desk just as the phone rang again.

"Thank you, Rhonda," I said as she handed mine back to me and she smiled again nodding as she picked up the phone. "Falling Waters Police Station. Rhonda speaking. How can I help you?"

I left satisfied that I'd handled it as best I could and started wondering what was on the day's special at Dinah's Café.

25

HONING IN

After a plate lunch of turnip greens, black-eyed peas, gravy and mashed potatoes, and pot roast, I needed two cups of coffee to get on with my job. The waitress whose name Fern was machine embroidered on the pocket of her blouse, was an older woman with gray streaks threading her ash blonde hair. She ripped off the green Guest Check from her pad and left it on my table by the window with a split second smile that was so brief I almost missed it. Falling Waters was not big on welcoming outsiders…with the stand out exception of Rhonda at the Police Station who was the only friendly face I'd seen so far that day.

As I placed the bills on the check and stood to take my leave, all eyes were upon me from the rear tables. The men and women customers appraised me with lidded eyes and disinterested expressions. One thing for sure: Falling Waters was not, nor ever would be, a tourist attraction. Nor did I expect to see a souvenir shop anywhere in town, although there was a lone tinted photograph of the dramatic waterfall that gave the town its name.

I left, closing the door quietly behind me. I had hopes of strolling around town and finding the town drunk. There's always at least one town drunk sitting on a bench somewhere trying to figure out where his next drink is coming from. If there isn't one, you can be sure he just died, and a new one will be taking his place shortly. I opened the tiny package of minted toothpicks the Café handed out at the register, and stuck one in my mouth hoping it gave me a nonchalant look and started walking down the one sidewalk in the town that ran along in front of the café and on down toward two blocks of buildings.

There was a feed store constructed of corrugated tin sheets with a wooden dock at the side; another corrugated tin building that housed a mechanic's shop with two pickups and a Jeep parked outside with *For Sale* signs on them; the vintage building with an *Irena's Place* sign in the yard; a boarded up video store; and a coin laundry all on that side of the street.

I rented a room for a week at the boarding house from a woman who stood behind a cluttered counter in the front sitting room. I looked over the post cards for sale on the counter while Irena filled out the paperwork for my stay. A bearded white-haired man sat in an arm chair by a floor lamp reading a fishing magazine by holding it up so close to his face it made my eyes hurt just looking at him. An orange cat slept on his lap.

Irena, a slim woman in her thirties. with the longest hair I'd ever seen worn loosely down her back smiled, and invited me to follow her to my new room. I stared at her hair in wonder as she led me up the stairs to the second floor. There was a hardwood varnished banister all along the stairs and along the landing and the biting strong smell of pine cleaner all along the hallway. It seemed to come from a freshly cleaned maroon carpet runner tacked down from one end of the hallway to the sparkling clean sill window at the far wall.

As it turned out, my room was all the way to the end and as she unlocked the door for me, I looked out the window and could see the back yard that separated her building from houses on the next street beyond. An oak tree and a pear and a cherry tree took up much of the backyard, and a tire on a thick rope hung from the thickest branch of the oak tree. The property line was marked with a combination of chain link and roughly one hundred feet of board fence at the back.

My new room was clean and orderly. Irena kept a well-maintained place. The bed was neatly made with a quilt and two pillows. There was a small sink on one wall and a varnished pine bureau with framed mirror on the opposite wall from the bed. Two windows glowed with bright sunlight that beamed across an oval rag rug on the plank floor. There were two framed prints on the walls. One of that same forest waterfall and the other of a doe, ears alert, in the clearing of a woods.

"You like your room?" Irena asked, holding out the key to me.

"I like it," I assured her.

She pointed to the sink. "We're hooked up to spring water here. I know you're going to like that."

"Definitely. Thank you." I tried to give her a tip. She waved it away.

"No, keep your money. This is my place."

She kept her tone very business like. "Well then, let me know if you need anything. I'll bring you up some fresh towels in a few minutes. They're in the dryer right now. There's a shower and tub halfway down the hall and only one other guest staying here at the moment. I don't know where you parked your car, but there are spaces for guests to the side of the building. You can pull in there whenever you want."

"I'll do that. I have a Chevy pickup."

"Good!" She brushed the palms of her hands together. "Well, okay. I guess that's it then. I'll be back." As soon as she left, I crossed to the window, opened it, and breathed in fresh mountain air, looking forward to drawing a glass of clear spring water from the faucet. A slight breeze circulated in the room and rippled the gauzy curtains. Besides the oak, pear, and cherry trees in the back yard, there was a vegetable garden with field peas, vine tomatoes and greens looking ready for harvest.

I stayed at the window looking out as I called Rhonda to report that I'd checked in to Irena's if she or the Chief needed to find me. A few minutes after that, Irena brought me the warm folded towels. I washed up at the sink wanting to lie down and rest for a while but knew if I did lie on that comfortable looking bed, I might doze off, so instead, I shut the room back up and went back downstairs ready to start running down Rocco.

I was feeling confident that I'd be successful and my energy level was up from the good home cooked meal and the invigorating fresh mountain air. So far I'd done everything by the book...notified local Law Enforcement what I was doing and where I could be found. Now all I had to do was find some local who looked needy and thirsty, maybe even shaky, and I'd be on track.

I walked down the six block long Main Street, past more metal buildings, then turned at the corner onto Church Street, and a view of a few scattered houses along the blacktop leading out of town. Not wanting to go in that direction, I crossed back onto the opposite side of the street to walk all the way back through town. There was a vacant lot between two brick buildings. One of the buildings had a Thrift Store on the ground floor and boarded up second-story windows. In the window of the Thrift Store was an antique rocking chair with a pink ceramic basin and ewer displayed on a stand next to it. Leaning against the rocker was a guitar with only one string and three missing tuners, and an open blue velvet lined hard case lying on the floor next to it.

I passed the building and glanced at the vacant lot. There was a gnarled crabapple tree to the rear of the property and the grass looked recently mowed. Sitting on a folding chair tilted back against the trunk of the tree was an older man wearing a visor cap pushed back on his head. His eyes were closed, and I crossed over to him as he swatted a fly away from his face.

"Excuse me," I said as I approached. There were dark circles under his eyes and his bottom lip trembled.

His eyes snapped open, and he jerked awake. "Yeah? What you want?"

"You wouldn't know where a man can get a drink around here, do you? I just got into town and haven't seen a barroom yet."

He laughed. "If a man could get a drink in this town, I'd be drinking it."

"There's no saloon in town?"

"Used to be. Burned down."

"If you know where I can get a drink, I'm buying," I offered.

There was a long pause. "You from Louisiana?" He squinted at me.

"How'd you know?"

"Close your mouth, you won't catch flies," he advised laughing again. He enjoyed his wit so much he started coughing then spat to his right.

"Well, okay, then. I'll leave you to your nap." I looked up as a blue jay flew from the tree.

"How'd you get all the way up here from Louisiana? You lost?" he asked, wiping his mouth with the back of his hand.

"I'm on vacation. Wanted to see what the Ozarks looks like."

"What you think so far?'

"I like it," I said. "Easy on the eyes up here."

"Oh, yeah. I left and went out to California for a few years. Big mistake. Came back soon as I could save up bus fare."

"Well then, maybe I'll run into you again. I have to see about finding me a drink somewhere."

"How much you need?" He asked as I turned to leave.

"Just a jar. I'm not much of a boozer. But my back hurts from driving all day. I could use a little painkiller right about now." I put a hand on the small of my back and winced, hoping he'd buy my story.

"We talking a pint jar or a quart jar? I don't figure you for a jug."

"A quart would be good."

"I'll see what I can do. You'll spring for one for me too, right?"

"That's what I said."

"Name's Tom Perkins, by the way." He put out a thin hand. We shook.

"Mine's Harris Viator. "

"Okay, Louisiana. Meet me back here in about an hour. I'll see if I can scare a drop up for you. And it won't be nothing like that swamp water you got back home. This is High Test." His voice rasped, and he cleared his throat. He placed a hand on his neck to soothe it. "Sure could use some myself. I'm dry as Texas right about now."

"Sounds like you're dry all right, Tom. So I'll see you back here about…." I looked at my watch. "About one-thirty."

He looked up at the sky and pointed. "I go by the sun. If I ain't here, have a seat. I'll be back shortly. Nobody will run you off. My sister owns this property."

"Later, then," I said as I walked away, headed back to my truck. My plan was to sit in it and wait. So far, so good. I leaned back against the headrest with my cap pulled low over my eyes as though taking a nap of my own, crossed my arms and watched from beneath the visor. I had a clear view of most of Main Street, and hoped I'd be able to see if old man Perkins was going to do me any good.

Within five minutes, I saw him round the corner of the block to head into the Thrift Shop. Another ten minutes and a forest green pickup with a jerry rigged wooden bumper pulled up in front of the shop and waited at the curb until he came out. Tom hustled into the cab of the truck and they took off slowly up the street, passing me by without even a glance in my direction.

The driver of the pickup was leaning so far against the driver side of the truck that it was hard to make out his features. All I could see was he wore a flannel shirt and Western hat with the brim rolled. Tom was alert in the passenger seat and I was sure he could almost taste that liquor he was looking forward to. I watched the truck go on down the road and waited long enough for them to round a bend before cranking up my engine and following. This was something I'd always been good at in Louisiana, and I wasn't planning on falling down on the job in Arkansas, even though it was unfamiliar territory.

I had bitter determination going for me, and that put me on high alert. I could almost smell my quarry by that time.

As I reached the top of the hill a mile out of town, I saw the truck up ahead rounding another curve. By the time I reached that bend in the road, the truck had gone out of sight. I sped up, and after going another quarter mile, caught a glimpse of it once more. About five miles out of town, the truck turned off into some woods and I slowed, fearing they'd spotted me and were waiting up ahead. But by the time I reached the spot where they turned in, I saw it was a dirt road with five-strand barbed wire along one side and thigh high pigweed and thistle growing alongside the road on both sides. The road had dips and potholes, and it was easy to see that no county plows had ever resurfaced it.

I didn't see the pickup, so put the truck in reverse and pulled back out on the blacktop. I'd found a road of interest, and needed to get out of there before I was spotted following my contacts. I drove on back to Falling Waters and parked in the same spot I'd been in before. The whole trip had taken less than half an hour. I expected to be able to meet up with Tom fairly soon, so I locked the truck and went back into the Café for another cup of coffee while I waited.

"You still in town?" Fern asked.

"Oh, I'll be here all week maybe," I said.

"You want some pie with that? Fresh apple pie. Still warm from the oven."

"Sounds good," I said. She hurried away and I waited on my coffee and pie while keeping an eye out the window for Tom's return.

When Fern returned with my order, I kept my eye on the street while I attended to the flaky crust and the chunky apple filling. The coffee was piping hot and strong and I drank it black so I'd be ready for whatever adventures the rest of the day would bring.

By the time I'd finished and Fern had brought my check, I was feeling restless, so paid at the register, and left the café to walk over to the vacant lot and wait for Tom. He still wasn't back by the time I got there, so I sat on his folding chair and glanced at the sun and then my watch. According to both, he was due back.

I didn't have long to wait. Tom's ride dropped him off at the Thrift Store and he briskly crossed the grass to where I sat, one paper bag under each arm. He was smiling. "Told you I'd help you out," he said, with a crooked smile.

"How much I owe you?" I asked.

"Forty and one of these for me," he said. "No, make it forty-five and one of these. I have to give my partner some money for gas."

I fished in my pocket for my wallet and snapped out the bills. "Thanks, Tom. You did good."

"You want the red or the white liquor?" he asked.

"I like it clear."

"I didn't know, so I got one of each. And here you go." He handed me the paper bag from beneath his left arm. The top of the bag was twisted shut. I took it and handed him the money.

Tucking it under my arm, I started to leave. "See you," I said as I started to walk off.

"Ain't you gonna take a sip with me at least?"

"No, I'm going to go back to the room, lie down, drink some and hope it cures my aching back."

He laughed. "They all as trusting as you down there on the Bayou? That might be nothing but creek water in that jar."

"I'm sure it's just what you say it is, and I'm about to kick back with it." I took a few more steps away from him.

"Oh, it'll cure what ails you, mister. Of that I guarantee." He chuckled. "Just don't come back complaining cause it was too much for you to handle."

I raised a hand in farewell and continued on toward Irena's Place.

26

SEEKING ROCCO

I returned to my room, stashed the liquor under the bed, splashed water on my face and got ready to start my hunt for Rocco. When I got back to my truck I retraced the way out of town and traveled toward the dirt road where Tom and his friend had turned off. This time I stayed on it and followed it through mixed woods of hardwoods and pine on both sides of the narrow road. The road was so rutty I had to drive very slowly as it made my truck rattle and I wanted to approach wherever I was going as quietly as possible. I drove almost two miles through the woods before I saw any indication of people living anywhere around. Finally I saw something shadowy by the side of the road up ahead and slowed down to a crawl.

There was a man swigging a beer and leaning against a tree by a cattle gate, so I kept driving up the road another half mile and then turned into a dirt trail leading into the woods and parked the pickup.

I'd have to creep slowly back through the woods and try to approach the house from another direction, hoping there were no other lookouts on duty.

There were deadfalls and branches all over the ground left over from a recent storm as the breaks were a bright golden color and fresh, and the sap was still oozing on some of them. Pine needles blanketed the ground so my footsteps were muffled. I kept my head low wary of the possibility of fish hooks strung between trees to snag poachers. I also tread carefully near to tree trunks to avoid any traps that might also be set for trespassers. Camouflaged deer cameras could be watching me, but it was not much use keeping an eye out for them as they would be well hidden.

I kept scanning the area as I slowly moved ahead, on the lookout for anything threatening my approach. The property was dense with a mixture of different hardwoods. I recognized gum, ash, pin oak, and hickory trees plus some others that I couldn't identify, and a great multitude of thick vines twining all through those woods. There were plenty of orange and also mottled gray toadstools mixed in with the moss and fern of the forest floor. A crow called and then another answered. The sound was lonely and I felt kinship with it because I was very much on my own up there moving in on a completely unpredictable situation. The sky was getting darker and the cloud cover was dingy and heavy, warning of a pending storm.

When I had cautiously made my way to within fifty feet of the house, I stopped, hunkered down and planned to just observe for a while. There was a shiny black GTO and two beat up pickups parked in front of the house, all facing out toward the road. The house was a vintage frame circa 1920 set on blocks with a rusty tin roof and spacious front porch. On the porch was a green metal glider and several red tin chairs lined up against the front wall. The paint on the uprights was peeling, and there were two wooden barrels on each side of the warped front steps.

A man lounged on the glider leafing through a magazine, black boots propped up on an upended metal trunk. A Doberman slept on the deck underneath his stretched out legs. I circled around and tried to move toward the sill windows on my side of the house. It was then that the young blue pit bull scrambled from under the house howling, and the Doberman's head jerked up, cropped ears erect. He stared my way for a few seconds, then leaped off the porch headed toward me.

There were two choices: climb the oak beside me or shoot the dogs. I climbed the tree. If you haven't climbed a tree lately, you'd be surprised at how fast you can shimmy up one if there's a pit bull and a Dobie after you. I threw a leg over the lowest branch and waited as the pit bull carried on in full voice at the base of the tree, leaping and falling, leaping and falling. The Doberman circled the tree around and around, head raised and snarling.

The man on the glider sat up suddenly, the hat falling off his face and strained to see what the dogs were barking at. "Satan! Duke! Shut up!" he yelled, grabbing his hat before it fell off the glider.

Someone inside yelled, "What the hell are those dogs barking at?"

"Must be a coon they treed over there."

"Call em back so I can get some sleep, dammit!"

"Satan! Duke! Get over here!" the man ordered from the glider, his voice ragged. He slapped the hat on his head and stood.

The dogs kept on growling, barking and jumping. The man stood on the edge of the porch and whistled for them. They finally obeyed and turning around, headed back toward the house, still growling deep in their throats.

"Get over here, you!" the man called again, eyes narrowing as he watched the Doberman return to the porch. "Lay down over there!" The pit bull stood at the edge of the house looking back at the tree and then the house as though unsure of where to go.

"Get over here!" the man called, still standing at the edge of the porch. The dogs, although abandoning their prey, continued to growl.

"Shut those goddamn dogs up, can't you?" yelled the man from the house. "I've been up all damn night and I have to listen to this shit now? Put them in the back in the kennels, or I'll never get back to sleep."

"I got it," the man on the porch said. "Come on, Satan. Duke." He jumped off the side of the porch and the dogs followed him toward the back of the house. From my vantage point in the tree, I could see a long row of side by side kennels with a metal roof set about twenty feet from the back of the house. An excited black-and-tan paced back and forth in one of the chain-link kennels.

As the man put the dogs into their units, I studied the back area. A large metal building, approximately one thousand square feet, lay beyond the kennels and about fifty feet from the house.

I planned to wait it out in the tree until both men went back to sleep, but my legs were cramping. Easing myself into a more comfortable position, I leaned my head back against the bark of the tree, reminded myself I'd sat out many a surveillance in my time, and returned my gaze toward the house.

27

FRESH KIND OF HELL

My legs were cramping by the time I scored and finally got a look at Rocco. He came out on the porch, stretching and yawning, then stepped off the porch and looked up at the sky. He was wearing a white tee shirt with a black vest, jeans and boots. He ran his fingers through his hair, combing it back away from his face, then yawned again. He looked around briefly, then retreated back into the house.

My blood started to boil, bugs were making me itch, and I had a severe crink in my neck, but I contained myself, and waited. I'd learned patience from many an hour of surveillance, and knew how to bide my time. Somebody inside the house turned up the radio loud on some Megadeth, and then the dogs started howling again from the kennel in back. The unmistakable sound of beagles chorusing mixed in with the other hounds and pit bulls.

I waited another hour and then slid down the rough bark of the tree, skinning my hands, and half stooped, started the trek back through the woods to my truck. As I made my way through the shadowy woods, I kept down in case they had strung fish hooks or other booby traps set at a man's height. I watched where I put my feet as well, never knowing what kind of snares they might have set up for trespassers.

As the rock and roll and howling dogs faded somewhat into the distance, I began to relax, knowing I was fairly close to where I parked the truck. It was an instant later that the ground gave way beneath me, and I fell into a pit spiked with bamboo shaved to dagger like points sticking straight out of the bottom of the four-foot dugout.

Because I'd been zigging and zagging, I'd landed on a far corner of the pit, and only one spike went through my boot. It caught me on the right side of the ball of my foot and went straight through the leather boot to stick out of the top. The pain was excruciating, and my mouth was so full of dirt that my cursing was muffled as I folded crumpled on the dirt at the bottom of the trap. I spat and coughed and worked the dirt out of my mouth, but it still gritted against my teeth.

The sun had moved far to the west and I knew I had to get out of there while I still had daylight or I'd never find my truck and I'd be falling into another booby trap while looking for it. Either that, or I'd be spending the night under a blanket of pine needles until dawn. The crew back at the house probably let the dogs out at night on patrol duty...still another reason to waste no time getting back to the truck.

I checked for anything broken in the fall, but I was all right except for my right foot. I gritted my teeth, ground my jaw, and began to force my boot off the spike. I almost bit my tongue off with the pain as I worked my foot free. I can't describe the pain, but it was ferocious and burned like fire. Bad as it was, I knew it was only a matter of time before the shock of it wore off and the pain became intolerable. I had to move fast to get back to my truck or I'd be in that hell hole all night.

I hauled myself out of the pit and started crawling toward the road, until I could risk putting my weight on my left foot. I crawled like a baby for about twenty yards, then made my first attempt to stand. I fell back down three times, but finally managed to get halfway up so I was semi-mobile again. Half hopping, half limping, I made my way toward the truck as the daylight continued to fade. I was so pumped with adrenaline that I knew I could make it and such a fire burned inside of anger and determination that nothing at that point could have stopped me but a gun.

The music and the howling in the background finally died, and when I could see my truck through the trees, I was so encouraged I picked up my limping pace and made it through the last ten yards. I dragged myself along the bed of the truck and opening the door, fell against the seat of the cab, then hauled myself inside and let my head hang back on the neck rest as I fought to revive and get the hell out of there.

When I was finally ready to turn on the ignition and start back for Falling Waters, I had to arrange myself so I could work the gas pedal and brake with my left foot. I managed to work that out and took off, never so relieved to be leaving a place. I turned the truck around and started back to town. When I passed where I'd seen the sentry posted earlier, he was gone and I saw no other person when I drove down that dirt road. I hung a right and headed back to the rooming house with one thing in mind...to get back to the bed where I could lie down and drink some of that white whiskey that was sitting tightly capped underneath the bed back in my room.

28

REPORTING TO THE CHIEF

I parked the truck on the side of Irena's place in one of the marked guest spaces, and hobbled into the house, my foot on fire and jolts of pain shooting up my leg. Irena wasn't around, and I made my way through the entryway and dragged myself up the stairs to my room, hanging onto the wooden banister like a drowning man clinging to a piece of driftwood. When I'd managed to limp across the hallway and down to my room, I unlocked it and stumbled toward the bed.

I flopped down like dead weight onto the mattress and leaned back into the pillows, then with both hands lifted my right leg up onto the bed and with boots still on, stretched out and closed my eyes so I could rest enough to grab the cell phone and call the Chief to report what I'd learned. After lying there for about five minutes, breathing hard and fighting the pain, I reached under the bed and retrieved the jar of clear liquor.

I took the first mouthful and swallowed and it burned all the way down. I began to have hope that I could deaden the pain because the liquor was so fiery it almost took my mind off it for a second or two. I took a few more drinks from the jar and then set it carefully on the bedside table. My medicine for the time being. I slipped the cell phone out of its holder on my belt and called Chief Wooten.

"This is Harris Viator, Chief. Remember me? The guy from Louisiana?"

"I remember."

"I found Rocco Theriot. I saw him come out of a house back in the woods and I saw him go back inside."

"How long ago?"

"About two hours ago. He's out in the woods in an old house about ten miles from here. It's on a dirt road with no sign out at the highway. That's the place I told you about."

"You don't sound too good."

"I'm not good. On the way out of the woods, I fell into a booby trap they dug out there. Bamboo stakes at the bottom. One pierced my foot and I feel like hell or I'd have come by the station house. It was all I could do to drive back here."

"Where are you now?"

"I'm back in my room lying down."

"At Irena's Place?"

"Yes."

"So what landmarks can you describe to get to this place you're talking about?"

"I watched the mileage. It's nine and a half miles on Clark Road heading north. It's the only dirt road leading off around there. There's a hill and then an S curve right before you get to it."

"I know that road. It's out of my jurisdiction. I'll call the Sheriff. Do you need help?"

"I'll be all right for now. I'll go see a doctor to-morrow. But not today. I'm not moving from this bed for a while."

"Irena will help you. She's a good lady."

"I know it. I could tell when I met her."

"You sure you saw Rocco? I don't need to be send-ing the Sheriff off on a wild goose chase just cause a stranger drifts into town and says so."

"I know what I saw, Chief. I saw Rocco, and he still looks the same as in the picture I gave you. He might have lost a few pounds around the waist, but it's him."

"I'll be in touch. Don't go anywhere."

"That's funny," I said and he clicked off.

Having sent the posse after Rocco, I took another few drinks from the jar, and then closed my eyes so I could rest for a few minutes and gauge the effects of the liquid painkiller I'd drunk. About ten minutes later, Irena knocked quietly on the door.

"You decent?" she asked through a crack in the door.

"Come on in."

She came in bearing a tray and came over to the bedside. "I brought you something to eat. The Chief called me and told me to check on you. Said you'd hurt yourself."

I worked the pillow against the backboard and sat up wincing. "What's this?"

"I brought you some supper. You like beef stew with homemade biscuits on top?"

"Are you kidding? You're an angel of mercy."

"That's me." She smiled and set the tray beside me on the mattress. "What happened?" She eyed my torn boot.

"Stepped in a hole messing around in the woods."

"Anything broken?" She leaned over to see better.

"Stake went through my boot. How come the Chief called you?"

"He's a first cousin," she said. "You'd better get that boot off before your foot swells up."

"Too late for that."

"You can't just let it stay that way. You'll get infected."

"I'm not going to move from this bed until tomorrow."

"Okay…I know all about stubborn men. You better eat that while it's hot. I'll call my brother. He's a vet. We don't have a doctor in this town."

"Vet's good. We're all mammals. Same difference."

"Eat your supper and I'll go call him. He'll tell me what to do." She glanced at the mason jar on the nightstand. "I see you've been doing some doctoring on your own."

"Good for snake bite and whatever else ails you."

"Ozarks anesthetic," she smiled and then left the room.

29

NURSE IRENA

By the time I'd finished eating and dozed off for an hour, Irena rapped quietly at the door and woke me up. "You awake?" she called through the door.

"Come on in," I called and blinked my eyes open, still dazed from sleep. It was dark outside and the only light came from a lone streetlight from the street in back of her property. She clicked on the ceiling light from the switch beside the door.

She entered the room with a basin, some lethal looking scissors, and a brown glass bottle of something with a cork in it. "My brother said for me to cut that boot off and pour antiseptic on your wound. This here is wound medicine. He gave it to me last year for my dog. It's good stuff. And he said for me to get that boot off and put a clean sock out of the dryer on your foot."

"I don't know about that," I said, trying to sit up.

"I do. Just lay back down. I'll take care of it. He said you have to let me drive you to Stoneyville in the morning so you can get your foot looked at by a doctor."

"Horse doctor is fine with me. I'll go see him tomorrow."

"Are all men in Louisiana stubborn as you?"

"Most of them."

She came over to the bed and stared at the boot as if she could melt it off my foot by looking at it. "You going to let me do this or not?" She looked at me and waited with one hand on her hip.

"Make it quick is all I have to say."

"Brace yourself then." She started slowly trying to ease the boot off, but it wouldn't budge and I hollered when shooting pain ran up my leg.

"I'll have to cut it off," she said, twisting her mouth as she thought about it.

"They're all I brought with me."

"Don't worry. You won't need anything on that foot for a while. Just heavy socks." She pulled a thick white sock out of the pocket of her dress and held it up. "See. Fresh from the dryer. Still hot. Very sterile."

She went to work and produced some industrial sized scissors to cut the boot down the side. When she'd finished, she was able to slide it off my foot. My sock showed bright red bloodstains mixed with brown stains from the leather boot. "Now I have to peel off this sock before it sticks to your skin. You ready?"

"Go for it."

She peeled off the sock and it had stuck to the skin in a few places. What she revealed was a ragged rip in the flesh between my fourth and fifth toe that tore into almost three centimeters of flesh. "Now I'm going to have to pour this wound treatment on and it's a nasty color, so I don't want to get it all over the bed. I'm going to slide your leg over so I can pour the antiseptic over your foot so it drains into the basin. You up for this? Better take a sip of that white liquor you got over there."

"Let's do it and get it over with."

She slid my leg off the side of the bed, so I was turned on my side. Then she positioned the basin under my foot and slowly poured the purple antiseptic over the entire side of my foot. I was ready for it and bit my tongue so I wouldn't yell, then I reached for the jar and took another hit of it as the antiseptic did its work. The whole side of my foot was dyed purple but I knew the stuff was good. It wouldn't sting like fire if it wasn't working.

"There now see? We're done for now. I'll get a towel so you can rest your foot back on the bed. Hang on." She went over to the sink and took a white towel from the rack beside it.

"Your towel's going to be purple."

"Aw, so what?" She folded the towel on the bed, then lifted my leg so it was back on the mattress and gently laid it on the cloth.

"There now. At least you can sleep tonight without infection spreading into that hole you got there. In the morning I'll bring you up some breakfast and then I'll drive you to a doctor for some proper treatment."

"That was probably all the proper treatment I'm going to need."

"He wanted me to soak your foot in as hot water as you can stand, but I didn't think you would go for that."

"You're right."

"Maybe in the morning we can do that. After you get a night's sleep and have some breakfast."

"Thank you, Irena, for helping me out."

"You're most welcome. And another thing. I'm going to set a slop bucket by the door so you don't have to hobble down the hall to the bathroom."

"Don't bother with that. I'll hobble down to the bathroom when I need to," I assured her.

"Like I said, I'm setting a slop bucket inside the door. And you better not be all proud and stubborn about it, or you'll end up hurting yourself."

"I'm not doing that," I said and lowered my head like a bull. "Nobody is going to have to empty any slop bucket of mine."

She shook her head. "I figured you'd say that, but I'm leaving the bucket anyhow. Better to let somebody do for you than to end up losing your foot."

"Thanks anyway. But no thanks."

"I'm going to leave you alone now. I'll check on you first thing in the morning. I wake up before dawn. That's not too early?"

"No. Thank you."

"Good night then. Don't drink too much more of that stuff. You might decide to go out dancing." She laughed and left me for the night.

My foot was throbbing, but I still had half a jar. So I took another jolt of it and laid back to try to go to sleep.

30

NO DICE

I did sleep through the night with a lot of help from the liquor, and by the time Irena came back to check on me, grey light was filtering through the windows, and I awoke with more pain in my head from the liquor than was in my foot.

"You awake?" she called from the door. I saw where she'd left the enamel bucket by the door sometime after I'd fallen asleep just like she said she would.

"I am now," I called back. "Come on in."

"I brought you some hot coffee and breakfast. How's that sound?" She said with more cheer in her voice than before. She entered holding a tray and closed the door behind her with her foot. "Eggs, sausage, biscuits, and fried potatoes," she announced as she came toward the bed.

"Hey, you're too good to me," I said as I punched the pillows and sat up against the headboard.

"Don't mention it. I told people in my church about you being laid up and some of them are going to drop off some good things for you to eat later on today. Probably by the time we get back from Stoneyville."

"That's really nice of your friends," I said, arranging the tray on my lap.

"They're good people. Always glad to help someone who is in need." Irena glanced at the bedside table. "I see you did a good job on the pain killer last night," she said. "It's almost gone. You're going to have to make another run," she smiled.

"Like the man said, 'It's good for whatever ails you.'"

"I'll let you eat in peace then. I'll be back in a while so we can go see that doctor. I'm bringing you up a crutch I had in the back room somebody left here a long time ago. You can use it to get yourself on downstairs to my car when we go."

She left and I ate every crumb of that hot breakfast, then sliding the tray off my lap onto the bed I managed to get out of bed and hobble to the antique porcelain sink. I grimaced at the werewolf face in the mirror, splashed water on my face and hair, and washed up with the homemade tan soap bar Irena had placed in a soap dish shaped like a bathtub that said: *Having a tub of fun in the Ozarks.*

When I'd finished cleaning up as best I could at the sink, I hobbled back to bed and put my foot up again until she came back upstairs for me. As I was lying there with eyes closed trying to get rid of my headache, the cell phone rang and it was Chief Wooten.

"Thought I'd bring you up to date," he said.

"What happened?" I asked, suddenly alert, the headache forgotten.

"The Sheriff went out there...there's only one homestead down that road. Belongs to the same family for over a hundred years. Sheriff says he went with two deputies. One watched each entrance to the house. He knocked on the door, asked the man who answered the door about your man, Rocco, and showed him the photo I gave him. The man denied ever seeing a Rocco Theriot, ever hearing about a Rocco Theriot, and claimed whoever saw him there at the house was either drunk, hallucinating or lying.

"The man said the owner of the house, Floyd Metzger, was at work in his mechanic's shop, but he would tell him about this escaped prisoner, and if he heard anything about Rocco or if he showed up, he would alert the Sheriff right away. The Sheriff knows the family that's owned those woods all these years and that's as far as he's willing to go with it."

"So he didn't even search the house? Just took the guy's word for it? This Floyd Metzger? With me being an eye witness and all?"

"Sheriff said the man invited him in to look around. So he did pass through the rooms of the house. He saw nothing suspicious or out of the ordinary."

"What about illegal activity there? Why would they have a booby trap with bamboo spikes in it if they weren't doing something illegal back in that remote place?"

"Sheriff wasn't about to send his men hunting through the woods for marijuana or a still with traps scattered around….on a stranger's say so. Besides, like I said, he's known Floyd all of his life."

"This is crazy. I know what I saw."

"Look, Harris. If I hear anything, I'll let you know. Drop by the office before you go back to Louisiana and leave us your contact information down there. If I find out anything, I'll let you know right away. Meantime, is Cousin Irena looking after you?"

"She's an angel if that's what you mean. Don't know what I'd have done without her. Starved to death for starters."

"Irena's a good cook. You picked the right place to stay. How long you think you'll be in town?"

"Soon as I can drive home I'll leave. Irena's taking me to the doctor today, so I'll rest up until tomorrow at least."

"Call me if you need anything then," he said, "I'll see what I can do," and he clicked off.

I slipped the cell phone back into its leather holder and snapped it on my belt, then lay back against the pillows and tried to figure out what had happened when the Sheriff went out there hunting Rocco. I was still frowning and trying to make sense of it all when Irena came back to the room with the crutch to collect me for the trip to the doctor.

31

RECUPERATION

D r. Taylor, a lanky man with white hair combed straight back and a haggard face, cleaned the wound, put in a dozen stitches, gave me a booster tetanus shot, and three white envelopes loaded with antibiotics and painkillers. He sat at the rolltop desk of a ground floor office in his two-story 1865 home accessed by a side entrance. The doctor warned me to stay off my foot for a few days so the wound had a chance to heal without the added aggravation of putting weight on it. "This is a very nasty wound in a very bad place. You've got to give it a chance or you'll deeply regret it."

"I've got to get back to Louisiana," I said. "I know I can drive this way. I already had to do it coming back from the woods."

He frowned, all business and direct. "You mess around with that wound and you might end up losing part of your foot. Do what I'm telling you and stay off it. Catch up on your reading. Read some

Shelby Foote. You got any Shelby Foote at your place, Irena?"

"No, actually, I don't," she said.

"Do you have any Bruce Catton then? Cottrell?" he asked.

"No."

"Well, what do you have over there to read then?" he asked, lowering his glasses onto his nose and peering over them at her.

"I have a shelf of mysteries and Westerns that guests have left behind. He might like those. I don't think he'd like what I read much."

"And what is that?" the doctor asked.

"Oh, this and that. Gardening books mostly, and some biographies of people I don't think Harris would be interested in. Religious books."

"And it would be too much to expect Falling Waters to have a library wouldn't it?" He shook his head, then looked at me. "If I lend you some books, Irena can bring them back to me one day. Maybe I can keep you in bed for a couple of days at least.

"Do my part to save your foot."

He turned toward the door to his office. "Wait here. I'll be right back."

I smiled at Irena. "Bossy, isn't he?"

"Oh, he's always like that. But he's good. Everybody around here uses him, unless they won't see doctors because of their faith. We have quite a few around here that go to healing churches. Like the Holiness people." She raised her eyebrows at me. "And you better do what he says. He means what he says always. He's not just saying things to scare you."

"I don't know if I can stay in bed that long. I get too restless."

"Don't you worry. We'll help you stay off your feet. My church people and me."

Dr. Taylor came back into the room then toting a brown paper package wrapped in twine. "I put three books in here that will keep you busy for a while if you're not reading those Westerns and mysteries." He handed me the package where I still sat on his examining table. "These aren't just some bloody tales. You're going to learn something too."

"We had a Civil War battle right near here," Irena explained.

"And our great grandfather was in it," he said, jabbing a finger at the package I held. "You'll see. There's mention in one of these books about him. Cade Taylor. He's buried right here in the Stoneyville Cemetery."

"My great grandfather Jerome fought in the Civil War also, out of Lafayette, Louisiana. He's buried in St. Beatrice in the church cemetery. I'll be glad to read your books. Thank you."

"Always glad to help someone stay in bed when they need to. Part of the treatment," he said in a gruff tone.

After I paid him his nominal fee, we left and drove the ten miles back to Falling Waters. Irena helped me hobble back upstairs to my room, and I fell back onto the bed and leaned the crutch against the bedside table for later use. I opened the package Dr. Taylor had given me and saw he'd lined me up to read about Quantrill, Bloody John Anderson, and a book on the various battles of Arkansas. I was only able to read one chapter of the Quantrill book before the pills he'd given me made my eyelids so heavy, I couldn't keep them open to read even one more line. By the time Irena brought a tray with a hot dinner for me, I was sound asleep.

32

BEDRIDDEN

The pills didn't wear off until dark and when I woke up and saw how night had descended without me noticing, it was a bit eerie. The light on the back street cast a lonely cone of light and all else was black including my room. I stretched out an arm and turned on the lamp on the bedside table. There were my envelopes of pills, a glass of water, and on the other side of me on the bed was a tray with a plate of cold dinner and pie on the side.

I'd slept hard and felt groggy from what medicine was still in my system, but I decided to wait to take any more pills and make it over to the sink to splash water on my face so I could read for a few hours before going back to sleep. Irena came back upstairs to check on me a little later, and brought me some ice cream to go with the pie. I had just hobbled back with my crutch from the bathroom down the hall and was sitting on the side of the bed.

"You really slept. That's the best thing you can do right now. That cherry pie was made by one of the church ladies."

"Please thank her for me. Best I ever had. I'm going to read some of these books for a while then I'll take a couple more pills and go back to sleep. It'll keep me from going stir crazy."

"If you see Doc again, he'll probably test you on it. He heads the historical society up there in Stoneyville….and the Sons of the Confederacy chapter also." Irena smoothed my bed and fussed with the pillows. "Learn anything yet?"

"How about this? The Ozarks got its name from *aux arcs* after the bows of the Osage Indians… French trappers named it. The Osage orange tree…*Bois d'Arc*…has very hard wood that they used to make their bows. Did you know that?" I asked her.

"I did know that," she smiled. "Anything else?"

"Yes. We call those trees Horse Apple trees back home cause the horses like the fruit. We used to play games with those big orange balls the trees drop. The skin is nubby and they're big like grapefruits. You ever play with those?"

"Probably did," she said. "Your wound feeling any better?"

"Oh, yeah. It's coming along."

"Don't start getting hard headed and take off in the middle of the night for Louisiana just cause it's feeling better."

"Naw. I know what he said is true. I don't plan on being stupid."

"Good. That's what I want to hear." She watched me carefully as though I might sneak away and go home.

"I just hate that I'm such a lot of work for you is all."

She put a hand on her hip and tilted her head watching me as I got back into bed.

"When the Good Lord puts someone in my path who needs help, I know what I'm supposed to do. And if I don't, well, shame on me. That's how we do things in my church."

"What is your church?"

"Same as always. I was baptized and grew up in the Holiness Church."

"Well, you know I'm really grateful for all you're doing. If it wasn't for you, I'd have left for home hours ago and my foot would be turning green right about now."

"That's why the Good Lord put you in my path. He didn't want you to suffer needlessly. You better hurry and eat your dinner before that ice cream melts." She pointed to the tray, gave me a small smile, and left the room.

I watched her leave and thought about how opposite Irena and Lenny were. I would never have to lecture Irena about showing cleavage or wearing shorts that barely covered her. I smiled at the contrast between the two women. Irena wouldn't be caught dead anywhere near a strip club, let alone dance in one even if she did believe her father murdered her boy friend. I couldn't even work up a mental image of Irena in a thong up on the stage showing everything for the hungry men, because it was an impossible image.

This bit of contrasting made me realize I hadn't had much time to think about Lenny, and I wondered if she was all right. I was too stubborn to call her, but wanted to talk to her and tell her about all that had happened. I never would have found Rocco without her help. I missed her beauty and her sensational body, and her humor and her touch, but I wasn't about to call her. Stubborn. But then Lenny was stubborn also, so it was highly unlikely either one of us would ever call.

I ate the perfectly seasoned meat loaf and mashed potatoes and lima beans, and the pie and ice cream, then slid the tray away toward the edge of the bed and picked up the Quantrill again. By the time my foot felt well enough to travel, I was going to know a lot more about guerilla warfare and bushwhacking than I ever had before. I'd had a taste of guerilla warfare when I fell into that bamboo spiked hole, and it seemed like an appropriate subject for me to be studying after what had just happened to me, and what could even happen in the future if I was able to chase down Rocco still another time.

Later on, Irena came back up to take away the tray and bring me some hot chocolate to wash down my pills. "You sleep sound now, you hear?" she said as she left to go back downstairs for the night.

And I did just that, sleeping hard all through the night.

33

LEAVING ARKANSAS

After following Dr. Taylor's directions and staying on the bed reading and sleeping for two days, I woke up the third day after the accident with cabin fever and knew I had become too restless to remain there any longer. I got up and limped around the room gathering all my belongings and getting ready to go home. I told Irena I couldn't stand lying around in the bed any longer, and we argued about it, but after wrangling for a while, she realized she wasn't going to talk me out of it, so she reluctantly offered to fix me up with some sandwiches and a thermos of hot coffee for the long drive home.

She didn't want to even charge me for the room and board after I was hurt. "It's my Christian duty," she protested. "And I was glad to do it." My money was almost gone, and I told her I'd send her a money order as soon as I was able for all she'd done, but I wanted to save whatever I had left for gas so I wasn't pushing my luck and running on empty.

She carried my things down to the truck for me and gave me the crutch to take with me. When I'd settled into the cab, and laid the crutch on the passenger side, I looked over at her standing there by the driver's side and wanted to give her a kiss for all she'd done. I started to lean my head out the window to plant one on her cheek, but thought better of it, and instead nodded my head at her and said, "Don't know what I'd of done without you."

"Sure wish you'd stay just one more day," she said, wiping her hands on her apron, looking worried. "At least call me and let me know how you made out on the trip back. I wrote my number on the paper bag."

"I'll call you," I promised, and she stepped away from the pickup when I turned the key in the ignition.

As I backed the truck out to the street, she waved, and I waved back, then turned off on Main Street headed back down south.

When I passed the vacant lot where I'd met Tom Perkins, I thought to swing by and tell the old man goodbye. He was sitting on his chair beneath the apple tree, but he didn't look so well. Even from the street I could see his face was swollen and his eyes sunken. I parked the truck and called out to him from the curb.

"Hey, Tom."

He looked up and when he saw me he became visibly upset. "Go away!" he called. "Got nothing to say to you."

"What's the matter? You all right?"

"Go away! Go home. I don't know you," he rasped, and he flailed an arm at me like he was batting at flies.

"Tom. It's me. The guy from Louisiana." I thought he must be having some sort of alcohol related daydream.

"Go home!" he rasped again and this time agitated as he was, he swung both arms trying to get me to leave.

By then I could make out that his eyes weren't sunken, they were blackened. I realized suddenly with a shock that somebody had hit him. I felt instant tenderness toward the old man, and turned off the ignition, reaching for my crutch so I could get closer and find out what happened to him.

I managed to hobble out of the truck and around the side to go to him, but he became so agitated as I advanced that he leaped out of his chair and started trotting in the opposite direction to get away from me, his baggy trousers flapping. "Go! Go!" he called, and as I was upsetting him so much, I returned to the truck and got back inside the cab.

As I started the engine again, I realized what had happened. The poor old man had been beaten up for getting suckered by a stranger and leading me to their operation back in the woods...and also to Rocco's hiding place. And thereby bringing the sheriff down on them and right to their door. I felt intense remorse over causing Tom such trouble. I hadn't seen this coming, and would never have endangered him if I had.

The best thing I could do was to leave Tom alone and stay far away from him, or I'd get him into even more trouble. Reluctantly, I drove away from the curb and headed out of town. My foot hurt, but pangs of sorrow for the beating I'd caused that friendly old man hurt even worse. It hadn't taken them long to find out who had been talking to a stranger in town and how that had lined up time-wise with the Sheriff tipped off about Rocco. Either that or some-one had found out about me from Chief Wooten or the Sheriff himself. I didn't know the town or the county politics, and being an outsider and a flatland-er, there was no way I was going to find out how it worked around there either.

It was going to be a long, hard trip home, and all the more so having found out how Tom had gotten himself all banged up because of me. Another strike against Rocco. More misery he'd caused. Maybe he was not even gone from over there in the woods. Maybe he was still there hiding out and laying low. Now that he'd eluded the Sheriff even searching the house, why become a fugitive on the run? Way easier to just stay put and out of sight where he was.

The whole thing was such a lousy mess and my foot was throbbing again so much that I almost wanted to just go back and lie down in my old room at Irena's Place. Tempting as that idea was though, I continued heading out of town and didn't look back. My hunt for Rocco was a bust, and I was going home defeated. But what the hell, at least I hadn't lost my foot or worse.

34

HIGH CHAPPARAL

The trip home was tedious to say the least, as I had to use my left foot for the brake, the clutch, and the gas pedal. Each time I filled up the gas tank, I had to hobble in to pay and then keep going to use the Men's Room. Irena had stacked four wax paper wrapped sandwiches in a brown paper bag and thrown in a bag of chips. The food and the thermos of hot coffee kept me going hour after hour.

But by the time I got home seven hours later, my foot was so swollen and throbbing all I wanted to do was to lie down with my foot up and watch a movie until I fell asleep. But first I checked in with Celeste and hobbled into the back yard to hug Willie and Merle, brush them, and sit with them for a while. Celeste brought me over a red tin chair and I sat on it while the dogs messed with me and I threw balls for them. Celeste brought a footstool for me and an icy bottle of beer. Then she went into the kitchen to fix me a cheeseburger and thick home fries, knowing I could use a hot meal after that long trip home.

She served me the burger and fries at her kitchen table, and wanted to know all about my trip. I filled her in on all of it, and she sat at the opposite side of the table with a cup of coffee listening intently, elbow on the table as she supported her chin with one hand, not interrupting even one time.

"That's some story," she said when I'd finished. There was a pause as she thought about it, eyes half closed, fingers idly tapping on the table.

"What you thinking about?" I asked as I finished off the last crumb.

"I'm thinking about how you must have made some bad enemies while you were up there, it looks like."

"Yeah, but who cares? They're up there and I'm down here."

"I'll bet they're mad enough to come find you," she said, her tone flat.

"Rocco doesn't know where I live, and besides, he's probably three states away by now, now that he knows they're looking for him in Rock County. I'm the least of his worries."

"It's not Rocco I'm worried about." She got up from the table, cleared my plate, and went to the glass domed pie saver to cut me a piece of peach pie she'd just baked. "You want some coffee with this?" she asked as she served me a large slice.

"No thanks. I drank too much coffee on the road. I'm going to try to kick back and maybe even catch a nap with my foot up on a pillow."

"You don't want to play with that wound. You'd better go see my doctor tomorrow. Make sure it's not getting infected." She sat down again with another cup of coffee.

"I'm fine. I still have antibiotics the Arkansas doctor gave me. I just need to get off it and let it heal."

"You called that nice girl friend yet…let her know you're home? Let her come make a fuss over you."

"I don't think so," I said too fast. Celeste gave me a look, then raised her hands.

"Sorry. I'll butt out."

"It's okay. We're on the outs right now."

"Just temporary, I hope."

"Maybe. Maybe not. I don't know. And right now I have bigger problems than hardheaded women."

Celeste tried not to smile, and covered it with raising the coffee cup to her lips.

"I love this pie."

"Want some more?"

"No, no. I'm going to go lie down now. Maybe I can sleep through the night. Call me if you need me though."

"I'm not going to bother you. Go sleep." She waved me away and I carried my dishes to the kitchen sink. "Just leave it there. I'll take care of it. Go lie down before you fall down."

"Thanks, Celeste. I'll sleep a lot better after that good food. You're the best."

I hobbled back to my room, turned on the TV hoping to find a Western I hadn't already seen, and flopped onto the bed, propping my aching foot onto a pillow. Within ten minutes of *High Chapparal,* I was sound asleep.

35

LENNY IS ATTACKED

I slept like the dead and woke up the next morning before dawn with the TV still on and a rerun of an old Rifleman episode running. My foot had stopped throbbing and felt almost normal. I got up and after a steaming hot shower, decided to drive to a nearby truck stop for a big hot breakfast with a bottomless cup of strong coffee. Then, depending how my foot was holding up, I'd make my plans for the day.

The truck stop was jumping. There were four 18 wheelers parked in the side lot and a scattering of pickups and cars in the front lot. It was like high noon in there with the blazing neon lights and country music playing, the store and restaurant lively with people walking in and out, and it wasn't even fully light out yet.

I filled my plate from the buffet with almost everything they put out, and brought the heaping plate back to my booth as the waitress brought me my first mug of coffee. I went at it as though I hadn't eaten in a week and even after all that chowing down, wanted to go back for more, but allowed myself only one more biscuit before quitting. Three cups of coffee later, I was ready to check out when my cell phone rang and I was startled to see Lenny's number come up on Caller ID.

"Harris. You awake?"

"Yeah, I'm out eating breakfast. Where are you?"

"I'm up at the camp." She didn't sound good.

"What're you doing up there?"

"I came up to be alone and do some writing on that idea I told you about."

"That's good then."

"No, it's not. Something happened."

"What?" I felt a twinge on the back of my neck and shook it off.

"I was attacked up here." She spoke so softly it was as though she didn't even want to hear it herself.

"What do you mean?"

"I was attacked yesterday. I was lying out on the chaise writing in my notebook, and Junior sneaked up on me. Quintus wasn't even around. He'd gone into town. Junior grabbed me, force-kissed me and his hands were crawling all over me like a lunatic. He was all over me like a….like I don't know what. It was horrible."

"What'd you do?"

"I grabbed the little perv by his balls and threw him off me so he was lying on his back howling. Then I twisted him like a corkscrew so I thought he'd die he was screaming so hard. I kneeled on his chest while I was doing it, and he bit me on my leg."

"Drew blood."

"Good God, Lenny. Did you call 911?"

"Oh, you know I did. He's unconscious cause after he bit me, I really lost it and beat him over the head with the first thing I could get my hands on. My beer bottle. I cracked his skull, I think. I heard something crack. Meanwhile, Bijou bit him on the ass. He was out like a light. They hauled him off in an ambulance."

"Why didn't you call me before this?"

"I was afraid to. Cause you warned me about these freaks of nature."

"You should have called me. I'll come up."

"No. Don't come up. I'm driving back today. I'll come see you at the motel. I just wanted you to know what happened before I left in case…"

"In case what?"

"I don't know..in case they arrest me or something."

"Arrest *you?*"

"I don't know. I'm talking crazy. I couldn't sleep all night. My nerves are shot."

"Nobody's going to arrest you, Lenny."

"Maybe for nude sunbathing. Entrapment or some shit like that. Don't forget, his father's the Police Chief."

"His father doesn't seem to like him very much. And nobody's going to arrest you for sunbathing in your own backyard in the middle of a hundred acres."

"I know. Like I said, I can't think straight right now."

"Don't drive then. I'll come up there and get you."

"No. I'm okay to drive. I just want to get out of here. Like *now!*"

"What did Quintus have to say about all this."

"He was furious. He already hates Junior's guts. He made me a hot rum toddy and ordered me to take a hot bath and go lie down. Then he fixed a nice dinner for me and brought it up on a tray. He was great. He hopes they lock Junior up for a good while and get him out of our hair. He's a menace."

"Did the Chief come out to see how you were doing?"

"Yes, he did. He was so embarrassed his face stayed red the whole time. He interviewed me and apologized over and over for his little pervert. He decided Junior's gone mental and needs to be in a locked psycho unit somewhere. I kind of think he's afraid Daddy will have somebody work Junior over soon as he finds out what happened. Either work him over or make him disappear."

"A locked unit? That little dirt bag is lucky I wasn't there. He'd be glad to be in a locked unit after what I'd have done to him."

"It's all a lousy mess. But I'll be seeing you soon. Soon as I get there I'll come by your place."

"Tonight's one of the nights Celeste plays. I can take you over there to Acey's and we can eat dinner and listen to her sing. Get your mind off of it."

"That would be good. Anything to get that image out of my head of that little geek slobbering all over me. So gross."

"Okay then. Drive safe and don't drink anything for your nerves."

"I won't. "

I sat there for a few minutes glaring out the window, visualizing the scene she described and my jaw got so tight with anger that it cramped. I rubbed my jaw and stared out the window at the big rigs in the parking lot.

"Something wrong?" the waitress stopped and asked. "Bad news?"

"Yeah, but it's going to get better," I said and gave her a tight smile. "Thanks for giving a damn."

I paid my tab and left for home, very anxious to see Lenny again. I had steam coming out of my ears thinking of what I'd like to do to Junior, and to calm myself down I told myself that at least I was pretty sure Lenny wouldn't be running around without clothes on anymore.

36

ACEY'S BAR & LOUNGE

When Lenny picked me up, she leaped out of the car and ran to me soon as I came out of my room. She threw her arms around my neck and held on tight like she was drowning. I held her for a few minutes as she silently tucked her head under my chin. She was wearing a long sleeved pleated shirt with only the collar button open and navy blue slacks. She wore the shirt out over the pants and navy flats. A red and navy silk scarf covered her hair and she'd tied it under her chin. I'd never seen her so covered up. All she needed was a pair of dark glasses and she could go incognito.

"I'm so glad to see you," she said finally, letting go of me and realizing I had a crutch under my arm. "What happened to you?"

"It's been a rough week," I said. "For both of us. I'll tell you about it later. For now, let's go hear Celeste."

We drove over to Acey's Lounge in Lenny's Charger. It was only ten minutes away going back toward Ida and then driving west on the four lane toward Eustis.

Even though it was early, the surrounding parking lot was already half full with sedans and pickups. The building was a rambling old frame with metal roof and a red neon sign with a flashing arrow pointing toward the entrance. It said: *Acey's Bar & Lounge Cocktails Steaks & Seafood.*

A stout man in a white dress shirt and Western hat with his hand on the back of a petite woman wearing a denim skirt and boots was leading her toward the entrance. Another pickup pulled in after us and another couple got out as we slowly made our way toward the heavy front door.

"You hungry?" I asked because the smell of grilled meat was drifting from the restaurant.

"I could eat something," she said as we made our way up the wooden steps onto the wraparound porch.

"Probably after what you've been through, a hot meal will do you good."

"Along with about four shots of Black Jack with beer chasers," she said.

"Don't get loaded. You have to drive home," I cautioned.

"All right. I'll save my drinking for when we get back to your room," she said, and gave me a look that told me our first fight was history, and soon all would be like before once more.

Celeste was playing piano when we arrived at one end of the sprawling room. The ceiling was high, and there were rafters overhead with cone shaped metal lights hanging from them. Booths lined the walls and there were tables arranged in a semi circle around the dance floor. Celeste was singing and playing *Today I Started Loving You Again* as we entered and over a dozen couples were dancing to it.

I leaned my crutch against a booth near to the piano, and we settled onto the red upholstered seats across from one another. Lenny reached across the table for my hand.

"I missed you. You don't know how I missed you. And especially after what happened up there at the camp. I'm sorry for my big mouth."

"It's a good thing Junior is locked up. Saves me from going to jail, me too."

"I should never have been so stupid as to not listen to you. If I had, none of this would have happened. You'd have been up there with me, or we never would have gone up in the first place."

"What is, is," I said. "No use wasting time rehashing it."

"At least I learned my lesson," she said. "From now on, I'm not going to be quite as opinionated. I'll at least listen to you instead of stomping off all mad." She stroked my hand and turned her head to watch Celeste. "She's really good. That's one of my favorite songs by the way. Just so you know." She tilted her head and listened as the dancers glided by.

Celeste played a combination of slow songs and upbeat ones. The dancers waltzed and two-stepped as she continued through a songlist of Cajun ballads, Texas Swing, and vintage Country songs.

We put away platefuls of food and homemade rolls. but skipped the alcohol. Lenny because she was driving and me because of the medicine I was taking. An older man asked Lenny to dance to a waltz and she did. I watched them together, not surprised to find that Lenny could waltz along with the best of them. He brought her back to the booth and thanked her for the dance, then thanked me.

"I thought the lady might like a dance because I can see you're hurt and can't dance with her yourself," he said.

"You got that right," I told him.

Celeste took a break then and disappeared through double doors to the kitchen.

She came back after a few minutes with a man of medium height and gray hair combed straight back. He looked to be in good shape and had dark somber eyes. She took him by the hand and led him over to us.

"This is Acey Vidrine," she said holding up his hand in hers for emphasis. "And Acey, this is my motel security man, handy man, motel manager, whatever you want to call him, Harris Viator, and his friend, Leonée Badon."

I reached out my hand and shook with him.

"What happened to you?" Acey asked.

"Fell in a hole."

"Looks like it hurts to be you. You got to watch where you're putting your feet," he said.

"How do you do?" Lenny put out her hand.

"Pleased to meet you," Acey said. "You enjoyed your dinner?"

"It was all good. As you can see, we ate every last bite of it."

"Everybody likes the food here," Celeste said.

"That's why so many people are here….and your great music," Lenny said, smiling at Celeste.

"Thank you, Lenny. Glad to see you again." She held up a finger. "We're going to make an announcement tonight. Don't leave until we do, please."

"What're you drinking?" Acey asked. "I'm going to send over some drinks from the bar. Might help that foot." He pointed to my leg angled out from the booth.

"We're sticking to sodas tonight," Lenny said. "I have to drive us home."

"Well then, how about your dinners are on me," Acey said.

"Thank you. I didn't expect that," I said. "A very nice surprise."

"Oh, that's Acey Vidrine for you," Celeste said beaming at him. "He's something else, isn't he? Don't forget to stick around. I'm going to go freshen up and then I'll be right back." She turned and headed in the opposite direction toward the Rest Rooms sign at the entrance to a hallway at the far corner of the room.

Acey said he had to take care of something in the kitchen, and after we thanked him again, he headed back toward the swinging doors.

About fifteen minutes later, the two of them reappeared, and this time Acey had his fiddle with him. He joined Celeste at the piano and the two of them played *La Bague Qui Brille*. Many dancers immediately took to the floor, and all the couples looked like they had been dancing regularly together for years. Celeste and Acey were so good together that Lenny kept looking over at me and smiling, then took my hand and pressed it against her face.

"They're great!" she said when they finished and we clapped along with the crowd. It was then that Acey spoke directly into the mike. "Thank you, dancers. Thank you everyone for coming out tonight. Celeste and I have an announcement to make." Celeste turned on the revolving piano stool and looked up at him smiling.

"Celeste and I are going to be making a CD together very soon. We've been talking about doing it for a long time, and now we're ready to go ahead with it."

The crowd clapped and there were a few shouts of 'Yes!' and 'About time!'

Acey motioned for the applause to stop. "And there's still another announcement we have to make." The audience quieted and waited. "Celeste and I are getting married next month in the church. But we're having the reception here, and all you regulars are invited! You know who you are!"

There was a scraping of chairs as many in the crowd stood to show their appreciation of this. The applause and whistles went on for a few minutes and Acey gave Celeste a kiss on the mouth during all the commotion.

"That's lovely," said Lenny, taking my hand again. "And they play together so well too. A perfect couple."

"They've been friends for years. He lost his wife and she lost her husband, but all of them were friends for many years."

"So nice to see them so happy," she said as the applause gradually stopped and Acey and Celeste went back to making music. They started in on *Parlez-Nous a Boire,* and then Lenny suggested we go back to the motel, so we made our way out to the parking lot, the music following us through a loudspeaker installed on the porch. We crossed to the car and once inside, Lenny leaned into me and tilted her face waiting for me to kiss her.

It had been days since the dispute in her apartment, and the kiss was as electric and long lasting as the first time when we'd gone up to Wallace together almost a month before. She finally held her head back and ran her fingers through her hair. "Whew! That made me weak in the knees. Let's get back to your room quick!"

She drove quickly back to the motel and we wasted no time getting out of the car and crossing the twenty feet to the room. I fumbled with the key, but then we were safe inside and I let the crutch fall to the floor as we fell onto the bed laughing because it felt so damn good to be together once again.

Lenny, never the shy one, started undressing the second we hit the mattress, and I did the same. I took a moment to gaze at that incredible body, and then clicked off the light and grabbed her to me.

But things didn't go as I expected. Lenny didn't respond as she usually did when I ran my hands over that fabulous figure. As I smoothed her perfumed skin and drank in her beauty, she put a hand over one of mine halting what I was doing.

"Sorry to be like this, Harris. I'm still traumatized by that little geek pawing me and pressing on me with that gross little pecker of his. Can you just hold me tonight? Just hold me and give me a little more time to revive myself?" She raised my hand and kissed the back of it. "It's nothing to do with you. I love being next to you and feeling safe again. It's the sex part that turns me off right now. That little creep really did a number on my head."

"What I'd like to do is slip into that hospital room and finish the job you started when you beat the crap out of him," I said.

"And Bijou took a nice bite out of his ass too, I promise you."

"Like I say, I'd like to finish the job you and Bijou started."

"No, no. I don't need you to be arrested and put away. I need you here with me. He'll be locked up for a long time when I get done with him in court. I don't know what attempted rape charges are in Louisiana but I'm going to do a number on him. Wait until I tell my father what Junior did. He'll have one of his nastiest lawyer friends on the job immediately. Junior's going *down!*"

I held her in my arms and she pressed herself against me as though afraid I'd let her go. "Just hold me for a while," she said, "and then I'm going to get up and go home. Bijou is still upset from what happened. He's probably scared that I'm not home with him right now."

"I'll hold you as long as you want," I said, my voice hoarse from desire, and I did. We lay there quietly for at least another hour. I rubbed her neck and shoulders. The muscles were tight and she made little appreciative noises as I did that, like, "Ummm, that feels so good." Then I rubbed her back to relax her, carefully keeping my hands away from any area beyond her lower back, although my hands were itching to roam.

Lying next to her without putting sexual moves on her was not just difficult, it pained me, but I managed to do it despite my own body screaming to do exactly the opposite. As I lay there that night proud of myself for behaving so sympathetically and admirably, I began to wonder for the first time if I wasn't falling in love with Lenny. That must be the reason I was not trying to gradually break down her defenses as so many of us males are practiced at doing. Little by little, gradually working our way toward what we want. Maybe I was more than falling for her, maybe I was already in love with her. This made me nervous and I squirmed a bit in the bed as I wondered about it.

"This is the first time I've felt safe since the attack," she whispered.

I held her tighter. "You want to sleep here tonight?"

"I better not. I really need to get home. I haven't even unpacked yet. And I'm afraid Bijou will howl or scratch at the door and leave claw marks in the paint. He's been known to do that when angry or upset about something. He might wake up the neighbors.

I'm going to go home, have a few straight shots of Black Jack and go to bed. Hopefully I can sleep late tomorrow." She shuddered. "Anything to get that creep out of my head. But you still haven't told me the story about how you hurt yourself."

"You remember what you found out from Amber to help me find Rocco?"

"Sure. Of course."

"Well, right after that day at your place when I last saw you…." I started the story and continued until I'd related the whole Arkansas saga to her.

She silently listened until I'd finished with how Tom Perkins had run away from me.

"So…the Sheriff up there did nothing?"

"That's it."

"Hmm. That maybe explains something odd."

"What?"

"Amber called me on my cell yesterday. She was telling me how they all missed me at the club, and how Nick was in a terrible mood all the time since I'd left. And how the twins were really sad that I was gone and didn't seem to want to even work there anymore. And how the regulars complained about how I was gone and I was the main attraction in that dump. That made me feel good that people missed me anyway. But then Amber asked me about you. Sort of out of nowhere asked me where you live. I thought that was strange. I mean why would she care? I thought maybe she wanted to sneak over here and snag you away from me, but now I'm wondering if this ties in somehow to that ex of hers up in Arkansas."

"Like how?"

"I mean what if word got around in that little town up there about you being in town and tracing Rocco to their place out there in the woods…and who you were. What if he called her and pressured her to find out where you lived?"

I sat up against the headboard at that while still holding her. "Yeah. Pressured her whether anybody had been asking around about him or Rocco."

"And she pretended like she was just calling to chat, but he told her to find out where you lived."

"So what did you tell her?"

"Before I thought about it, I told her you lived in a motel somewhere." She quickly added. "I didn't say which one." She released me, clapped a hand over her mouth and sat up letting the sheet fall, then quickly covering herself with it. "Oh, my God! They might come looking for you! How many motels can there be around here?"

"Calm down. They're too far away for that. Besides, they're too occupied with business as usual up there. They're not going to be driving all the way to Louisiana to hunt me down."

"All the same…be careful. My nerves are shot to hell from that wannabe rape of Junior's. I don't know what I'd do if something happened to you."

"Lenny, come here." I held out my arms. "I'm armed. I'll be on the alert. Nothing's going to happen to me." She came back into my arms, and I held her another half hour before she left for the night.

37

UNEXPECTED COMPANY

I fell asleep that night shortly after Lenny left for home, feeling no pain, and slept like a rock until a noise outside woke me up. The bedside clock said 3:30, and I sat up, quickly alert. I knew the Mexicans had turned in even before we returned from Acey's, so they wouldn't be stirring around until near dawn. Feeling uneasy, I opened the drawer of the nightstand and retrieved my pistol, before going to the window to see.

I lifted one slat of the blinds and peered through. The outside spots angled to show the Magnolia Motel sign gave enough light for me to see a man leaning over doing something to my truck. He was doing something on the passenger side. I unhooked the chain and opened the door and yelled, "Hey! What you doing, you? Get away from my truck!"

He jolted up, stared at me for a split second, his face in shadow, then took a shot at me where I stood framed in the doorway. The bullet hit the frame of the door, splintering wood. I ducked back inside, raised the .38 and waited for a clear shot, not wanting to hit my truck. Merle and Willie started outraged barking from the fenced yard in back of Celeste's house. At that moment, the Mexicans opened their doors just enough to see out.

"Hey, Harris. *¡Cuidado!* We got you covered!" Jorge rasped in a semi whisper.

The intruder was hunkered down by the running board of the truck. "Get back in your rooms and nobody gets hurt," he called to us.

"*¡Cabron! ¡Pendejo! Vayate* and *you* won't get shot!" shouted Jorge.

"Call 911!" I called to him.

"I already did!" Ismael called back from the next room down.

At that, the man emerged from the shadow of the truck and ran like hell in the opposite direction, zig zagging across the property towards the back fence line. where Merle and Willie were now barking in a high pitched fury and rushing the fence, leaping up and almost scaling the six foot chain link. The man rounded the fence into the shadow of the trees and was gone from sight. Celeste's front porch light came on casting a cone of light over her front yard, and she emerged from the house yanking the belt of her robe tight. "What the hell is going on out here?"

The dogs barking changed to howling and the Mexicans all started rattling off rapid Spanish in their doorways to each other. I caught the words *pistole, rata,* and *ladron.*

"Somebody was trying to steal my truck," I called to her. "He shot at me. We ran him off. The law is coming. Go back inside and make sure all your windows and doors are locked."

"Don't worry. I lock up tight at night."

"Well go back inside anyway. I'll handle it when the cops get here. I'm going to put some pants on." I went back inside and pulled on a pair of jeans, just as I heard the patrol car pulling into the driveway. He pulled up abreast of all three of our trucks and rolled down his window. "You called in a shooting?" He asked from the car.

"Yes."

He got out of the car, looking around, and then walked toward my truck where the passenger door was still open. He shined his Maglight into the cab, waving the beam slowly all around. Then he examined the door with the flashlight and clicked it off. He stomped toward me. "So what happened?" He looked around at the Mexicans who were hovering in their doorways.

"I heard something that woke me up. I look out and a man is doing something to my truck. I couldn't see what. When I yelled at him, he shot at me. Hit the doorway right there." I showed him the splintered wood. He clicked on the Maglight again and examined the damage, but didn't touch it.

"Anybody hurt?"

"No."

"You all witnesses to this?" He looked over at the Mexicans. They all nodded, "¡*Si!* ¡*Si!* Yes!"

"You get a good look at this guy?"

"No. His face was in shadow. He ducked and ran like a shot that way." I pointed toward the far edge of Celeste's fence.

"So what do you think? He was looking to steal something in the truck, or wanting to steal the truck?"

I shook my head. "I don't know what he wanted. He was doing something over there by the door."

"Come with me and look. Tell me if anything's missing." I followed him toward the truck and when we got there, I looked in the cab and he held the Maglight so I could see. I bent the seat forward from the rear steel wall of the cab. That was where I stored an assortment of bungee cords, spare quarts of oil, coiled rope, and various other paraphernalia. There was even a thermos back there. I looked through the things I'd stashed. "I don't see anything missing. Maybe he was just getting started when I interrupted him."

"Seem like an unlikely place to be hunting for loot," the deputy said. "And hardly worth shooting you over it. Something else maybe going on here?" He trained the light on me.

"Like what?"

"Like is there some other reason he might have been shooting at you? This some kind of drug deal gone bad maybe?" He frowned.

"Drug deal? I was sound asleep! So were those guys...my neighbors! They have to be at work in a couple of hours!" I was so frustrated, my voice croaked.

"Okay. Take it easy. It doesn't make any sense yet. If he was stealing the truck, he'd be on the driver's side. And there's nothing in here worth bothering with. Don't you lock your truck?"

"Usually, yes. But tonight I was out with my girl friend and we went in her car, and when she dropped me off I didn't think to check it before going to bed."

"You should always keep your vehicle locked," he said. "All right. I'll go sit in my car and write this up. Somebody will come by tomorrow and retrieve that round from the doorway. Don't mess with it. Don't touch the wood. Understand?"

"Sure. Understood."

"Then give me your driver's license, so I can take down your information, and I'll write it up and you can sign it when I'm finished. You got me?"

"I'll go get it." I started back to my room as he asked the others to show him their IDs as well. When I came back with my driver's license, he was busy checking out their green cards. When he was satisfied the witnesses were all legal residents and had finished his notes, I thanked them all and told them to get back to bed knowing they had to get up in a few hours for work. "*Muchas gracias, amigos.* I owe you."

"Oh, no, no. ¡*Niente!*" they chorused, waving such an idea away with their hands. With a final ¡*Niente!* they went back inside and closed their doors.

I waved at Celeste still standing at her front gate. "Go on back to bed, Celeste. We got it. It's all taken care of. He's just writing up the report."

"You sure you're all right?"

"I'm fine. Go back to sleep. Sorry all this woke you up."

"Sleep? After all this?" She laughed. "Don't think so. Good night." She turned and headed back for the front door.

I walked back to the deputy and gave him my license. He was already making out the report and he took the license from me without looking up from his clipboard. "Okay. I'll come get you when I'm done and you can sign it. You can go back in there and wait on me if you want. But first lock your truck up." He continued writing and I did what he said, my mind so alert, I was like Celeste. No way would I get back to sleep that night.

38

THE SPARE TIRE

I was still jumpy after the deputy left, so to calm down, I turned on the TV and found a crime movie I'd never caught before. It was already half over by the time I tuned in, and I tried to pick up the plot enough to figure out what was going on. Doing so helped to distract me and I managed to gradually relax enough to doze off briefly, and then suddenly it was dawn and I woke up through habit and lay there half asleep. I should have been able to have delicious memories of my time with Lenny the night before, but all that was overshadowed by the thief in the night that took a shot at me.

Trying to make sense of what happened was hopeless, so giving up on that, I got up, showered and dressed and went outside to the truck to go find some breakfast. As much as I wanted a hot cup of coffee and something to eat, I took a minute to walk around the cab and look around in the early morning light to see if there was something the deputy and I had missed in the dark of night.

The stepside Chevy truck had a kind of side saddle indentation for the spare, and it looked like it had been messed with. The tire looked like it had been loosened somewhat from its concave space, and then it hit me that the guy had been trying to steal my spare. I frowned as I wondered why anyone would go to all that trouble to steal a tire…and then shoot at me over it. Now the episode was even more confounding and mysterious.

I had a tingling on the back of my neck as I continued staring at the tire, and because my inner alarm was going off, I didn't touch it. I took out my cell phone and punched in the number for my old boss, Chief Ira.

"Hey, Chief. This is Harris. I'm up here in Ida, but I need to drive over there and talk to you."

"Hey back at you, Harris. What you waiting for? Come on over."

"Soon as I grab a cup of coffee and a roll, I'll be there. Got something for you."

"We got coffee and sweet rolls here, Harris. Come on."

"Ten minutes." I clicked off and drove on out to the road heading south for St. Beatrice. The Chief sounded glad to hear from me, and that was a good thing because I had a strange story to tell him.

It was the first time I'd been back to the St. Beatrice Police Station, and it made me wince as I drove up to see the old workplace. It dredged up painful memories that I hadn't forgotten but had shoved to the back of my mind.

There was a receptionist I'd never seen before, and I asked to see the Chief. She told me to go on in that he was expecting me. I went down a short hall and turned into his office. "Hey, Chief," I said. "How you doing?"

"Well, look who's here," he said smiling and coming around from behind his desk. "Come on to the coffee room. Let me fix you up." He led me to a narrow room with a coffee machine, mugs, and a plate of sausage biscuits and cinnamon rolls.

"Get you something to eat and grab a coffee, then come back to the office and we'll talk," he said clapping me on the shoulder.

I poured a much needed coffee and took a roll back with me on a napkin and joined him in his office. He was tilted back in his wooden swivel chair. "How you been? Thought I would have heard from you before this."

"It's been crazy. And that's just the half of it."

"Go on. I'm listening." He put his boots up on the desk and settled back with his fingers laced over his stomach.

I filled him in on my job at LolliPops and how I'd met Lenny who had recognized Rocco's name from hearing Amber mention it. Then I outlined the entire Arkansas trip, and how all that had gone down.

"And so you're getting around on that foot all right?"

"It gets easier every day. I'm getting used to it."

"So now what? Sounds like the Sheriff up there isn't going to go any further with this."

"No, probably not. But the story doesn't end there. Last night I woke up to a noise outside my room at the motel, and when I looked out there was a man doing something to my pickup. I yelled at him to get away from my truck, and then he shot at me. Missed me, but splintered the doorframe."

"He what?" The Chief sat up at that and leaned forward planting his elbows on the desk.

"It's true. He took a shot at me, then my neighbors opened their doors and he decided to run. He took off toward the back of the landlady's house and disappeared.

I called 911 and a deputy came out but nothing was missing and we couldn't figure out what he wanted or what he was doing. The deputy filled out a report and said he'd send somebody around today to dig that round out of the doorframe. So I go back to bed and this morning I'm going out for breakfast and I take another look in daylight. I could see where somebody had been working at the spare on that side of the truck. So it hits me that one of those boys up in Arkansas might have packed that tire with some goodies for me to deliver down here for them. Make a mule out of me. Just a theory, but it's worth checking out. So, I didn't touch it, just came straight over here. What you think?"

"Maybe the guy was just trying to steal your spare."

"If that was all, why did he shoot at me? I told him to get away from the truck. All he had to do was run. But here's something else. Lenny told me last night that the same woman who had mentioned Rocco's name to her before, called her up day before yesterday and asked where I lived."

The Chief frowned and absently fidgeted with his moustache and stared off at a corner of the room as he thought about all I'd said. While he went over this in his mind, I ate the roll and finished the coffee. Finally he brought his eyes back to me.

"How do you figure they stowed a package in your spare?"

"When I was laid up in the rooming house, my truck was parked to the side of the building. There're no lights out there. All they had to do was sneak up during the night, remove the tire, and take it somewhere to pack it. Nobody's around that late at night. It's a one horse town. Nothing goes on there."

"Sounds like quite a bit goes on there."

"That operation is out in the county. Some miles out of town."

"How do you figure they knew who you were?"

"That town is so small, word is bound to get around about a man coming up from Louisiana, and then all of a sudden the Sheriff is knocking on their door looking for Rocco. All they had to do was ask around at the Café or look for a truck with a Louisiana plate."

Chief Ira nodded, then worked his mouth back and forth as he thought. "Let's go have a look at that tire of yours." He stood and came round the desk then led me out of the office and down the hall to the front entrance. "We're just going out to the parking lot for a minute, Renee," he called over his shoulder as we passed through the glass and steel door.

We crossed over to the truck and he stared at the tire for a minute, then nodded and waved me back inside. "Tell you what," he said, as we filed back to his office. "I'll call in Woody, he's on duty, and have him take that tire over to the garage, take the air out of it, and check it. If your theory's correct, and there's contraband in there...that same man will come back to the motel for it. So then we can set him up through the Sheriff's Office. But first we have to see if your theory is correct. Meanwhile, why don't you go walk down the street and eat a hot breakfast at Miss Josie's, and I'll call you on your cell phone when we know something."

"Thanks, Chief."

He raised his bushy eyebrows. "For what?"

"For believing in my crazy theory."

"Doesn't sound crazy to me. Makes perfect sense if that's what they wanted to do. Pack the tire while you're laid up. Easiest and cheapest transport they could have arranged for a dope run."

39

THE SET UP

Miss Josie made sure I put away enough breakfast for two people. And after I'd finished and paid the check, I walked back the two blocks to the Police Department. Renee told me to go on back to his office, and the Chief was all smiles when I entered.

"Have a seat, Harris." He laughed, shaking his head. "They can't keep a good man down."

"What you mean?"

"Last time I saw you I told you I knew you were a good cop. Remember?" He waited until I settled myself into the chair in front of the desk. "Your theory was right on time. After they let the air out of the tire, and took it off the rim, there it was….a baggie full of what looks to be cocaine. If that's what it turns out to be, that thief is most definitely going to figure out a way to come back for it. The Baggie weighs twelve ounces."

"Where is it now?"

"I called Sheriff Quebedeaux right away. He had a detective drive right over to check it. The detective determined it was cocaine, so he directed Woody to put it back into the tire, fill it up again with air, and replace it on the truck. The Sheriff will get back with me when he's got his plan worked out as to how they're going to coordinate this. My guess is, he'll have a deputy watching your place tonight."

"I'll be watching also from my room."

"I think you'd better stay out of this one. Let them handle it. Just lay low and stay safe. It would probably be better if you stayed in a different room tonight."

"They're not interested in me. I just got in the way is all."

"That's what you hope," he said. "Just stay safe. You've had enough grief to last a lifetime."

"Yep," I said. "That's sure enough true, Chief."

"If this goes as planned, the guy will show up again and take the tire. The deputy can follow him to wherever he takes it to retrieve the dope out of there and maybe get more than just the one man. He's bound to have somebody working with him. And they can arrest both or all of them."

I nodded.

"And if that all goes as planned, and they're able to bust these people...well, then, that would go a long way toward vindicating you, don't you think?" He sat up straight and cocked his head looking at me with an amused look in his eyes.

"You mean like..."

"I mean like maybe getting your old job back. Who could deny you that if you were able to sniff out this operation? The people of St. Beatrice would be grateful to you for stopping this Arkansas connection. We have enough troubles around here as it is without them bringing in more grief from out of state."

I just looked at him. I hadn't foreseen this development, and I was speechless.

"Well, we'll see. Let's wait and see. But in the meantime, you be careful."

He stood and we shook hands and then I left his office, said goodbye to Renee, and went out to my truck and drove back to Ida feeling energized. I was unofficially on a case, my theory held up, and I was anticipating some action as soon as that night. Not only that, but Chief Ira had pretty much offered me my old job back if this all worked out as planned. All that and I had one of the world's most beautiful women as my girl friend.

Not bad for someone who had hit rock bottom just a few months before. "Thank you, Jesus!" I said aloud and turned onto the four lane back toward Ida.

40

MIDNIGHT CREEPER

I warned Celeste to stay in the house that night and not come outside for any reason, and explained to her that the police were watching and waiting for the intruder to come back without going into any of the details. She wanted to know more, but I made up something about how they'd been looking for someone who was going around looting people's vehicles in the area and since we knew now he was armed she needed to stay locked up and out of sight.

"Oh, hell," she said. "I leave it all in your hands. Just make sure he stays away from the Lincoln, please."

When the Mexicans came home from work all worn out, sweat bands streaked and gray, I took them two six packs of Coronas as thanks for watching my back the night before. They were weary and dull-eyed from roofing all day and appreciative of the beers. I then tried to explain in my broken Spanish how important it was to lay low that night and stay inside while letting them know just enough to get my point across.

That made their eyes glitter and come to life as they gazed at me with questions. "*¿Que? ¿Porque?*"

I put a finger to my lips and shook my head. "*No preguntos, por favor. ¡Pero, oigame, eso es muy importante! Peligroso afuera esta noche. ¡Policia! ¿Comprende? ¡Silencio! ¡Muy necessario!*" I dragged a make believe zipper across my lips to get the idea across.

They all nodded in unison and set their lips in a firm line showing that they understood the importance of this. Jorge shook his finger like a school teacher at the others to show he would make sure they did what I said they must.

"*¡Vaya con Dios!*" Cornelio whispered, as he made a sign of the cross. The other three echoed him and also made signs of the cross over their work stained tee shirts.

When I returned to my room, I called Lenny and asked how she was doing.

"I'm better. Just being near you for a few hours helped more than you know," she said.

"Same here," I said. "But look, no matter what…. do *not* under any circumstances, come anywhere near this motel tonight."

After a moment's pause she asked, "Why? Would I be interrupting something?"

"Not in any way you think. But hear me. Do *not* come by here for any reason.

"Don't call either. I'll fill you in later when I know more."

"Tell her hello for me."

"Lenny, this is serious. Quit playing around."

"Okay, okay. Sorry. Are you all right? Is something wrong?"

"I'm all right, and I'll be a lot better after tonight I think. Don't worry, everything is under control."

"I'm not so sure about that. You sound funny."

"Lenny! Everything's good. Just stay away. I'll talk to you tomorrow."

"How about coming over here in the morning, and I'll make breakfast for you. You can put the suspense to rest then."

"That's good. I'll come over when I wake up. Have the coffee ready. I'm going to need it."

"Coffee, O.J., and a mushroom and cheese omelet. How's that sound?"

"I'll be there."

When we clicked off, I thought to make a pot of coffee in the room's coffee maker to help ensure I could stay awake for the night's long haul. I had a good feeling about it…like the whole thing would go down as planned. If I'd only known what it would lead to, I would have called the whole thing off. But everybody knows hindsight is 20-20. So what's new?

Shortly after midnight, I'd watched two and a half Westerns, a crime movie, and another Rifleman rerun. I'd finished two pots of coffee and was wired on caffeine. I kept the lights off and routinely got up and peered out between the slats of the blinds at the truck. If he kept the same timetable as the night before, I had a long wait. But I figured he would not want to follow that same timing a second time since it had gone so badly the night before.

Knowing what was in that tire, I knew he wasn't going to let it sit there for long.

Just a little more patience was what was called for, and I knew how to wait. I clicked off the television and pulled the one chair in the room up to the window and prepared to sit there until he showed.

* * *

By two o'clock nothing had happened. The caffeine had worn off, my eyelids were drooping and I had to keep getting up to splash cold water on my face to stay awake. Then finally, a half hour later, there was action. A shadow crossed from behind the trees at the far boundary of the motel property. The shadow came slowly forward until I could make out the outline of a man headed for my truck.

I'd made it easy for him and parked it exactly as I'd parked it previously. He sneaked up on the passenger side and although I couldn't see it, I knew he was fumbling around with the spare, so stealthily that this time no sound could give him away. I breathed in deeply, secure in the knowledge that the deputy who was no doubt viewing this would be watching his every move from some position across the road angled for a clear view of the truck.

It didn't take him long to release the tire and suddenly he reappeared crossing the property back toward the tree line rolling the tire ahead of him as he went. I smiled at how beautifully this plan was playing out. A few minutes later, a pickup passed in front of the motel with its lights turned off, and then shortly thereafter a sedan, lights on, passed by. The pickup was bound to be the thief. As to the sedan, who knew?

Now that the thief had fallen into the trap, I quit the long vigil, stretched my aching back, and crawled into bed. I turned it over in my mind to the deputies and fell asleep almost immediately with a great sense of relief.

41

CHIEF IRA REPORTS

The next morning, I hastily dressed, drove over to the truck stop for breakfast, then drove to St. Beatrice for a report on what went down the night before. Although I was most anxious to hear, I didn't bother calling for information because I knew Chief Ira would never tell me anything over the phone.

I knew the minute I entered his office that the plan had gone well. The Chief had a wide smile on his face and waved me to the chair in front of his desk. "Sit down, Harris. You're going to love this."

I sat as ordered and settled myself into the chair. "Can't wait to hear, Chief."

"They nailed three of them. Two deputies followed the pickup that left your motel with the tire to a shade tree mechanic's garage out on County Road 27. There were two men waiting on the arrival. Maybe three. What I heard is that maybe there was a third man, and he might have ducked out when he caught a whiff of what was happening.

What they did was, wait until they got the air out of the tire and retrieved the package. Then they went in. It was beautiful. They caught them not only with the package, but also with guns in the garage, so that's more counts for guns around a controlled substance." The Chief rubbed his hands together in glee. He shook his head. "It all was so *clean!*"

"Great news, Chief. They're going away."

"Oh, yeah. Not only that, but after Detective Mitch Lanclos gets done with them, they'll be ratting out that bunch up in Arkansas. And you can count on that."

"Juicy, Chief, juicy!" I smiled and did a thumbs up.

"I made sure Sheriff Quebedeaux knew we never could have done this without your trip up there looking for Rocco and then your quick thinking after that first attempt to steal the tire at your motel."

"What did he say?"

"He was pleased with your work. He says you have vindicated yourself."

I nodded, feeling a sweet rush of justice accomplished racing through my veins.

"So, at least we've shut down one pipeline for the damn drugs around here, thanks to you."

"Glad to help out, Chief. I've got to get going. I have some errands to run for the motel and a date besides."

"You managing the place over there now?"

"I've been doing maintenance. Carpentry. A little plumbing. Yard work."

"I know that place. Rosemarie and I go to Acey's to hear Celeste and dance now and then. You're lucky you fell into that arrangement."

"I know it. I was in bad shape when I stumbled in there."

"Just remember what I told you that day. Anybody tells you they never made a major screw up is either lying or too boring to pay any attention to."

He stuck out his hand and we shook. "Thanks, Chief," I said and then I left for the motel to clean up for the date with Lenny.

42

IRENA CALLS

Soon as I walked through the door to my room, the cell phone rang and it was Irena. She spoke so softly I could barely hear her. "Something terrible happened."

"Are you speaking into the phone? I can barely hear you."

I strained to hear her. There was a pause, and then her voice went up a notch above whisper level. "My house burned down two nights ago."

"What? Say what?"

"Somebody set fire to my house. It was arson. The Fire Marshall found where it started. Somebody poured gasoline around the outside of the building out in back in the middle of the night and set fire to it. The old house went up like….like it was made out of cardboard! It was horrible! You wouldn't believe how fast it all burned to the ground. I barely got that old man out who was staying in the room down the hall from you." She paused then for a muffled cough.

"It was all the Volunteer Fire Department could do to keep the house next door from burning too."

"Irena! Who would do this? I can't believe you have any enemies in that town….in any town!"

"Word got around I took care of you. I don't know." Her voice trailed off.

"Took care of me! So what? What would that matter to anybody?"

"Some people around here didn't like that. Like I said, I don't know. I just hear things."

"What did Chief Wooten say? Does he think this is all my fault?"

"He's furious. I pity the ones who did this when he gets hold of them. He promised me he'd find out who did this. He says he thinks you stirred up a hornet's nest in our county, but he has no evidence of that…yet. I haven't talked to him since. Don't worry. He'll find out who did it. He's good."

"If it's because of me bringing the heat on that crew in the woods, I wish I'd never gone up there looking for Rocco. You'd still have your house. Finding Rocco definitely isn't worth you losing your home."

"Don't blame yourself. You had no idea what your trip up here would lead to. God takes care of His own. I'll be all right."

"Where are you now?"

"I'm staying at Doc Taylor's. I got scorched while getting that poor old man who lived upstairs out of the burning house. I had to drag him out, he was half asleep, poor thing."

"Where are the burns?" My voice rose and I felt the heat of anger rising over me as surely as if I was standing near the house watching it burn down. My face felt so hot I walked to the sink and wet a wash-cloth to cool my face down.

"I'm burned on my arms and hands and face. Doc says I'll have scars but that's better than dead."

"Your hair? Your beautiful hair?"

"I had it wrapped up tight like I do every night when I go to bed. My hair didn't get hardly any of it…just a little singed where some stuck out of the kerchief."

"And the old man? He's okay?"

"He's suffered some burns too, but mostly smoke inhalation. He'll recover just fine, Doc Taylor said."

"Now where's he going to live?"

"I'll buy something else with the insurance mon-ey. And I'll rent him a room just like before. I can maybe buy the house next door. It's been vacant for a while. We're looking into it. Or I might even reno-vate a hundred year old house in the country about a mile from Doc's house. It used to be his aunt's, but she has passed on."

"I'm driving up there. Just as soon as I can get away."

"There's nothing you can do. The house is gone. Nothing but the fireplace and chimney is still stand-ing. It's too depressing. Just a black charred mess soaked from the fire hoses. Don't drive up. You just barely got yourself back down there."

"I'm in the middle of some things down here right now. But soon as I can, I'll come up and help you."

"Don't trouble yourself. Like I said, there's nothing you can do. What's done is done."

"Oh, this isn't finished yet, not by a long shot. I will come up there when I can and help make things right again. None of this would have happened if I hadn't come into your life and you stuck your neck out helping a stranger when I was down and out."

"Anyone in my church would have done the same thing. Don't feel guilty. There is evil in the world, and we know that. Be careful down there. When these people get angry there's no telling what they'll do."

"Don't worry about me. I'll be fine. It's you I'm worried about."

"They've done their worst by me. They sent their message. That was enough."

"Enough for now maybe. Keep me posted, please."

"I will."

"And say hello to Doc Taylor for me."

"I will. God bless."

"And the same to you." After that conversation, my face was still so hot with anger, I stood at the sink and repeatedly splashed cold water on my skin. Along with the anger was a good helping of guilt for bringing this evil over to such a good person. First old man Perkins and now Irena. All because of helping me out. It seemed I had brought nothing but misery to Falling Waters. Just as Rocco had brought misery to me, I'd gone and spread it around to other people. I felt rotten and low down as I looked in the bathroom mirror. "Chump!" I said aloud, then left the room in disgust, hands clenched.

I was still worked up when I got into the truck to go meet Lenny, and telling myself to calm down didn't help at all.

Lenny answered the door wearing a silk scarf around her neck and a long sleeved top over loose jeans and low cut furry boots. "Come on in. Glad to see you." She leaned over and pecked me on the cheek. "I made some special treats for you. Come on into the kitchen. Everything will be ready in about five minutes."

She led me into the narrow kitchen and I sat at a small round wrought iron table laid with mats and silverware. She brought over a glass pitcher of Mimosas and set it down on the glass tabletop. "That O.J. is fresh squeezed." She poured this into our stemmed glasses and then returned to the stove. "I made crawfish pies. One of my mother's specialties. Made the crust from scratch this morning."

"You've gone to a lot of trouble."

"Keeps my mind off that creature from outer space up in Wallace. Besides, I wanted to do something special for you. You deserve it." She opened the oven door and peered in.

"Looking good," she announced, turning off the oven. "I better serve these up in a minute. Let me get the salad out of the fridge first." She took a glass salad bowl out of the refrigerator and brought it to the table.

"Wild green salad with pecans," she said. "Help yourself." She returned to the stove, put on an oven mitt, removed the lightly browned pies from the oven and served them on light green plates. "And now," she said as she brought them to the table and sat down across from me. "I think we're ready."

We toasted one another, "Cheers!" and then I took a bite of the best crawfish pie I'd ever eaten…. and I've had quite a few in my time. "Fabulous," I told her after the first bite. "Best I ever had."

"My mother is a great cook. You'll get to see when you meet her."

"I'm going to meet her?" I said, surprised.

"Yes," she said, but didn't explain, instead taking another bite of the pie.

We ate in silence after that and when we'd finished the small pies, she brought two more out of the oven and we ate those, finished the salad and also the pitcher of Mimosas.

"And now, we're going to have our coffee in the living room. So, why don't you go out there and make yourself comfortable while I just clear these dishes and bring out a tray of desserts?"

I went out into the living room and sank into the couch, leaning back and feeling much better than when I'd arrived, but still carrying the heavy feeling of Irena's news from Arkansas. I stared out the sliding glass windows at the clouds and the tops of the sunlit trees in back of the apartment building in a bit of a fog from the Mimosas, but not enough of a haze to shake the gruesome picture of the burned and charred foundation of Irena's building.

"Here we are," Lenny said, as she carried a tray of coffee mugs and sherbet dishes filled with pecan ice cream. I quickly moved some magazines and she laid the tray on the coffee table. "Help yourself," she said, and I did with no hesitation.

As we leaned back against the couch cushions eating our ice cream, Lenny began to hesitatingly fill me in on what she'd started in the kitchen. "I had six messages from my father by the time I got home last night." She licked the back of her spoon.

"Only six?"

"Only six! And he was ranting and raving on each one of them."

"So I take it he heard what happened."

"Heard about it? I thought he'd stroke out he was so angry."

"Sounds like the safest place Junior can be right now is in jail."

"Huh? I doubt he'll even be safe in jail. The way my father sounded, I don't think he'll ever make it out of the hospital let alone be safe in jail."

"Is he going up there?"

"No. He's demanding I go home. He says if I don't go home, he'll send people for me and take me home by force."

"So what did you say?"

"I started to remind him that's kidnapping, but then remembered my mother. She knows now too, and he says she's distraught, and I have to go home or something bad will happen to her because she's so upset and worried about me."

"So what did you tell him?"

"I gave in. I can't stand to have my mother sick with worry. She just wants me safe. My father wants Junior dead. And knowing my father I would say that means Junior is not long for this world."

"It won't be a big loss." I was starting to like her father.

"By the way, Quintus has the whole attack down on video from the deer cameras he put up. But we're not letting any of this get out. Let Junior tell his lies and whatever he comes up with to try to get out of this. Then we'll unload the videos."

"That's great that Quintus got those cameras up in time."

"Yes, but no way am I going to watch any of it." She made a face. "No way in hell would I watch a rerun of that nightmare."

She took another bite of ice cream as she let all this news sink in. I drank my coffee and waited, glad that she was going home as after the news from Arkansas I now had two women to worry about.

"So, what I said in the kitchen…about you meeting my mother? Well I hope you come to see me at their house."

"When do you plan on going?"

"He insists I'm there by dinnertime tonight."

"You okay with that?"

"I told him I'd be there just as soon as I could… but I had some things to take care of first." She looked closely at me.

"You need help with something?"

"Yes."

"What?'

"I got a phone call from the twins this morning. Amber didn't show up at their place today. They were all going to the casino. Sometimes the twins take her and they all go eat lunch at one of the restaurants over there in that mammoth building, then go to the off track betting at the racetrack at the far end, or else play the slots at the casino."

"Maybe she's sick."

"No way. Amber is not sick. She's not even home. They went over to her place to check on her. She was supposed to be there early so they could do some fittings for some stage outfits of hers. Amber's not like that. To not show up like that or call. That's not Amber."

"Maybe she went home with somebody last night and crashed."

"Not Amber. After work, it's either gambling or she goes right home and gets her sleep. The casino is her life. Men come in way second to gambling. I told you she's an addict."

"So what do you want to do?"

"I want to check out the casino. Just in case she got mixed up and is waiting for them there. Not likely, but I'd feel better if we did. Sometimes she even gets so carried away, she'll stay at the hotel next door to the casino if she's on a gambling binge. But she never mixes her gambling up with her work nights. She's got to keep that money rolling in. Protect her habit."

"You want us to drive over there now?"

"Would you?" She looked at me with pleading eyes and I wanted to pull her to me and assure her

I'd do anything she wanted, anytime, but I resisted the urge and just nodded my head. My hands were itching to touch her though. I covered my desire for her by reaching for the tray.

"Let's go then. I'll help you clean up the kitchen first."

43

AT THE CASINO

The casino was only a half hour away and a quarter mile off the four-lane heading north. By the time we got there the vast parking lot was a third full already. We had to park at least a dozen rows away from the immense building. Lenny kept looking around for Amber's car. "She drives a cherry red Firebird. Remember?"

"Sure, I remember."

"She has a ratty looking purple flag kind of thing on the antenna so she can find the car."

"I remember that too. It's faded." As we made our way toward the six front doors, we passed others coming in and going out. I held the door open for a group of women as Lenny waited at my side. Then she stepped on inside and I followed, the clamor of the slot machines immediately assaulting our ears. We passed by the attendant and through the entrance to the giant, carpeted room where hundreds of slot machines were whirring, ringing and dinging and bright lights of all colors were flashing and blinking in the subdued lighting from above. These machines were steadily worked by a great multitude of people, so intent on feeding the slots with a continuous flow of cash that they wouldn't have noticed if Lenny was doing one of her strip club routines.

We passed by row after row of somber people concentrating on the machine in front of them, their eyes glazed, as we searched the crowd for Amber. I stopped to look over the shoulder of a man with a rolled rim Western hat who was feeding a machine with a brilliant, hypnotic display of exploding color and images of creatures from outer space, but Lenny pulled me away. "Come on," she said in my ear, "They don't like people standing nearby. Bad luck."

We left the noisy room, and the relative quiet of the twenty-foot wide hallway toward the restaurants and racetrack brought immediate relief. "My ears are still ringing. How can Amber stand that for hours at a time?"

"Are you kidding? She lives to feed those machines. And she has plenty of company as you can see. But she liked to play the slots around three in the morning. She always said they pay off much better that late cause people have been pumping money into them all day. She always said she had her best luck at night. Especially on the high end slots. Five dollars. Ten dollars. Even twenty dollar machines gave her the best results."

She took my hand as we passed restaurants and barrooms on our way toward the far reaches of the building and the off-track betting room at the track.

I glanced over at her with pleasure at this, but she kept her eyes directly ahead as we moved along behind dozens of couples and loners sauntering through the huge building as though they were deciding where to eat or what to do next.

When we got to the track, we entered a giant room with banks of monitors displaying all the races going on at the moment across the nation. Men and a few women were leisurely sitting all around the room watching different races, consulting their forms, and occasionally getting up to bet at the machines or at the windows.

Beyond all this action a bank of glass doors opened to the dramatic sprawl of the track beyond. Brilliant sunshine outside contrasted sharply with the artificial lighting within. Despite their attention to the races, many men glanced at Lenny as we walked around the room looking for Amber. It made me laugh because even when covered up to her chin she drew attention.

"What's so funny?" she asked, jerking my hand.

"Nothing," I said, and stopped to watch a race going on at Belmont.

"If you want to watch it, let's sit down," she said. So we sat at a long table among half a dozen others and watched the race going on in the rain.

"Sloppy track," said the man sitting next to Lenny to no one in particular. He had a New Orleans accent that could also have been a New York accent.

"I love racing," Lenny whispered when they passed the finish line. "Amber does too. I'm disappointed she's not in here."

The tracks in Louisiana take turns during the year, and right then it was Lake Charles' turn, and we saw another race was coming up there on a monitor far across the room, so we moved over closer to it.

"I'll go get a form," I said and went over to buy one for us. We studied the race coming up and Lenny wanted to bet her lucky number 8 and I picked a filly with the name of Fugitive Sal, probably because I had fugitives on my mind, so I figured that would count for something in the betting world.

We went over to the windows and placed our bets with a smiling gray haired woman. We each bet a ten and returned to our seats with five minutes to go. She took my hand and leaned against my shoulder. "You know, despite worrying about Amber, I'm really enjoying our trip over here." Her perfume drifted around her as I took a chance and lightly stroked her hair. She moved closer to me, and I began to sense she was recovering from her ordeal, and we'd be able to pick up fairly soon where had we left off.

"I know what you're thinking," she said, looking up at me and smiling.

"Sssh. The race is starting." I put a finger to my mouth and we raised our faces to watch the overhead monitor.

This quarter mile race was in bright sunshine, and her horse got boxed up in the rear and couldn't break out. Fugitive Sal, however, was a different story. She started out on the rail, got crowded, then breezed ahead of the pack after the three quarter mile pole. She tore it up and roared into first position with another filly pulling ahead and gaining on her at an alarming rate. But Fugitive Sal crossed the finish line almost a full body length ahead of her rival, and the odds were so good, she made me a fast hundred dollars.

"You lucky son of a gun!" Lenny said, and pulled my face to hers and kissed me.

The move was so sudden, she caught me by surprise, and I almost dropped the winning ticket.

"Come on," I said, and pulled her to her feet. "Let's go cash out and get going. We're either going to have to look for Amber or go back to your apartment. I have no will power when it comes to you."

"Understood," she said. "But I think we can do both."

We left the casino, then drove around the parking lot to the hotel next door to check their parking lot for Amber's Firebird, but no luck there either.

"She sometimes plays low ball or *bourrée* at a little country bar about five miles out of Ida. They have a back room there for card games. Big pots there, you'd be surprised."

"Is it Fast Fred's?"

"Yes. You been there?"

"I hauled shell for their parking lot. Played a few games there too."

"You get around, don't you?"

"Enough."

She drove south back down the four lane then turned off onto a stretch of country road, passing a few farms, then a trailer park and a section of unworked fields, high with native grasses and young chicken trees. Just past all that was the ranch style bar with a pea gravel parking lot. She turned in and circled the building to check in the back, but there was nothing there but a pickup with a buckled hood, an abandoned chicken coop and a green dumpster.

"She could have been picked up by a friend and driven here. We better go in and check just to be sure."

"You're grasping at straws."

"I know but we've come all this way. Anyhow, I'm getting thirsty. How about you?"

"I could drink a beer."

She took my hand again as we crossed the lot and then entered the bar through a heavy metal red door. We had to stand in the doorway for a few seconds and adjust our eyes to the dim light. A vintage jukebox stood in the corner with spiraling red neon lights. One of those antiques with the songs listed in ink, penned in by hand. The song playing was Dewey Balfa's *Parlez Moi a Boire*. Lenny started tapping her foot and turned up her face to me. "Wanna dance?"

"Let's look for your friend first." I started to lead her toward the back room.

There were a few patrons sitting at the bar who turned their heads to watch us as we passed through the swinging doors to the rear. The back room was narrow and the game was going on at a table against the wide horizontal boards of the left wall. Five people sat around the round table and an overhead cone light was suspended from the beaded ceiling by a chain. Each player had a stack of bills and a drink in front of them and a game was in progress. A dark haired woman sat with legs crossed on a metal folding chair across from the table watching the game.

We stayed back well away from the table long enough to see Amber was not there either. I looked over at Lenny and motioned with my head for us to go back to the bar.

We left the players knowing they wouldn't appreciate us hanging around, and returned to the front room.

Don't Get Married was playing when we returned and we slid onto barstools a few feet away from a group of three men who were playing dollar poker.

The bartender, an older woman with hair piled on top of her head came over and we ordered drafts.

"We're looking for a friend of ours. She comes here and plays cards a few times a month. Have you seen her? Amber? She stands out. Very beautiful. Long blonde hair," Lenny asked.

The bartender laughed, shaking her head. "Even if I had, I wouldn't tell on her."

"We're worried about her. Her friends are all out looking for her."

The woman shook her head. "Sorry. I can't help you."

"But you would if you could. Right?"

The woman walked away still smiling and drew the beers from the tap then returned with the frosted mugs and set them down on round cardboard coasters. "I haven't seen her, *chère.*"

I paid for the beers and touched my mug to Lenny's before we drank. "So where do we go next?'

"Maybe we should swing by her place again. Maybe she'll be back by now and all this was for nothing."

"Hope so." But I had a dismal feeling come creeping over me, and my stomach tightened. This wasn't going to end well. The timing of it was too close to not suspect it had something to do with the bust of the night before. Amber's link to Lenny and then me wasn't too hard to figure out. I didn't say anything to Lenny about my fears on this. She'd just been through a lousy experience, and there was no point scaring her. But I was relieved she was going to go stay with her parents where I knew she'd be protected from any further harm.

44

REUNION

After we left Fast Fred's, we passed by Amber's apartment building and drove through the paved parking lot, but still no Firebird.

"We've gone everywhere I can think of. I'll call the twins and see if they've heard anything." She paused at the exit to the lot and made the call on her cell phone but the twins had no news to report.

Lenny slumped in her seat, discouraged, a forlorn look on her face. "Dammit. This stinks. I can't think of anything else we can do right now."

"Let's go back to your apartment for a while. You can get packed to leave for your parents' house. If there's any news, they'll call you."

"Okay. I guess that's all we can do." She eased out of the lot and we drove back to her place. Neither of us spoke, the corners of her mouth were downturned, and I was wondering if she'd read my mind and was visualizing the worst.

By the time we made it up to her apartment, the sun was fading fast, and the living room windows were already taking on the look of dusk. "What time do you want to leave for your parents' place?" I asked her as she passed into the kitchen.

"I don't know. I'll get there when I get there, I guess. My mother goes to bed early. Lucien stays up late. He has insomnia. Probably cause he's such a frigging crook," she called.

"Didn't you say he wants you home for dinner?"

"He knows I'll show up when I'm good and ready. He gets to boss my mother around, but he knows he can't boss me."

She brought two beers from the kitchen and handed me one. "Let's go into the bedroom and have these. I have to pack and you can relax on the bed while I pull things out of the closet. It'll get our mind off this wild goose chase we've been on today."

"Whatever you want."

I followed her through the living room to the bedroom and setting the beer on the bedside table, kicked off my shoes, stacked the pillows against the satin padded headboard and made myself comfortable, stretching out my legs and leaning back.

She slid open the mirrored closet doors and started picking through the hanging clothes. She'd pull out a shirt, examine it, then hang it back, pull out another, then hang it back. After repeating this half a dozen times, she slid the door shut again and turned around. "The hell with it. I'm not in the mood for this." She picked up her beer from where she'd set it on the floor and started toward the bed.

"Go ahead and move over. I'm going to take it easy too."

I moved over and patted the space beside me. "Come on over here."

She rounded the bed and began unbuttoning her shirt as she moved, revealing a pale pink lace bra. Then she came to the bed, set her beer on the nightstand and slid the blouse off nonchalantly without meeting my eyes as if she didn't know she was driving me crazy.

Then she flicked the straps a few times and unhooked the bar with a slow smile and flipped it off like she was doing a routine. And there she was again. My beautiful half naked girl friend. It was all I could do to remain calm. A few seconds later, she was slowly stepping out of her slacks like she was on stage, and then she laughed at me probably because I looked like one of the clientele at LolliPops by that time.

She did a number with her pink lace thong and then still laughing, she slid onto the bed to curl up next to me.

She reached for her beer, took a long drink, set it back again, wiped her mouth with the back of her hand and said, "You know what? Junior can go to hell. He's not screwing me up any more, and he's not turning me into The Snow Queen. You and I can pick up right back where we left off, cause I think I just got cured."

45

THE FIREBIRD

That night after getting back to the motel, I watched maybe ten minutes of a movie, then fell asleep with the TV on again. A habit of mine. I slept like a rock after the steamy reunion with Lenny. When I awakened though, the first thing I thought of was not Lenny, but was the crisis I'd caused for Irena.

I took a quick shower, shaved, made a pot of coffee, and got ready to get back to work on some things I had to do at the motel. Jobs that I had postponed because of all the disruptions. I grabbed the broom out of the utility room and started sweeping down the walkways that ran out to the front landscaping.

As I reached the end of the walkway, I saw some litter a passerby had tossed in the front flower beds and went to retrieve it. The usual fast food bag with a ketchup smeared cardboard box inside, and the usual soft drink with plastic lid and straw sticking out of it. Some melted ice sloshed inside as I tossed these into a low trash barrel I kept hidden in back of one of the azalea bushes by the building.

As I went back to retrieve the broom I'd left leaning against the building, I glanced at a passing car with a noisy muffler that passed, and then I saw it. The cherry red Firebird, glossy in the morning sun. It was parked a little ways down the road, maybe thirty feet from the motel sign. I stood there blinking like a dummy as I stared at the very car Lenny and I had been hunting all the previous afternoon. There it was in all its 1979 glory. Glinting in the light, the faded purple flag hanging limply from the antenna. No doubt that it was Amber's.

For a minute, I actually felt relief. She was somewhere around. I was about to find her. And then my stomach dropped like a lead weight, and I knew there was no finding Amber. Her car was there to tell me something, and it wasn't anything I was going to like.

I dropped the broom and started walking fast toward the Firebird expecting to see her slumped in the front seat. But as I got closer, I could see there was no one in the car. I came up beside it without touching the metal and peered inside. The interior was clean. Nothing inside. I walked around the car looking for something, anything that could give me a clue about what was going on. And then I stopped short by the rear bumper. The smell of Lysol was rising from the trunk. I went dead inside and fished my cell phone out of my jeans.

46

SHERIFF QUEBEDEAUX

Ten minutes after my 911 call, there were five vehicles surrounding the Firebird and a deputy was blocking off that lane of the road with orange cones, and another was wrapping neon yellow Crime Scene tape around the perimeter of the area.. A row of cars was parked on the opposite side of the highway and a dozen gawkers had already gathered, trying to see what was going on. I recognized Detective Mitch Lanclos when he arrived to head up the investigation.

The body was wrapped inside double black trash bags and soaked in Lysol. The bags were taped mummy style round and round with duct tape. The crime scene techs were snapping pictures of the car and trunk from all angles. The grim looks on all the personnel at the scene told any passersby all they needed to know, There was a body in that trunk and it wasn't alive, and this was a murder scene.

Workers were all over the car outside and in, dusting for prints, and the E.M.T. people were going to have a long wait before they would receive permission to remove the body.

Lenny had to be told, but I knew she'd probably be sleeping late, and I didn't want to wake her with such nightmare news, so I put off calling her. I stood on the motel property and watched the professionals, knowing I could do nothing to help, but not wanting to leave the scene either. My roofer neighbors had long since gone off to work way before knowing anything about this, but Celeste came out fully dressed to see what was going on and I filled her in on what I knew.

"Oh no, that poor girl! Why would anyone kill her?"

"I don't know. But she was a nice person. She was popular at the Club. Everybody liked her."

"Being a stripper is not safe," she said, shaking her head. "Too many psychos out there."

"I think it would be a good idea for you to go stay at Acey's for a while. You're going to be married soon anyway. Maybe you should just speed things up and move over there now."

"Why? I didn't have anything to do with all this," she asked, frowning.

"I know, but who knows how these people think." I didn't want to tell her the details of the bust two nights before, but I did want her out of there.

"Why should I be worried? I've lived here safely for years and years."

"Just call Acey for me and tell him I think it would be a good idea. Will you do that for me? Please?"

"Well, all right. But I don't see why I should."

"I'll take care of everything here at the motel. You know that."

"I'll see what Acey says about it. I'll do that much at least."

"Thank you. I wish you would." I placed a supporting hand on her shoulder.

"I'm going into the house to make breakfast. You come along when you're ready. No point in standing out here gawking. There're plenty of other people doing that for us across the street. Let's stay out of the way so those people can do their job."

"Yeah, okay. I'll go feed the dogs and be right there."

Before I left, I caught up with Lanclos, a stocky man in his forties, and told him I was the one who called it in, and I had to get back to work. He said he'd be in touch when he had a minute, and gave me his card. I had met Detective Lanclos a few times before when I was working for St. Beatrice, and he remembered me, but thankfully said nothing about the Rocco matter. He was busy with the crime scene and kept glancing over there, so we only spoke for a few minutes.

"A lot going on around this motel lately," he said. "All linked somehow to you." He flicked his eyes back and forth between me and the crime scene techs doing their job. "You see any connection between this and the drug bust we just did?"

I didn't answer at first, just shook my head. "Who knows with these people?"

He nodded. "So you smelled Lysol and got suspicious, that it?"

"Yes."

"Good thing you did. Ever see this car around here before?"

"No."

"So what made you suspicious enough to walk over there close enough to smell the Lysol?"

"It belongs to a woman I know who works at LolliPops. Amber. Don't know her last name. Her friends have been looking for her. I know that much."

"LolliPops, huh?" He looked back at the men milling around the Firebird. "You have any kind of relationship with her?"

"Never saw her outside of the club."

"You sure about that?" He watched me closely.

"Definitely."

"All right, Harris. We'll have to wait for a positive ID on the body before we know anything more. I'll give you a call. I have to get back over there now. As soon as possible, I need that car towed and secured where we can really go over it. Don't go on vacation. I'll want to talk again with you."

"I'll be around."

I left the scene reluctantly and went about my chores with a heavy heart. Now I had another person to add to my list of people who would have been a whole lot better off if they'd never met me. A bitter pill to swallow and it felt like lead in my stomach. I felt so lousy and so discouraged, I wanted to just go back to bed and sleep it all off like a bad hangover. But when life sucks you can't let yourself do that. Lying around just makes it all that much worse.

47

ROCCO

A gruesome event like that will really throw you off. Rather than stay around the motel brooding about it, I decided to get some chores out of the way to take my mind off the horrors of a dead body dumped off right in front of where I live. A body that might as well have had a note pinned to it with my name on it. For what reason, I could only speculate. Certainly the Camaro was not dropped off there accidentally. It was no coincidence either that it was in front of the motel. A warning? If so, of what? That I was next? Or was it a clumsy attempt to implicate me somehow in the murder? Nobody could be dumb enough to believe that merely parking the car there was any kind of evidence incriminating me.

I could have allowed these kinds of thoughts to ricochet around my brain for hours. I needed distractions to avoid all that. So the rest of the day I ran errands to the hardware store, the feed store, the auto parts store, the grocery store, the plumbing supply store.

I left a message for Lenny to call me, and by the time I got back to the motel, it was fast growing dark. By that time, the Camaro had been towed and the road was clear of all the personnel and activity that had taken place earlier. I put all the purchases away, toted what was for Celeste to her house, fed the dogs and returned to my room to take it easy for a while.

I pushed some pillows up against the headboard and clicked on the TV, hunting for a movie. No sooner had I landed on a movie with a car chase through the desert, then my cell phone rang with an undisclosed number. "Yes?" I asked, my tone weary.

"Hey, man. It's Rocco. I can't talk long on this phone, so listen hard."

"Rocco! You son of a bitch…where are you?" There was a ding, ding, ding sound like a gas pump in the background and a horn beeping.

"Nowhere. I'm nowhere, man. And don't try to find out about the cell phone I'm using. I borrowed it from a biker. We're both on the road. I told him it was an emergency. I always say, if you need help ask a Cajun or a biker. Works every time. But listen. I know I messed up your life, and I'm real sorry about that. I did a bad thing. So to make up for it, I gotta tell you something urgent. Get the *hell* out of town! Those guys in Arkansas are furious and swear they'll get you for what you did. They're going after you for fucking up their entire sweet little operation."

"Rocco! Who the hell are you talking about?"

"Who do you think? You got the law after them up in Arkansas. The law after them in Louisiana. These people are some nasty freaks of nature….they don't play around. They will *kill you for that, man!* Listen to me! Get out of town. Go somewheres. If you do what I say, I saved your life. It's because I owe you."

"Relax, Rocco. Nobody's going to drive all the way down here from Arkansas and go hunting for me just because I was looking for you. That makes no sense."

"Harris! Your hunting for me is what started all this shit. You think they're hanging around up there now after all that's gone down? They're already across state lines and they took their goods with them. They have to set up somewheres else now and it's all because of you sticking your nose into their business."

"And them hiding dope in my truck. That almost got me put in jail. So who did worse, me or them?"

"Whatever. Just do what I'm telling you. I gotta give this phone back."

"And so they had to go and burn down Irena's house up there? What kind of crud have you been hanging with, Rocco?"

"Don't know nothing about that."

"*They set fire to Irena's house up there!*" I raised my voice like I was talking to a deaf man.

"Don't know the lady," he said. And then the line went dead.

"Rocco! ROCCO!" I yelled uselessly, holding the phone in my hand and looking at it as if it could tell me something. I laid it down on the bedside table and got up to get a beer out of the cooler I kept in a corner of the room.

If it's never happened to you, let me tell you, it is unnerving to hear that people want to kill you. The last time I heard someone wanted to kill me was from a kid in the sixth grade named Randy Tauzin who hated my guts but never followed up on his threat. Playground threats. I had an icy feeling that this threat was the real deal. But I hadn't any ideas of what to do about it except to report it. Maybe the Sheriff's Office could hustle me up some protection.

As I took the beer back to the bed and tried to get comfortable again against the pillows, I figured probably the best thing to do was call Detective Lanclos because he was already investigating Amber's murder, and I didn't want him to have to investigate mine also. I'd also call Ira and let him know about what Rocco said. I fished Detective Lanclos' card out of my pocket and pressed in the numbers for his cell phone.

He answered by growling his name into the phone.

"Detective, this is Harris Viator."

"What you got, Harris?"

"It's a long story."

"Why don't you come over to the office tomorrow then if you've got something for me."

I paused and thought about it for a few beats. "That might be too late."

"You don't sound too good."

"I just received a warning that someone is trying to kill me. One person or more, that is."

"This have anything to do with all that's been happening over there at the motel?"

"That and more. I'll tell you about it, but not over the phone."

There was a pause on his end then. I heard someone talking low in the background. "Okay, Harris. I'm leaving here in a few. I'll come by there before I go home. Give me half an hour. That work for you?"

"I'll be here." I cleared my throat. "I hope."

* * *

I swilled down another beer before Lanclos pulled up beside my pickup. It was twilight, and he had his lights on so that they swept across the windows of my room as he parked his truck. I peered out the window to make sure it was him. As he got out of the truck, he saw me looking and raised a hand in greeting. I went to the door and opened it before he knocked.

"Come on in, Detective. Thank you for stopping by. You want a beer?"

"No, I'm good." I locked the door and put the chain on, then showed him to the one chair in the room. I pulled it over beside the bed and sat on the edge of the mattress and turned the TV sound all the way down with the remote.

Lanclos wore a denim shirt with an unzipped gray nylon jacket, chinos and scuffed, but polished brown boots. As he settled into the chair, he pulled a small spiral notebook and pen out of a jacket pocket and flipped the notebook open.

He clicked the pen and wrote something on the pad, then looked up. "We have a positive ID now on the body. It is Amber." He drew a deep breath and paused for a moment.

I didn't respond, just nodded, feeling even more lousy.

"So, what did you call me about?" He looked tired, but interested.

"You want the long or the short version?" I asked.

"Try me," he said.

I started off by telling him how the Rocco saga started and how he'd ruined my life, but he held up a hand. "I know who you are. And I know all about Rocco and what he did to you. Pick up the story from after all that mess was over, and in the present time. How did you get involved in the Arkansas end of this?" He leaned back in his chair and waited.

So I told him how I went to work at LolliPops and finally got wind of Rocco through something Amber said to one of her girl friends, and tracked him on up to the Ozarks. Lanclos stopped me by holding up his hand again. "So who's the girl friend?" he asked.

I immediately wished I could backtrack and leave Lenny out of it. On the other hand, it might be good for him to know. It was a stretch, but she could be in some kind of danger as well. So I gave him her name and explained that it was because of her telling me about Rocco's possible whereabouts that I drove up to Arkansas.

"This woman, Lenny. She a close friend of Amber's?"

"I wouldn't say that. They saw each other at work mostly. She went with her once in a while after the club closed to the casino. Amber was a gambling junkie. That's about it, far as I know." I quickly changed topic and told him about the farm in Arkansas, and the booby trap and how a spike of bamboo went through my foot and how the Sheriff up there didn't do anything more at the farmhouse than ask a few questions and get a few lies. I told him about Mr. Perkins getting beat up because of leading me to them. I told him about Irena's waiting on me when I was laid up and the visit to Dr. Taylor, and how I'd struggled to make it home all the while unknowingly smuggling the stash of cocaine.

I pointed toward the door. "You can still see the splintered wood in the door frame where their pick-up guy shot at me when I caught him messing with my truck. Haven't gotten around to filling it in with wood putty yet. Too much going on around here lately."

"That's a fact. Way too much going on around here." He stood and walked over to open the door and examine it. He ran his fingers over the damage, then closed the door and put the safety lock on. He settled himself into the seat again and repositioned the notebook on his lap. He tapped the pen on his knee. "You're lucky the guy has poor aim."

"Yes, I'm damn lucky."

"So go on with your story," he said.

"And after all that went down, I got a phone call from Irena that they burned her boarding house down because she helped me." I shook my head. "That was like a knife in the gut to me. Her building was this great old place from the 1800s. Built before the Civil War. Her great grandfather built it. One of those bastards burned it to the ground. And Irena got burned because she went upstairs to drag out this old man who was staying there."

Lanclos wrote on his pad, then raised his head and brought his eyes back to mine.

"Burned her house down? Just for helping a wounded man? That's a ruthless bunch up there. They know who did it yet?"

"No, but the Police Chief in Falling Waters is her cousin, and he knows everybody, so it's just a matter of time."

"I'll bet she wishes she never met you," he said, shaking his head.

"You got that right. And I wish I'd never met her. She'd still have her boarding house."

"Don't get hung up on blaming yourself."

"I do though. That's a real nice woman up there."

"Yeah, sounds like it. But what's done is done."

"I'll make it up to her….somehow." I looked away because I had no idea how that was even possible.

"So, that brings us to why you called me tonight. You were threatened?" He watched me carefully narrowing his eyes.

"Yes. Rocco called me tonight. He talked fast. Said he only had a few minutes time on the phone. Wouldn't tell me where he was. Said the whole crew up in Arkansas had bailed and left the state when they got wind of what happened down here. Said they were furious that their sweet operation was blown because of me, and I was targeted. Like I have a bulls eye on me."

"Why would Rocco take the risk of warning you?"

"He said he knew he'd ruined my life and he owed me. He wasn't with them anymore and they were long gone, but he wanted me to get out of town and save myself."

Lanclos continued to watch me without speaking, waiting for more.

"I asked Rocco if he knew anything about Irena's house burning down. He said he never heard of her. Could be true. He stayed way out of town."

"How did he even get your number?"

"He didn't say. How did they even know where I lived in the first place? Maybe through Amber. I don't know."

"Maybe Amber was killed because it was through her you found out about where Rocco was." He raised his eyebrows and watched for my reaction.

"It's a possibility."

I got up and fetched another beer from the cooler, but first held one up in silent question to see if Lanclos had changed his mind about having one. He shook his head. I brought the icy can back and sat back down on the bed, tearing off the flip top, and wiping my wet hand on the sheet. "She might have owed somebody some money though, She was a gambling addict. But then that doesn't explain why they'd dump the Camaro in front of where I live. That's just too much of a coincidence."

Lanclos nodded absently, and had a faraway look in his eyes as he thought over what I'd reported. I waited just as quietly to hear any conclusions he came up with. The only sound was the faint whisper of water running through the pipes, most likely from one of the Mexicans showering two doors down.

Finally he spoke, "Probably be a good idea not to stay in here. Move to another room. Leave your truck where it is though…parked in front of this room. That's one precaution that's easy to pull off."

"I can do that."

"We'll keep an eye on this motel. We may get lucky and grab some more people who are involved in all this."

"So I'm a decoy now?"

"You can put it that way if you want." He gave me a sideways smile. "I'm going home now. I'll make a couple of phone calls from the house. See what I can do."

He flipped his notebook closed and slid it into a jacket pocket. "Go get comfortable in another room, but let me know the room number."

"I'll tell you right now. I'm going into the next room over." I pointed to the wall in back of the TV and the dresser. "Anything closer to the Mexicans and I'll be hearing Ranchera music through the walls."

He smiled again. "Okay. That's it for now. Call me if you see or hear anything you don't like."

"I will, Detective. Thank you." I stood to walk him to the door.

Lanclos stuck out his hand before he left. "Be careful," he said, as he gave me a firm handshake. Then he was gone, and I started looking around the room for what I would need to take with me next door. As I turned off the television, the last thing I saw was a scene with a cowboy going to sleep by a dying campfire, using his saddle for a pillow. A shadow was sneaking up on him from behind a boulder as his horse whinnied. I didn't have a campfire, a saddle or a horse, but I definitely could relate to the shadow lurking around in the middle of the night. Not a good feeling. I grabbed another beer out of the cooler, considered that it might slow down my reactions if something happened during the night, weighed the pros and cons of this, and ended up tearing off the flip top anyway.

48

LENNY NEEDS A FAVOR

I finally got settled in the next room and slept fairly well considering all that was on my mind. The next morning, I busied myself with chores around the motel, working extra hard to keep my mind off all that was going on.

Mid morning the cell phone rang. I was glad to see it was Lenny.

"You okay?" she asked.

"Sure."

"I'm not. The twins saw the news this morning. They're even worse off than I am. They knew Amber for much longer than I did. They can't believe it. *I* can't believe it."

"Me either."

"Poor Amber. I can't bear to think of what she must have gone through." Her voice broke.

"It's bad all right."

"Let's hope the dirtbag who killed her made it quick."

"Yes." I waited, not knowing what else to say.

"The news said they have no leads."

"No."

"But you're okay?" she asked again.

"Yeah, I'm okay. Shouldn't I be?"

"If there was a dead body left on my doorstep I wouldn't be doing okay."

"The car wasn't on the motel property. It was parked out on the street."

"Same difference. No way I would have been able to sleep last night."

"I'm getting used to trauma here lately."

"I can see that. You're getting a lot of practice. This is all tied in somehow, I believe. Nothing else makes any sense. Too coincidental."

"Right."

"Why didn't you call me when all this was going on yesterday?"

"I did call you. Left a message."

"Oh, sorry. I didn't listen to my messages. I've been on the move. Look, I need a big favor," she said. "I know you've just been through a lot, and you must be worn out, exhausted really. But this is really, really important or I wouldn't ask you." She was breathless like she'd been running. "And I'm embarrassed to ask you when you have so much on your plate."

"What is it? Why are you out of breath?"

"Am I? I guess I must be. This news came out of nowhere."

"What news?"

"I'm at my parents' house. I told you my father was furious about what happened to me up there at the camp. Well, the Chief called down here and said he was so angry he wouldn't bail Junior out. He's out of the hospital now and in the little Wallace jail in back of the police station. He worked it out with the Sheriff up there that he could stay in his jail instead of the Parish jail. The Sheriff is glad not to have to feed another prisoner and this way Junior's mother can send his home cooked food over from the house. Cozy, huh?"

"Crazy. But at least he's locked up."

"Anyhow, the Chief said Junior has something he wants to tell me. He won't even tell the Chief, which makes him mad, but Junior is mad at him for not bailing him out. And he has no friends, so no one else is going to do it, that's for sure."

"So what's this about wanting to tell you something?"

"Yeah, he has something to tell me, and I'm like…what's he going to do, write me a letter? And the Chief says, no, he wants to send a message with someone I trust."

"I get it. That would be me. Right? You want me to go up there and find out what he's talking about."

"Would you? Could you? The man is going to drive us all nuts before this is over. I don't have a clue what is on his mind. But he says it's very important and I need to know something that I'll be glad to know, and will really want to know. I don't know what the hell he's talking about, but he's got me really curious….and…well, I want to find out."

"What about your father?"

"What about him? The Chief said someone I *trust...*"

"Sure. I'll go up there and see what's on his mind. Anything else you want me to do while I'm up there?"

"No. It's a long drive up. After you find out what he wants, go stay at the house. I'll call ahead and have Quintus fix you a delicious steak dinner for as soon as you get to the camp. Then sleep over and I'll tell him to fix you a big breakfast so you can drive home without having to stop anywhere to eat. Or stay at the camp as long as you want. I'm sure you could use a little R & R after what you've just been through. People come from all over just to relax there for a weekend. That's what it's made for.... relaxation."

"Sounds good, but I can't stay overnight. Too much going on here, things are so crazy. So I'll leave soon as I can get out of here...today."

"Oh, that's wonderful of you. Thank you so much. I'm so glad you'll go for me. And I'll make it up to you big time. Just wait til you see what I'll do for you!"

"Looking forward to it. I'll call you soon as I know something then."

"You don't know how much I appreciate this." She blew some kisses over the phone and clicked off.

When she called me, I'd been playing with Merle and Willie, so I changed the water in their bowls, raked their area, and went on to the back door to tell Celeste I had to do something important for Lenny back up in North Louisiana.

"I'll be back late tonight. And please start packing to go to Acey's house. I don't think it's safe around here for you any longer."

"So dramatic you are."

"Celeste." I gave her a look.

"Okay, okay, I'm packing up. Don't rush me. There is a lot I have to take care of before I close up the house."

"That's good. I see Acey talked some sense into you."

"He's delighted about it. Says he can't wait to get me under his roof so he can boss me around." She laughed and wiped her hands on her apron. "Drive careful, *cher*."

49

JUNIOR

The Chief walked me down a hallway and showed me to a drab little room with cement block walls painted gray where Junior sat on a gray metal chair with his face turned to the wall.

"Junior. Wake up. You've got company," the Chief said, his tone rough.

Junior slowly turned his head to look at me and nodded.

"Yeah," he said, his voice flat. The lower lids of his eyes drooped and his color was sallow.

"Have a seat," the Chief said to me and indicated the only other chair in the room.

"I'll give you a few minutes alone, then I'll be back to get you. Junior, look at me," he said. "Watch yourself, you hear me? You act up and you'll be in shackles next time you want to talk to somebody."

Junior's eyes were bouncing all over the room, looking anywhere but at the Chief.

"You deaf all of a sudden? I said, do you hear me? Hello!" The Chief made a mock megaphone with both hands around his mouth.

"Yeah, yeah. I hear you." Junior finally spoke, glanced at his father, then settled his eyes on me.

"Act like a man then." He pointed a finger at his son and then abruptly turned and left the room.

"You wanted to send a message to Leonée, so she sent me. What you got?" I sat very still, ready for anything, hands on my knees. I watched him carefully as I spoke. His eyes kept darting back and forth like he was watching a tennis game, but he didn't speak for several minutes as I waited.

Finally he cleared his throat and shifted in his chair, then looked at me. "I know something she would like to know."

"Okay. What you got?" I leaned slightly forward.

"She used to have this boy friend. But he disappeared. She tell you about that?"

"Yes."

"How much do you know?"

"Not much. What should I know?" I was on high alert by then, and trying not to show it.

"There's something she doesn't know....that I know, but I want to trade in exchange for it."

"You know something about her missing boy friend? Renard?"

"Yep."

"And you want something in return?" My fingers itched. I could have punched him right then if I didn't keep a short leash on myself. "If somebody goes missing, a normal person would say what they know. They wouldn't hold out for some kind of a bargain."

He sniffed. "Maybe you would cause you're some kind of a chump, but I'm in no position to be nice here. I'm already real tired of being locked up. This shit gets old."

"So what do you want?"

"I want out of here. I want her to drop the charges. She lays around in the back yard butt naked and then goes ballistic if a man gets near her. I'm lucky she didn't split my skull open the way she was going after me."

"She's in her own back yard and you're out there lurking around her house again…when you just got arrested for trespassing over there. That make sense?"

"I wasn't trespassing. She invited me over." He looked at the floor, mumbling.

I cupped my ear. "Say that again. I couldn't have heard you right. You say she invited you over? You did get some brain damage, didn't you?"

"She did invite me! Prove she didn't."

I started to rise from my chair. "You want to talk crazy or do you want to talk straight? Who do you expect will believe that? I'm leaving if you're going down this road."

"Wait a minute. Sit down. Sit down."

"Only if you stop lying to me. I've come a long way and I'm tired out. I want to go eat somewhere."

"Whatever. Just tell her I know something about when her boy friend disappeared that maybe she needs to know. But like I said, I want something for it. Get me out of here. I want to go home."

"Look, I want to help Leonée find what happened to Renard. If you know something, I want to hear it. As far as trading for it, the whole thing is way out of her hands now. Maybe you can get somewhere with the prosecutor. I don't know. But whatever happens with it, you need to give any information you have to your father. Let him figure out what to do. I'm going to go find a restaurant now." I stood and turned toward the door.

"Wait. Maybe she could change her story. Say it didn't happen like that or something. That she overreacted, got all hysterical on me."

"That ain't going to happen. Give it up, Junior." I started toward the door again.

"How about I give you a hint." He narrowed his eyes.

"A hint of what?"

"Of what happened not too long before her boy friend disappeared."

"And?"

"She might like to know something I saw that afternoon."

"Something you saw…like what? Give me something."

"Somebody sniffing around. That's all I'm saying til *I* get something." Junior's eyes flicked back and forth around the room like there was something to see other than gray cement block walls, and he drummed his fingers on the table.

"And how would you know? You were slinking around out at the camp again?"

"I like it over there."

"You like looking at Leonée you mean." I took a few steps back toward him. "Isn't that right?"

"Who wouldn't?"

"Yes. Who wouldn't is right. But the point is, she doesn't want perverts hiding in the bushes trying to get a look at her on her own private deck in her own back yard. That's why we have no trespassing laws. People don't like being spied on. Are you dim?"

"Just tell her what I said and leave off the phony outrage act." He licked his lips. "You just want her all to yourself. You're jealous."

"Jealous of you, Junior? You're a comedian, right?"

He smirked and crossed his arms. "See? You're angry. Like I said…jealous."

"The lady decides who she wants to spend her time with. Meanwhile do you have a theory about what happened that night?"

"My theory? I look like a detective? How should I have a theory? Far as I know, he's coyote meat by now." He turned his gaze back to the wall.

"Come on. Everybody has at least one guess as to what happened. What went through your mind at the time?"

He ran a finger along a black streak on the wall.

"I might have figured he ran away cause he didn't know how to break up with her. I don't know. Or maybe she murdered him." He smiled and looked at me again. "Now that would be a twist, wouldn't it? Ha, ha. Joke's on everybody." His eyes were dull as dishwater and his stiff smile wore thin. "I wouldn't put it past her. Look what she did to me. She beats me up, but I'm the prisoner, locked up in a cell I can't turn around in, and I didn't do nothing."

"Save it, Junior. Nobody's buying your crap." I watched him fall into a sulk so fast, I could tell he'd been sulking half his life, he did it so well. "You like to sneak out there to the camp. Hang around in the background watching what goes on…right?"

"I got better things to do."

"Maybe so, but you are in a nasty mess now and you've been arrested in the past for being out there trespassing."

"She invited me out there. That's trespassing? Since when?"

I clenched my fists and it was all I could do to keep from knocking him off his chair, but I hid my anger as best I could and coached myself, *Come on, man, don't blow this. Get a grip!*

"So I drove all the way up here for nothing. Is that what you're telling me? Just some bullshit story about something so insignificant you never bothered to tell anybody before….and now another ludicrous whopper about your attack on Leonée? That it? Anything else? I'm going to need hip boots to wade out of here as it is."

"I told you she invited me out there to the camp. The whole thing was her idea. I get out there and she's lying there bare assed naked. What would you think if someone looks like her and invites you out and then she's buck naked lying out there in the sun? No jury will convict me."

"Junior, I hate to break it to you, but no jury is going to believe you over her. Your life has been one long screw up. How many times have you been arrested for shoplifting? Trespass? Peeping Tom? So if you do have something that will help her find out what happened to Renard, then spill it, and it will do a lot to change the long dismal future in Angola you've got staring you in the face for attempted rape. But drop the charges she has against you? No way."

He sniffed and wiped his nose with the back of his hand. "Okay, now I'm getting bored. I'm done talking to you. I told you I don't know jack about her boyfriend and why he disappeared on her that night. All I know is what I said. And I won't tell her unless she gives me something."

He walked to the heavy metal door and banged his fist on it. "If I did know where he went, don't you think I'd be trading on it?" He winced and rubbed his knuckles. "Damn, that smarts."

The Chief opened the door, shook his head in disgust at the sight of his son, glanced at me and jerked his head to indicate it was time for me to leave, and then led Junior away down the short hall to one of the town's two cells. I stared after them for a few minutes and watched the Chief shove Junior into his cell. He slammed the door shut with a loud clang, then turned and saw me watching.

"You got what you came for?" I didn't like his tone, but I never argue with a man with a gun, so I shook my head and turned away, the interview pretty much of a washout. I doubted Junior had anything worth the price of gas for the round trip, but I'd deliver the message to Lenny. You never know what will turn up if you don't try.

50

DINNER AT
WHISPERING OAKS

I called Lenny on the drive home to report what
Junior had said. She told me to come by her
parents' house for dinner so I could tell her all
the details.

"It's going to be past eight by the time I get
there," I warned.

"No matter. We'll wait dinner on you. It'll be
better this way. And you can meet my mother and
sister."

"Tell me how to get there then," I said. And she
gave me directions to Sweet Olive Place, a private
road that dead-ended at their house. "When you see
the snooty bronze plaque out front for Whispering
Oaks, you'll know you found us."

Sweet Olive Place was a good deal east of Eustis,
and on a solitary side of a lake that had been cut
off from a loop of the Mississippi River when it
had changed course thousands of years before. As

I approached the house, twilight was on the edge of nightfall. All the lights were on at the house. Floodlights low to the ground lined the driveway, and some of them were tilted to light up giant sprawling live oaks that lined the long gravel drive to the house. Some of the lowest and longest branches defied gravity by extending up to thirty feet with Resurrection fern covering the bark. After seeing the size of their camp, I expected their main house to be large, but when I saw it I did a double take. It sported the obligatory white columns, four of them, and all the upper windows were lighted...all six of them.

As I pulled up, I was disappointed that no valet came trotting out to park the pickup, so I left it there in front of the brick walk to the gallery. The bricks were mossy and no doubt made on the premises in bygone days. They were carefully tended and weeded. Banks of flowers lined the brick walk and the hundred foot wide gallery. And there were cement urns overflowing with flowers at each end of the wide brick steps leading up to the porch. As I approached the glossy black front door with a huge brass knocker, Lenny opened the door laughing and bouncing up and down with excitement. "So glad you found us! Come in, come in. I'll bet you're starving."

She ran to me and gave me an energetic hug, kissing me repeatedly.

"Quite a place you've got here," I said.

"Oh, isn't it though. Lucien stole it from an old lady who thought the world of him. It's Antebellum of course. Her family tried to fight it, but he bought it from her for about half what it was worth the year before she died and there was nothing they could do about it because she was in her right mind. I told you my father was a bastard." She didn't even lower her voice as she said this, and I looked past her toward the open front door but there was no one around. "Come on in and meet Mama and Mimi."

She took my hand and led me inside the foyer. A black drop leaf table stood near the door against the wall with a tall vase filled with yellow iris, a long gilt framed mirror behind it. The wide plank floors were highly waxed and a Turkish runner ran the length of a long hallway that passed on by a staircase on one side and a series of doorways on the right.

Lenny led me down the passageway to the wide doorway to the living room. Two tapestry couches faced one another in front of a fireplace with a carved wooden mantel. Two women sat on the sofas and smiled as we entered.

"Mother, this is Harris Viator. Harris, this is my mother."

Her mother sat forward and offered her hand. I stepped toward her and lightly shook it. "Please call me Lenore," she said. "So glad to meet you after all the wonderful things I've heard about you."

"And this is my sister, Mimi," Lenny said, guiding me toward the other sofa.

"Hello," Mimi said and her hand was so delicate, I was afraid I'd hurt her by shaking it. "Very pleased to meet you," she said primly. She looked nothing

like Lenny. Where Lenny was tan and strong looking, Mimi looked pale and frail. Her brown hair
was thin and hung straight to her shoulders. A tiny
rhinestone clip held it neatly in place. She wore a
sleeveless blue dress with an open white collar and
low-heeled blue sandals. When she was done greeting me, she folded her hands still in her lap and sat
quietly against a needlepoint pillow as though but-
ter wouldn't melt in her mouth. Like I say, she was
the opposite of Lenny.

Lenore patted the seat next to her and invited
me to sit. "We'll have our dinner in a minute, but
first won't you have a glass with us? What would you
like after that long drive that you were so good to
make for us?"

"We're having some white wine but you might
like something stronger?" Lenny nodded at me as
though to say I was going to need it.

"Okay. How about a bourbon and water?"

"Black Jack coming right up," she said and
crossed to a wooden trolley set up with a silver ice
bucket, a silver pitcher and three bottles of liquor. I
settled next to Lenore and when Lenny handed me
my drink wrapped in a napkin, I toasted all three
women with the glass before taking a sip. "To your
health," I said.

"To your health," Lenore echoed, raising her
glass to mine. "So glad you're here with us this
evening."

We made polite small talk until the housekeeper opened the sliding wooden doors to the dining
room and called us for dinner. Lenore led the way

to the long dining table and directed me to a high backed chair next to her end of the table. A crystal chandelier made all the stemmed glasses sparkle and gold edged china plates picked up the light as well. I stood blinking at the sight of all that shimmering dinner table, and then remembered my manners and pulled out Lenore's chair for her. Lenny and Mimi seated themselves and then a cheerful young woman in a white blouse and black skirt poured water for us. It wasn't until she returned with an oval tray of appetizers that Lucien joined the party. He entered through still another door leading to the rear of the house.

"Hello, hello," he said as he nodded to each of us. "Sorry. Was on the phone. Some irritating business I had to take care of." He immediately furled out his napkin and arranged it on his lap, then made a hurry up gesture with his fingers toward the young woman who was setting a small plate of stuffed mushrooms before him. "Let's have that wine now, please."

"Yes, sir," she said and tipping the empty tray to fit under her arm returned to the kitchen through a swinging door.

He ignored the mushrooms and looked directly at me. "I hear you have some news for us, Harris. That right?"

"Give the man a chance to eat his dinner, Lucien," Lenore said.

"We can eat and talk at the same time, can't we?" He kept his eyes on me.

"At least wait for the toast," Lenore said.

The young woman returned with a bottle of wine wrapped in a white napkin. She poured Lucien's first, and he took a sip and made the impatient gesture again with his fingers. "It's good. Let's go, Sherry."

Sherry went on and poured for all of us, and then Lucien raised his glass and made a toast to our health that we all echoed.

"We're so glad you could join us for dinner," Lenore added.

Lucien nodded, then drank some wine and went to work on the mushrooms before starting in on me again.

It wasn't until Sherry had taken up our plates and refilled our glasses that he brought up the subject again.

"So, Harris, what do you have for us? What did that idiot have to say?"

Lenore lowered her head and glared at him. "Lucien, please. There's plenty of time for that. We have a guest."

"Of course we have a guest. That's why he's a guest! He did us a big favor." He raised his eyes to the chandelier.

Sherry returned with a tray of salad plates and the housekeeper followed to help her. This slowed Lucien's impatience for a while longer while we were busy with that course, but it was obvious that he was restless because his mouth got tighter and his eyes flicked back and forth around the room as he ate.

It wasn't until the third course and he'd carved the roast for all of us and we'd started in on the perfectly cooked dinner that he brought it up again.

"So now….can you tell us finally what happened up there in the big town of Wallace?" He held his forkful of potato halfway to his mouth and waited.

I looked at Lenny. She shook her head. "Go ahead and tell him or we'll never have any peace."

I put my fork down wishing I didn't have to because the food was outstanding and I was hungry. Maybe I could make this quick so I could get back to my dinner. "Basically, he wants to trade some information for Lenny dropping the charges against him."

"What information?" Lucien's voice changed from semi-polite to hostile, like we were in a courtroom all of a sudden.

"He wouldn't tell me. He's saving that for Lenny."

"That's it? That's all he told you?"

"He said something about seeing something the day Renard disappeared."

Lucien frowned. "Playing games now? He always was a little son of a bitch."

"Lucien, please. We're trying to have a nice dinner party," Lenore said, then patted my arm. "I'm sorry, Harris. Don't mind Lucien. He has a lot on his mind. He's tired."

"Oh, for God's sake, Lenore. Stay out of this!" He glowered at her, then turned back to me. "That's it. That's all you have to report?"

I nodded. "That's it."

"So then what? Did you talk to Quintus before you left?"

"Lucien. Harris is surely hungry. He's been driving most of the day. Let him eat his dinner!" Lenore curled her fingers into a fist.

"Leave him alone!" said Lenny, and she rapped her knuckles against the table.

Lucien looked back and forth to his wife, to Lenny, and then back to me. "Don't mind them. I have to put up with this all the time. Just tell me. What did Quintus say?"

Lenny half stood so that her napkin started sliding from her lap to the floor. She grabbed it in time. "Dad. Lucien! We're eating here. Stop it!"

He pointed his fork at her. "Sit down, Lenny! This all started because of you in the first place."

"Oh, really? So now this is all my fault?" She sat fuming and picking up her wine glass, drained it in one gulp, then held it up for more. "Sherry, please, refill!"

Lenore looked close to tears. "I'm so sorry, Harris. I wanted this to be a special dinner for you."

"It's all right. Really. Your dinner is delicious."

"Yes, it is, if you could be left alone to eat it," Lenny said, glaring at her father.

Lucien raised his hands. "All right, I'm sorry to be so interested in what the little creep has to say who tried to rape my daughter."

"Lucien! For God's sake. Why don't you go to your study and calm down. Let us eat in peace."

Sherry refilled Lenny's glass and then topped off everyone else's.

Lenny raised her glass. "I have an idea. Let's start over. For Mother's sake." She looked at her mother with a sad expression. "Sorry, Mommy."

"Good idea, Sweetheart. We'll start over," Lenore said, her expression changing quickly as she smiled at Lenny, then me.

"This is a wonderful dinner," I said. "And I thank you."

"We have the best cook. She's a wonder. We're so lucky to have her."

Lucien was eating again, still frowning, but silent this time.

When we'd finished that course, Sherry cleared up the table and brushed off invisible crumbs into a small silver dustpan.

"You're going to have a treat now. Get ready for one of Tillie's famous pies," Lenny said. "Right, Missy?" She looked over the table at her sister who remained as still as a statue, arms tight to her sides, hands in her lap.

"Oh, yes," Missy said in her little girl voice. "You're going to love Tilly's dessert, whatever it is." She blinked as though she'd been daydreaming. "I hope it's strawberry." She gave me a timid smile. "With ice cream."

By the time the coffee was poured and the desserts served, I figured Lucien had held his tongue as long as he'd be able to. I wasn't off by much. We were only halfway into the pie, not strawberry, but the best blackberry pie I'd ever tasted, when he started up again.

"Now, may I ask again if you saw Quintus while you were up there?" His voice was strained. He was keeping himself on a leash, but with difficulty.

"Yes, I saw him."

"And did you tell him what Junior said?" Lucien spoke slowly as if talking to a child.

"No. That's Lenny's business."

He looked at me for a long moment, eyes narrowed, as though I'd threatened him. Finally he spoke. "That's my camp and my man Quintus. And this whole thing is *my* business. Quintus is the caretaker. Lenny's my daughter. And the little bastard did this at my camp! Soon as we're done here, I'm calling Quintus and then I'm going up there tomorrow to find out what this little bastard, *Junior*... has to tell me."

"No, *I'm* going up there to find out. First thing in the morning," said Lenny. "Not you."

"Bullshit. You're not going near that little animal. You've already done enough by lying around sunbathing with no clothes on. I'm going."

Lenny tossed her napkin down on the table and stood. "Come on, Harris. We're leaving. I can't stand any more of this!"

"Oh, please, darling. Don't go. Lucien! Why don't you go relax in your study and leave us alone. You're obviously tired. Go on now."

"You're telling me to leave my own dinner table?"

"Yes, I am. You've ruined our lovely dinner with your stubbornness."

"No, Mommy. I'm sorry. But he's impossible. Quit making excuses for him." She stood in back of me and tugged my sleeve. "Come on, Harris. Let's go."

I took Lenore's hand and kissed the back of it. "Thank you so much for everything. I'll never forget it." Lenore's eyes shimmered with tears.

"Goodbye, Harris. Nice to meet you," said Missy, giving me that same thin smile as though nothing out of the ordinary had happened.

"You have a lot of nerve doing this to your mother's dinner party," Lucien said, his face dark.

Lenny laughed at him. "So sue me!" She led me away from the dining room, through the living room and to the front door. "Go on to your place. I'll be right there. Just want to grab my things from upstairs before I leave."

51

HIRED HELP

I drove back to the motel and waited for her. All the rooms were dark. The Mexicans had gone to bed already. Celeste was still at Acey's house where I'd sent her. The dogs were even asleep and didn't hear me pull up from their shed in the back. I cut my lights before swinging into the driveway, and after parking in front of my room, I waited and looked around before getting out of the truck. There was enough light from the motel sign and the walkway fixtures for me to see that there was no one waiting to spring on me in the shadows or around the corner where the ice machine stood.

I went inside and changed clothes, putting on jeans and a tee shirt. The dress shirt and slacks I'd worn to Whispering Oaks went into a laundry basket I kept in the shower stall. I straightened up the room while I waited for her to arrive, wondering what she would decide to do next, now that she'd told off her father and stormed out of there.

Lenny was still fuming when she showed up at the motel. I heard her pull up and opened the door before she had time to knock. Her hair was wind-blown and her eyes were glittering with anger.

"I'm ready to drive right back up there to Wallace now so we can be there first thing in the morning to call the little bastard's bluff as to what the hell he thinks he knows. You with me?" She flopped onto my bed and crossed her arms in anger. "It's all some sort of trick that he's cooked up in that feeble tiny brain of his, but I have to make sure."

"Let him stew a little. Make him worry you're not coming."

"I would if I could, but I'm too curious."

"I have work to do here and I have to get out there and find a job. I have hardly any money left."

She scoffed. "I need you on this for moral support. I'll pay you. I have plenty of money, don't worry. Why can't I hire you to help me? Nothing's more important to me than finding out what happened to Renard. Nothing."

"I don't know. It doesn't seem right to take your money. You know I'd help you any way I could for free. It would be like taking money for doing a good deed."

"Oh, the hell with all that. You need money. I've got plenty of it. I need your help. End of story. What if I was to give you a thousand so you could help me even more than you already have? That way you wouldn't have to spend time looking for a job and we could maybe get somewhere with all this." She slid onto her side and punched the pillow to support her head. She frowned. "These pillows are hard."

I thought about how I could take her money and still feel right about it. I wanted to help her. I was almost as curious about what happened to Renard as she was. And her going up there to talk to Junior without me was not a good idea...not at all. She was too much of a hardhead....and Junior was too much of a creep for them to meet without a witness to their conversation. No telling what he was likely to pull on her. And no telling what she was likely to do to him if she lost her temper in that little gray cement block room.

"Well? What about it?" She punched the pillow again, trying to get comfortable.

"All right. I'll take your money. As long as you know that I would do it for free if I wasn't so damn broke."

She smiled, let go of the pillow and sat up, then her cell phone rang, and she lunged for her purse and dug it out. She held up a finger to me, and mouthed, "It's Jo-Jo." Then she rearranged herself back against the headboard and pillows as she listened.

While she was on the phone, I realized I was glad to be going out of town. If you've never gotten a warning that someone is trying to kill you, then you wouldn't know how it feels. To say it puts you on hyper alert is understating it. Leaving town and driving up to North Louisiana again was a plan I welcomed. And of course any time spent with Lenny was high on my list. Being on salary to the woman I was sleeping with? I started to rationalize the situation. So what? I was a trained cop. Why the hell not? Maybe I could even figure this thing out before it was all over. If I was able to, then it was worth every cent of her thousand dollars. One thing sure, I did need money, and she did need my help. Bottom line: I found a new way of looking at it, and it was okay by me to take her money. I relaxed.

"Okay, Jo-Jo. I understand. What if I ask Harris to go? That be all right? You met him at my place. Remember?"

She nodded and said, "Yes," all at the same time, then clicked off and tossed the phone back into her purse.

"Change of plans."

"Okay, what?"

"Germaine. Renard's ex? The one Jo-Jo was talking about at my apartment? The Swamp Lady?"

"I remember."

"She wants him to come out there to her family's camp. She sent word she wants to tell him something."

"And?"

"I would like you to go with him."

"Me? Why?"

"I'd like you to be there, that's all. You might learn something. Who knows? She's weird. Who knows what she'll do or say?"

"But you were just champing at the bit to drive up to Wallace to hear what Junior has to tell you."

"I know, but you're right. Let him stew a while. It won't hurt him to do that."

I shook my head. "All right. If that's what you want, I'll go with Jo-Jo."

"It'll be a learning experience. Ever been deep in the Atchafalaya?"

"No. Just around the Basin."

"We're talking serious Swampers here. From what Jo-Jo has told me, you're going to have the experience of a lifetime."

"You're the experience of a lifetime."

"Yep! That I am," she said, and patted the space next to her for me to join her in the bed, smiling all the while.

52

GERMAINE

The next morning was cloudy and gray. It was so somber even the birds were silent. I had sent Lenny off to her apartment the night before. It was hard to do because holding her close to me all night would have been my first choice, but I couldn't take any chances that somebody hunting me would show up during the night and endanger her.

As soon as I made a pot of coffee, had a mug of it, and showered and dressed, I headed out to drive over to Leveetown and meet up with Jo-Jo. We ate breakfast together at a café near the levee, and then we drove up onto the levee and over it to a boat ramp next to a long row of boat slips and a restaurant. I parked my truck at the public ramp as he backed his truck and trailer to the water's edge. I helped him slide the skiff into the water, and then kept it steady while he parked his truck.

We putted our way out of the area, passing houseboats and people working or sitting on their decks, until we made our way into somewhat open water. Traveling through the Atchafalaya Basin is confusing because everywhere looks familiar. Once we had passed along La Rose Bayou and turned off, I was totally lost, but Jo-Jo knew where he was headed and skillfully navigated us onward. Unless you're with the most seasoned Swamper, it's best to have a GPS with you for this reason. Very easy to get lost and many sportsmen who think they can find their way have gotten lost out there and required rescue. It's the better part of a million square acres of drowned cypress forest, and whether the water levels are high or low, it still all pretty much looks the same.

However, with Jo-Jo, no GPS was needed, and we traveled on south through the swamp to the Stelly camp within an hour. He silently pointed to the rise where the family compound was spread out. Encircled by cypress trees and willow, the family was camouflaged and yet still had visibility in all directions. No one could sneak up on them. Their privacy was assured.

Jo-Jo had already told me that the brothers guarded their territory of traps constantly. No one dared poach any of the Stelly traps for fear of the worst kind of punishment. It was rumored that some had tried, and some had never been seen again. The family had moved up from further South close to a hundred years before, and they had had plenty of time to stake out their own territory. It was rumored also that although they came down hard on anyone fooling with their traps, they were not as fussy about other people's territory.

Although suspected, none of the brothers had ever been caught raiding another Swamper's traps. As for Fish & Wildlife, the Stelly brothers had seldom been caught breaking the rules, although seasoned Swampers were known to keep bricks in their boats to weigh down any illegal catch they might have to throw overboard, should they see a Fish & Wildlife boat approaching.

Moise Angelle of Fish & Wildlife had put Caleb in jail twice, but Moise was well known for having some sort of uncanny sixth sense, and Swampers stayed as far away from him as possible. It was rumored that Moise's father Lucky stayed close by his side and directed Moise from the Spirit world.

"People have actually seen Lucky's ghost right there in the boat with Moise," Jo-Jo called over the rumble of the motor. "Caleb saw it too. He swears the stories are true. Every trapper knows about Lucky Angelle. And they're all afraid of what he might do to them. It's rumored an outlaw hunter murdered Lucky years ago, and left him for dead in the swamp, but nothing was ever proved."

"No wonder Moise has an attitude," I called to him.

"Swampers believe Moise suspects who did it. Knowing Moise, it's just a matter of time. He's like a dog with a bone when he's on a mission."

"Sounds like somebody is sleeping with one eye open," I said.

"If Moise Angelle was after me, I wouldn't be able to sleep at all!"

By the time Jo-Jo slowed the boat to land, there was only one skiff hauled up on the bank of the camp.

It was tied to the slender trunk of a willow tree and overshadowed by low hanging branches. Jo-Jo and I hauled his skiff far enough up on the bank next to it so that he didn't have to secure it. We stood for a minute looking around before we advanced toward the compound.

"All three of the other brothers are still out checking traps or fishing. They each have their own boat," Jo-Jo said.

There were three shacks on the rise. All three were covered over with sheets of corrugated roofing metal serving as siding. They were all supported by and built into tree trunks on the four corners of each cabin, so they could be elevated more than six feet up off the ground. All three roofs were metal as well. The metal siding was not uniform. Some squares of new metal had been nailed over in patches, giving the cabins a thrown together appearance. Most of the metal was a rusted brownish red, yet was shiny in places where newer material had been overlaid. A hound started barking and then a man's voice instantly silenced him.

A ten foot tall cypress cistern was positioned near the center of the compound. This giant barrel with metal support bands towered over the cabins and perfectly expressed the family's self-sufficiency and survival skills. The staves of the cistern were a weathered gray and the metal bands a dull black. There was even a small smoke house and an outhouse on the compound. The smoke house was not much bigger than the outhouse, and they were positioned at opposite ends of the area.

The windows of the cabins were all outfitted with green louvered shutters that were raised up to a ninety degree angle from the window frames by use of support poles. Someone was looking out from one of the windows in the nearest cabin to us, but the interior of the cabin was too shadowy to make out the person's features.

The cabins were staggered in a V layout with no more than thirty feet between them. As the available land on the rise was not even a half acre, available space didn't provide much privacy for any of the family members. From our position on the bank, I could see a bare space in the center of the layout that looked like a cooking area. There was a fire pit and a black cooker on legs that had once been a propane tank, but had been sawed in half lengthwise and hinged. The lid was open and steam rose from the cook fire. The instant a breeze changed and brought the smell of grilling fish toward us, I was hungry. The screaming of millions of swamp insects was so loud we had to talk over it.

"I hope whatever Germaine invited us here for includes some of that fish they got going over there," I said to Jo-Jo.

"Don't worry. These people know how to eat, and they will make sure you don't go away hungry."

Whoever was at the window disappeared and then a woman appeared at the door of the cabin closest to us. She stepped out onto the high warped steps and waved us toward her.

"Come on. That's Germaine there," said Jo-Jo. "Let's go see what she wants."

We walked quickly toward the cabin and as we got closer she disappeared back into the shadows of the cabin. "She shy or what?" I asked Jo-Jo.

"Shy?" he laughed. "That's a good one. Come on." He led me toward the steps and stopped on the top one. "You want us to come in there or are you coming out?" he called.

"What do you think?" she answered, her voice low. "Come on in."

Jo-Jo stepped inside the dark cabin and then I followed him across the bare wood threshold that was worn down in the center from many years of wear.

"Come on and sit," Germaine said and she beckoned us to a grouping of chairs in various shapes and sizes. There was a ladder back chair, a rocking chair, a chair cut out of a barrel, a cowhide chair, and an upholstered chair where she already sat, arms and legs crossed.

Toward the back of the long room was a long plank table. On shelves was a row of large black pots, mixed with some smaller white enamel bowls and pans. There was another shelf with nothing on it but empty gleaming glass jars and bottles. A blue pit bull puppy was sleeping in a basket by Germaine's chair. He was fat and twitched as he dreamed.

After taking a look at the room, I brought my eyes to Germaine and then couldn't help but continue to stare at her. She had long black straight hair falling all around her like a cloak. She was beautiful in such a way that I forgot to breathe. Dark eyes and a face out of a picture book, but her expression was as dark as her eyes, and her somber manner was not welcoming, but rather carried some sort of a warning such as *Keep your distance*, or better yet, *Caution: I bite!*

She wore jeans and heavy black work boots, practical for living in the swamp. However, on top she wore what looked like a blouse that had been cut off into a halter. The sleeves were cut off and left with rough edges and the bottom of the blouse was cut off showing about six inches of her flat tanned midsection. She wore no jewelry unless you could call a woven leather bracelet jewelry. But then, Germaine was such a beauty that jewelry could not possibly add anything to what was already there. When I finally realized I was being rude by staring, I looked away, but not before she gave me a whisper of a mocking smile out of the side of her mouth.

We each selected a chair and settled into them, waiting to hear why we had been summoned. If Jo-Jo was telling the truth, then neither of us had a clue why she wanted us to come all the way out to her lair. And lair it was too. There was heaviness in the air that was not just the humidity, but had something of her in it. It was as though her personality had saturated the cabin and the air itself was full of her somber personality. It was almost immediately evident why Renard had left her. As beautiful as she was, it was hard to believe Germaine was ever fun or easy to be with. To come to that conclusion so quickly gives you an idea of how close the atmosphere in that cabin was. It was almost hard to breathe in there, yet all the windows were wide open and a light breeze carried the delicious aroma of the grilling fish through to us. A mosquito buzzed around her and she smacked it dead on her arm and casually brushed it off along with the blood it left on her skin.

"You will eat with us," she said. It was not a question, but a statement, and the way she said it made clear that it was not up to us to decide whether we would or not.

"Now, Germaine. Only a dummy would ever turn down your cooking," said Jo-Jo. He rubbed his hands together in anticipation of what was to come.

"I'm not cooking today. My brother is making a dinner for all of us. We'll all be eating soon enough, but first I wanted to tell you something."

"Go," said Jo-Jo, holding out his hands. "Let's have it."

She swung her hair back and then raked it with her fingers and took a deep breath, pausing as if she might change her mind about saying what was on her mind.

Through a window to the side of her I could see a man wearing shrimper's boots come out of the middle cabin with a long handled steel spatula, a Redbone hound at his side. He crossed to the cooker and inspected the fish, then flipped them over with the spatula as steam drifted around him. The hound sat keeping a close eye on the grill.

"I haven't talked to you for a long time," she said to Jo-Jo. "I wanted to, but I kept waiting."

"Waiting for me to come see you?"

"No. Waiting to hear from Renard." She turned her head away from us and closed her eyes. "I was so sure he'd show up. One day just show up. I *knew* he would."

"Yeah, I know what you mean," said Jo-Jo. "Me too."

"So many nights I'd hear something and then I'd think, *that's him out there!* But no, nothing. It was always just one of my brothers coming in from fishing, or some night animal nosing around. I stay in here alone and I'm a light sleeper...so you can imagine what it's been like...not knowing."

"You should have told me. You know where I live," Jo-Jo said shifting in his chair. "I'd have come out to see you, but I never thought you wanted company."

She shook her head. "It's not that. I have plenty of company. My parents are over there." She held a hand out to her right. "My brothers are over there," and she moved her hand toward the window to her left. "It's that I couldn't believe he would stay away like this."

"He wouldn't," said Jo-Jo. "He'd have let me know something....where he was, what was going on."

"I know that!" She tightened her lips. "And I knew you'd tell me if you did hear something."

'Of course I would."

"Well, now things are different. That's why I called you out here." She moved her shoulder back and forth to loosen her back, then slowly draw a hand across her forehead.

"You've heard from him?" Jo-Jo sat up.

"No! Well, yes! But not like you think."

"What then?"

"I dreamed about him. And I have had no dreams about him at all since he disappeared. This is the first time."

"What? What did you dream?"

'I dreamed that he just stood and looked at me. He was outside staring at me. Nothing but woods behind him, and he just stood there at the edge of the woods, not saying anything…just looking at me. He looked bad. Like he was hurt. His face was messed up."

"And then what?"

"And then nothing. He was gone. That was it." She brushed one hand against the other as though to end the story.

"That's it? That's why you wanted us to come out here? For a dream?"

Her expression changed from somber to anger. "Don't you see? He must be *dead!* I often dream of people who have died. And that's how they all do. They just look at you or they don't even look directly at you, but they *do not speak!*"

Jo-Jo looked at me and then looked back at Germaine shaking his head. "I don't know anything about all that."

"Well, I do! I've dreamed of people who have passed on all of my life. Since I was a little girl. And that's how they all come to visit me. Silent. Always silent."

"So what does the dream mean then?"

"It means he wants me to know he's in spirit, but it also means he wants me to do something."

"Do what?"

"What do you think? He wants me to find out what happened to him. Find out why he disappeared. Who did this to him."

"You? You're supposed to do that?"

"I don't think he cares who does it. But he wants it done!"

Jo-Jo nodded. "I see what you mean. He wants us to know something happened to him. He didn't just take off somewhere, and we're supposed to go from there."

"That's right. Figure it out. Somehow."

"So where do we begin?"

"Right up there at that woman's place where he disappeared from in North Louisiana. That's where. I don't mind telling you, I despise that woman…and I never want to lay eyes on her because I don't think I could control myself."

Even in the shadows of that room, it was clear that Germaine's face was changing. A look of deep sorrow dragged down her brow and the corners of her mouth, and her voice became even deeper. She paused and looked away from us but not in time to hide the sudden tears that made her dark eyes go wet. She didn't cry outright, and the tears didn't spill over, but there was no mistaking her grief. She paused for a few minutes and Jo-Jo and I waited quietly before she spoke again.

"And I don't want to do something where I'd be locked up for the rest of my life in Angola, so I don't want to be anywhere near to her."

"Renard and you were broken up way before he met her," Jo-Jo reminded.

Germaine narrowed her eyes, pointing her finger at him. "That's true, but he would have come back here where he belongs if it wasn't for her. He belongs out here in the swamp where he was born and raised. He understands the swamp. Life in town is not for our kind. It's poison for people like us." She took a deep breath and withdrew her hand. "But that's where to start looking for what happened to him. Up there in North Louisiana. So go. Do it!" She made a grand sweeping gesture with her arm.

Jo-Jo looked at me again and then frowned. "Okay, Germaine. But I don't have any ideas about how to go about it."

"You'll think of something. Or *you* will." She focused on me and pointed a finger then at me too. "You're a cop. Do something."

"Used to be." I corrected her.

"What difference. Once a cop, always a cop."

"How come you know anything about me?" I asked.

She looked at me and smiled. "Until we know what happened to Renard...anything that has to do with that woman I will make it my business to find out about. So to both of you...find out what happened to him. That's what he wants. And that's what I want."

I saw no point in telling her what Junior had told us, so I kept it to myself, and I was feeling restless, wanting to get away from her. I looked over at Jo-Jo as if to ask, *We ready to go yet?*

But just then her brother yelled from the cooker. "Germaine. You got the plates ready? You all better come on now."

She rose from the chair. "Come on. Time to eat."

53

THE COOKOUT

By the time we walked outside to eat, all the brothers were there and Germaine introduced us to each of them: Minus, Caleb, and Aldus. The parents came slowly out of their cabin then and we met them as well. The mother, Elvira, was thin, her long white hair twisted on top of her head. She wore a long dress, the hem overlapping the top of her white shrimper's boots. She motioned for us to sit at one of the picnic table benches. Her husband, Alcide, grizzled and bearded, was not as friendly. He nodded his head at the introductions, then looked me up and down suspiciously. I held out my hand to shake, but he ignored it and turned to find himself a place to sit at another of the cypress picnic tables.

Minus served the tin plates at the cooker and then handed each of them to Caleb who delivered each one, starting with the guests, Jo-Jo and me. "Eat, eat," Germaine said. "Don't wait on us. It will get cold." The hound was already eating his dinner from a bowl by the grill.

We ate *sac-a-lait, choupique boulettes, goujon,* blue catfish, frog legs, and white beans with *tasso* and deer sausage. I had some of all that on my plate, but my favorite is the blue cat, and I don't get to eat it often enough, so I was really happy with that feast. Minus brought out a glass jug of homemade white liquor. "Homemade hootch," he smiled.

"You all have your own still out here?" I asked.

"Course not. Don't you know that's illegal?" he laughed.

The rest of the family laughed along with him as Germaine passed the jug and tin cups all around. She paused in front of me, eyes half-lidded like a snake. "You better take it easy on this at first. It's volatile." She poured just a half cup of the liquor into my cup and handed it to me.

"Warning noted," I said, raising the cup to my lips.

"We smoked that deer sausage right there," Minus said, pointing toward the smoke house with his fork.

"It's probably the best I've ever eaten," said Jo-Jo.

I took a bite of it. "Definitely the best I've ever eaten," I said. After that first drink of their moonshine that burned all the way down, I was already in a generous mood, but it really was the best sausage I'd ever tasted.

Germaine looked over at me and gave a hint of a smile.

As we ate and drank, I watched a blue heron stalking something at the water's edge near the boats as a hawk cried in the distance. The air smelled fresh and with my eyes closed I could have told you I was near the water as it smelled like my childhood bayou home. By the time I finished the half cup of liquor, I was totally relaxed and wished I could have stayed on there in their camp not just for the day, but for years. A light breeze stirred and a few wisps of Germaine's long hair fell onto her face. She moved them back with the back of her hand and then caught me looking at her. She looked away with indifference, and picked up a frog leg to munch on.

Two of the brothers went back for seconds, and helped themselves to everything all over again. "Filling up for the long night ahead out checking your traps, huh?" asked Jo-Jo.

"Yeah. Right now we'll go grab some sleep and then come dark we'll be at it all over again," said Minus.

"Never take a day off?" I asked.

"Can't. Gas for the boats costs too much now to get lazy," said Minus.

"We appreciate your hard work. This was delicious. One of the best meals I've ever had," I said.

"You're welcome. Glad you came on out," said Caleb.

When we'd finished eating, the parents excused themselves and crossed back over to their cabin. The brothers slowly disappeared one by one to take their afternoon naps preparing for the night's work. Only Germaine was left to pick up the plates and clean up the area.

"We'll help you," Jo-Jo said, standing.

I was basking in a spot of sunlight and enjoying my liquor haze and the peace of that great meal, and didn't want to break the spell, but slowly rose to my feet.

"No. I'll do it. You two just go and find who killed Renard. And don't come back until you know who it is and where his body is buried. Don't worry about justice once you find who it is. We'll take care of that."

"No, Germaine. *I'll* take care of that. He's my brother," said Jo-Jo, handing her his empty plate.

"Hmm. We'll see about that."

I did the same, handing her my plate with a nod of thanks, and then we made our way back to the boat. A crow cawed at us from an overhanging branch as we pushed it off the bank, sliding it into the water. He sounded annoyed, like he also wanted us to not come back unless we'd done our job.

"I hate to leave," I said as Jo-Jo cranked the motor. "Great place to live."

"Little bit of heaven," said Jo-Jo.

"Wish your brother had stayed out here. He'd be alive today," I said.

"Unless Germaine had slit his throat in the middle of the night while he was sleeping," Jo-Jo said, his face grim.

"I don't know. I kind of think she could slit a man's throat in broad daylight when he's wide awake," I said.

"Now that's a fact. You're a fast learner!" said Jo-Jo, as he circled the boat back toward Leveetown.

54

JUNIOR BARTERS

Once back at the motel, I called Lenny to tell her I was back and we could leave to see what Junior had to report. I showered, changed clothes, left plenty of food and water for Merle and Willie before she arrived to pick me up with Bijou riding along in the back seat. I reported on the trip through the swamp to the Stelly camp, leaving out the part about how much Germaine hated her.

"Well, did you tell her we're trying," Lenny asked, adjusting the radio to a country station.

"I didn't tell her anything. Best to keep quiet around that lady."

"I'll bet."

"Food's great though."

"I'm sure it was. You're talking some serious Cajuns out there in the Atchafalaya. Renard is a great cook, by the way. Or was. Jo-Jo is too."

As good as the camp dinner with the Stellys was, I was already starting to feel hungry again, and this conversation made me even more so. I'd made the trip so many times, I knew where the best stop off places were for breakfast, hamburgers, or home-made pie. We stopped for strawberry pie and coffee halfway through the trip at a truck stop I'd discovered the last time through. We walked Bijou around the parking lot and Lenny gave him her French fries before starting out on the last two hours of the trip.

By the time we reached the camp, Quintus had gone to bed and the lights at his trailer were off. But he'd left the floodlights on at the main house and when we got inside, we found a tray with a bottle of blackberry wine and two glasses. He left a note that said the wine was homemade by some neighbors down the road.

Weary from the long drive, we took the tray upstairs with us and got ready to turn in. We wanted to be well rested the next day so we could better drag out from Junior whatever it was he thought he knew.

"And I don't want to be tired when I see him, or I might punch his lights out," Lenny said. "So don't wake me up in the morning til I wake up naturally." She put her arms around me. "Good night. Thank you for everything you're doing."

I slid my hands down her back and pulled her to me without speaking. A whippoorwill called outside the window. In Louisiana it's said that when a whippoorwill calls they're carrying a message from someone who has passed on. I couldn't help but wonder if there was a message from Renard in that lonesome call.

"Do you believe in spirits?" I asked Lenny.

"Of course," she whispered. "Don't you?"

"I think so. But I've never seen one."

"I have. But I was only eight or nine and nobody would believe me."

"Who was it?"

"My grandmother. She stopped me from running out in the street. Then a car came speeding by. She was standing in front of me with arms stretched out to stop me."

"And nobody would believe you?"

"Nobody. They smiled that little smile that says you're so cute with your make believe. Made me mad. I knew my grandmother had saved my life."

"How do you know it was your grandmother?"

"Cause I could see her plain as day. Like she was really right in front of me. Just as real as you can imagine. I have a photo of her in my bedroom at home. I'll show it to you sometime."

"Well, I believe you."

"Glad to hear somebody does," and she pushed herself against me ending the conversation. But the whippoorwill kept calling, even though we stopped paying attention to the night music.

* * *

Once at the jail, the Chief led us back to the same room he'd used for my visit with Junior. Junior looked like he'd put on a pound or two overnight. His face was bloated and his eyes were cloudy from being shut away from sunlight for so long.

There were two chairs for us, and Junior had his chair leaned back against the wall, his arms crossed in front of him. His chair was tilted so far back, his feet dangled off the floor. The bruising under his eyes was almost gone and the bruising around his neck had faded to a mustard yellow.

"Put your chair back down, Son," his father barked at him.

Junior gave him a black look, but did set his chair back on four legs. "There. Satisfied?"

"Watch your snotty little mouth, hear?" The Chief pointed a finger at him.

Lenny sat, and I moved my chair in between Lenny and Junior because I wanted to be able to grab her if she went for his throat.

"Yell if he acts up. I'll hear you." The Chief left the room.

"Well?" Lenny said.

"Well what?" Junior leaned his chair back against the wall again.

"You called me all the way up here. Now what?" Lenny leaned forward. I kept my eyes moving between the two of them in case of trouble.

"All right, all right. I have something you will want to know," he said, his tone less hostile.

"So give it. We don't have much time."

"What are you going to do for me?"

She made a face like she was smelling something putrid, but didn't speak, just looked at him.

"I need something in return," he went on to say. "Otherwise why would I tell you?"

"Why would I give a psycho who tried to rape me anything but another punch in the face?" she asked, her hands forming fists.

I put my hand on her arm. "Take it easy, Lenny. This wasn't a good idea. Let's get out of here." I rose halfway out of my chair.

"Drop the bogus charges, and I'll tell you what I saw that afternoon," he said, paying no attention to me.

"Bullshit. I drop nothing. Even if I did drop the charges, in a sexual assault case you can't just drop charges...the state takes over. Dumb ass! Everybody knows that. Otherwise creeps like you get to scare victims into changing their stories. Try and keep up, Junior. Quit playing all those video games. They're rotting your brain." She pounded a fist on her thigh for emphasis.

There was a long pause and I sat down again, but I stayed hyper vigilant and kept my eyes back and forth on both of them. Junior kept his chair tilted against the wall and swung his feet like a kid in school while he decided what to do.

"Come on, Junior. Out with it. We've got things to do," Lenny said.

"What about this then? If what I tell you leads to anything, you'll make sure it helps my case."

Lenny looked at me, then back at him. "Sure, sure. Don't worry. If what you say helps me find what happened to Renard, I'll make sure everybody knows it was you tipped me off."

"You're my witness on that?" he asked, looking over at me.

"Of course."

"All right then. Here's the deal. That afternoon, the afternoon before the night your boy friend disappeared...a man came through town. He came over to me where I was hanging around out in front of the store drinking a soda. He wanted to know if I knew this friend of his from home....and he showed me a photo of somebody who looked a lot like a younger Quintus. Only the name he gave was different. I don't even remember what the name was now."

"What did you tell him?"

"Nothing!" Junior blinked and looked surprised that she asked that. "I don't go around telling strangers shit about people I know."

"So that's it? That's what you're peddling today and all you dragged us up here for?"

I held up a hand. "Hold up, Lenny." I kept my eyes on Junior. "Keep talking. What did he look like? About how old?"

"He looked to be kind of old. Gray hair and beard. Scruffy, but strong like he worked outside. He had deep lines in his face. Face like old leather."

"What kind of vehicle?"

"An old GMC pickup. It was green with one door gray primer."

"Did you catch the plate?"

"Didn't pay all that much attention. The truck was mud splattered. Could have been Kansas, but I'm not sure. I wasn't even positive it was Quintus he was looking for. The picture wasn't that sharp."

"So what happened next?"

"He moved on. Went on into the store and I left out of there. I didn't even think about it again until I've been holed up in here with nothing to do but sleep or stare at the walls bored out of my mind. Now it's got me wondering." Junior's voice had lost its edge.

"Can you remember anything else? Anything at all. Even the slightest detail?"

"You sound like a cop," Junior said.

"He IS a cop, you dimwit," Lenny said.

"Used to be." I motioned for her to back off, and kept my eyes on Junior.

"Remember? Like what?"

"Like what was he wearing for instance?"

Junior looked up and to the right as he reviewed the memory for a minute or two. "A plaid shirt with cut-off sleeves. He wore it out over his jeans. Open over a white tee shirt. And work boots. He wore work boots."

"That's good. You're doing good. What kind of work boots?"

"Just work boots. Like those brown ones construction guys wear."

"Were they worn and muddy? New? What?"

"I can't remember. Scuffed up."

I nodded. "Good, that's good. Keep thinking. Did the tee shirt have anything written on it?"

"You sure ask a lot of questions."

"Look back at it. See what else." We waited quietly while Junior angled his eyes up and to the right again. He set his chair back down on all four legs abruptly. "No. The tee shirt was just an old white tee shirt. He wore a visor cap. John Deere."

I smiled. "Okay, Junior. That's great. You did good. And don't worry, we won't forget this." I stood and turned to Lenny. "You ready?"

"I've been ready." She stood, scraped the chair back, and headed for the door.

"Aren't you even going to thank me?" Junior asked.

"No," she said. "I'm still too pissed at you."

"Aren't you even going to say goodbye?" he asked.

In answer she banged on the door.

"Bye, Junior," I said for her, and then the door opened and as the Chief let us out, Junior called, "Hey! Don't forget to put in a word for me."

"Yeah, yeah," Lenny called back. "Don't worry. If this means anything."

"He behave himself?" The Chief asked.

"Not bad for Junior," Lenny said.

"His mother always spoiled him. Still does. She's at the house cooking his dinner now," he said, shaking his head.

"Thanks, Chief," Lenny said.

"No problem. Take care of yourself." Then he nodded at us and turned back to his office, and we filed on down the hallway and out into the bright sunlight. We headed for the car blinking at the bright light.

"Well, what you think?" Lenny asked as she started the engine.

"I think we better find out more about your bud-dy Quintus."

"That's not going to be easy. Quintus never has much to say," she said, as she backed out of the park-ing lot.

"Then we'll just have to be smarter than he is," I said, as she turned onto the road leading back to the camp.

55

NOSING AROUND

Once back at the camp, Lenny made some sandwiches while I put together a salad. For a change, we took our plates into the dining room and ate at the dinner table for the first time. Lenny put out a big bowl of potato chips and we each had a beer while I mulled over what we could do with the information Junior had given us.

"I don't think I'll get anywhere asking Quintus about the man," I said.

"Go ahead and ask him, but one thing I know for sure," Lenny said, "is that Quintus would never hurt Renny. They liked each other. They even drank and played cards together sometimes when Renny couldn't sleep. Renny didn't sleep near as much as I do. Neither does Quintus. They were a good match. Both very good poker players. Renard would lose a lot to Quintus, then he'd win it back again the next time. Back and forth like that they'd go."

"Well, what the hell...I'll go down there and ask him about it after we eat. See what he has to say."

"You want me to go with you?"

"Not really. He might hold back something if you were there."

"What makes you think he'd tell you anything anyway?"

"I'm good at reading people. Even if he has nothing to tell me, I can tell if he doesn't like the question."

"Suit yourself then. We're going to have ice cream for dessert. Take him a bowl. It might soften him up."

* * *

So after we'd finished bowls of pecan ice cream, Lenny filled a heaping bowl and I headed down to the trailer with it. There were some rumblings of thunder and the clouds began looking ominous, but there were no raindrops yet. I knocked on the trailer door, and the dogs started barking. Quintus quieted them and opened the door.

"Brought you down some ice cream," I said handing him the bowl. He rubbed his eyes with one hand and took the bowl with the other.

"Thanks. I fell asleep on the couch watching a hunting show. Come on in if you want."

"Just for a minute. Got to get back home soon." I stepped inside and the dogs eyed me from the kitchen where they sat at attention, ears forward.

He motioned to them to relax and they lay back down, resting their heads on their paws, but keeping their eyes on me.

"Come on and sit down while I eat this before it melts."

He sat against a bed pillow at one end of the couch, and I sat on the other. "You want a beer?" he asked.

"No, thanks. Just had one up at the house." I waited until he had a few bites of ice cream, wondering how best to start. Then I plunged right in.

"We came up to talk to Junior over at the jail."

"Junior?" He put his spoon down in the bowl, and looked at me in surprise. "Why?"

"He had something he wanted to tell Lenny."

"And she was able to even talk to him after what he did?" He moved his body so he was facing me directly.

"He said it had something to do with Renard's disappearance so she came up to find out what he had in mind."

"So, what did he say?"

"He said a man in a pickup came through town that afternoon looking for somebody. He showed Junior an old photo." I tried to appear casual, but I watched him closely.

"A photo? Of Renard?"

"No. Junior said the man in the photo looked like you."

"Looked like me?" He hesitated, then twisted to place the ice cream bowl on the end table. "I don't get it. Who was he?"

"Junior doesn't know. He never saw him before or since."

"So what did Junior tell him?"

"Nothing. Then the man went on into the store and Junior left."

"Did he catch the license plate?" Quintus picked the bowl back up and took another bite of ice cream.

"Could have been Kansas. He wasn't sure."

Quintus didn't comment, just stared down at the bowl as he swallowed.

"You know anybody in Kansas?"

"Don't think so." He took another bite. "Never been through there."

"Okay then. Just checking. I've got to get ready to hit the road. Day's going fast."

"Sure." He put the bowl back down on the end table and stood. "Thanks for keeping me up to speed on Junior. He's a nasty little fucker."

"He is that."

"Anybody messes with Lenny, they're messing with me." We shook hands, and I crossed to the door as the dogs got to their feet to see me out.

Quintus stood at the door with the dogs flanking him as I walked slowly back up to the house, going over our conversation in my mind. Lenny opened the sliding door to the kitchen to let me in.

"Well? How'd it go?" she asked.

"He's lying," I said. "Grab us a beer and come on in the den while I tell you about it."

* * *

After we were settled on the couch in the TV room, I filled Lenny in on the visit to Quintus' trailer.

"What makes you think he's lying?" She set her beer can on a coaster on the coffee table in front of the couch, kicked off her sandals and swung her legs up over my lap and lay back against the cushions.

"I told you, I'm good at reading people. Had a lot of experience doing it while I was a cop." I sipped my beer with one hand and lightly massaged her ankles and feet with the other.

"So what's he lying about?"

"The stranger coming to town looking for him maybe. Maybe the part about never being to Kansas. Don't know."

"One thing for sure. Don't get any ideas that he had anything to do with Renard disappearing. He really, really liked Rennie."

"It's all a mystery. At this point, who knows? But I need to dig around."

"Dig around where?"

"If Quintus isn't going to tell me what I want to know, then I need to explore around here. Somehow find out more about him."

"And how can you do that?"

"That house on the back acreage. The old farm house where you said he used to live. I want to get in there and look around."

"Why? Nothing there but old stuff."

"Yeah, and if I nose around that old stuff I might find out something. It needs to be checked anyway. You have a key for the house?"

"All the keys for everything on this property are hanging on hooks in the laundry room closet. They're all labeled. I'll find it for you."

"That's good. So what I want you to do is in about an hour run on down to Quintus' trailer and tell him there's a moccasin got in the house somehow and you're scared out of your mind. Tell him I left to go home somehow. A friend picked me up. I hitchhiked, whatever you can come up with. While you're keeping him off guard, I'll be down at the farmhouse seeing what I can dig up."

"He won't fall for that. That you hitchhiked out of here."

"Then tell him I got a ride. If you act frightened enough, it won't be an issue."

"I don't know, sounds bogus."

"He's very protective of you. Moccasins have been known to come up from septic tanks into toilets. I know two people that happened to, believe it or not."

She looked at me with skepticism written all over her face. "Well, okay, it might work. Worth a try. There's not much he can say about your snooping around in that farmhouse. It's not his. It belongs to my family. And there's definitely old junk of ours in there. As a matter of fact, I think that's where my childhood toy box is stored. I saved it for my children, in case I ever have any."

"Okay then. We'll start the plan when it starts getting dark. I'll need a good flashlight."

"We have plenty of those around here. You'll find whatever you need in that same closet in the laundry room." She picked up her beer and raised her head to drink.

"There is one more very important thing though," she said.

"What's that?" I asked as I pressed my thumb into the high arch of her foot.

"Don't stop what you're doing." She closed her eyes and sighed with pleasure.

56

QUINTUS SPINS A TALE

I looked inside an old Army trunk, but could find nothing but two men's coats, a pile of sweaters, and a few loose items in a plastic bag. The smell of mothballs bit my nose. I closed the trunk back up and secured the brass catch back in place, then turned to a cardboard box of crumpled newspapers, protecting glassware or china. I closed that back up, but as I moved toward another box against the wall, Quintus spoke from the doorway.

"You won't find what you're looking for," he said in a low voice.

Lenny ran up on the doorstep just then. "He didn't believe me about the snake in the house. I tried to tell him." She pushed in beside him and ran over to my side. "Sorry, Harris."

"Like I said, you're wasting your time looking through all this old stuff. There's nothing here."

I was still on my knees, and I put up my hands to indicate I believed him.

"Why make up that story about leaving town? You didn't have to do that," he said.

"Sorry, Quintus. I didn't believe what you told me about that man who came through town looking for you...or someone."

He remained in the doorway, then began walking toward a chair covered with a sheet to protect it from dust. "Tell you what," he said. "I'll tell you a story that may interest you. So why don't both of you just make yourselves comfortable and relax for a few minutes." Lenny looked over at me.

"All right. I'm game." I sat down on the wood floor, crossed my legs, and leaned back against a corner.

Lenny unfolded a metal chair, dusted off the seat, and sat, crossing her legs. "Whatever you got? I want to hear it."

Quintus swept the sheet off the chair, letting it fall in a heap onto the floor, then settled into it and stretched out his long legs.

"I'll tell you this story, but that's it. No more, no less. Agreed?" he said, looking in turn from one of us to the other. The lantern light flickered and made the shadows of the room slide up and down the walls. Moonlight streamed in through the window, but outside that ray of cool silver light, the room remained dim.

"Agreed," I said.

"Tell us the story, Quintus," Lenny said.

Quintus bowed his head, thinking for a minute or two, then taking a deep breath, he began. "A long time ago, many years back, in a very small rural town, two men got in a fistfight at a local bar. It was over a pool game. There was considerable money on the game, with a lot of side bets, and one of the men sank the eight ball without calling the pocket. The loser was angry, but when it looked like somebody's head was going to get split open with a cue stick, the bartender yelled to take it outside, so they fought in front of the bar by the street.

"The cheater was knocked out and left lying on the sidewalk. Nobody paid him any mind and he lay there for a while in the rain, people stepping over him on their way in or their way out, until he came to. When he tried to come back into the bar, all wet and angry, the bartender wouldn't let him back in." Quintus rubbed his hand back and forth over the gray stubble on his chin.

"Some people bought the other man a few shots for his nerves, and then he left for home. By the time he got to the house he rented miles away out in the country, it was after midnight. He sat out on the dark front porch having a last smoke before going to bed. There was a full moon and everything looked peaceful and silvery gray. Owls were hooting and silently flying from tree to tree, and the crickets were loud.

"The man washed a few aspirins down with a beer while he unwound enough to go to sleep. After about half an hour, what looked like a dark green pickup drove very slowly by, then braked next to his field. The man left the porch and walked to the road to see what was going on. A rifle barrel slowly slid out of the window of the truck and a shot rang out. The man yelled, '*Hey*!' and the driver of the pickup gunned the engine, popped the clutch and roared off down the road.

"The man's stomach clenched in dread, and he hurried out to the field. His favorite horse, a beautiful brown and white Paint, was lying on her side in the grass. He felt ice run up and down his spine as he ran to his horse's side. The horse was dead with a bullet through the head." Quintus stopped talking and tightened his mouth.

"Good God!" Lenny said, hand to her mouth.

There was a pause as the two of us sat quietly waiting for him to go on. A whippoorwill called close to the window, and a wind stirred in the trees outside. A rat or a squirrel scurried around above in the attic.

"It wasn't long after that the man who was knocked out outside the bar that night disappeared. They found him three days later sprawled out in the woods and very dead. Chewed up by some varmints. Maybe a coyote or a wildcat had been gnawing on him. Never did figure out what he was doing out in those woods. People said he must have been hunting out there. But there was no shotgun found with the body. The dead man's two brothers accused the man who knocked him out that night at the bar. But there was no evidence to support that. Word spread about the dead horse, and public opinion was pretty much that if the dead man had been the one who shot the horse, then he got what he deserved. The brothers let it be known since the Sheriff wouldn't arrest the man they accused, that they would take care of it themselves. They made public threats and vowed revenge."

Quintus rose from the chair and walked to the window looking out. "So what happened?" Lenny asked.

"Nothing happened. The man they threatened to kill left town soon after that, and the mystery has never been solved to this day, all these years later."

"Where did this story happen?" I asked.

"Somewhere out in the Midwest, I believe." He slid his hands into his pockets. "It's a very old story. Ancient history."

"What happened to the brothers?" Lenny asked.

"One of them took sick and died about ten years later."

"And the other one?"

Quintus shrugged. "Who can say?"

We sat in silence for a few minutes while I thought about what Quintus had told us. I frowned as I reviewed the tale trying to make sense of it. Then out of nowhere, I made the connections and details started coming together for me. I snapped my head up as it all fell into place and a picture formed in my mind. "So the surviving one finally tracked down the man he believed killed his brother," I finally said.

Lenny looked at me. "Huh?"

Quintus breathed slowly as he continued to stare out the window without speaking. "Yes, you could say that. He never let go of it, and he finally tracked him down."

"But he attacked an innocent man by mistake…. case of mistaken identity. Isn't that true?" I asked, watching Quintus as closely as I could in the flickering light.

"What are you talking about?" Lenny asked, leaning forward in her chair.

"No," Quintus answered. "That's not true. He had the right man when he attacked. He knocked him down, then drew a knife to finish him off. But fortunately the victim's good friend intervened right at that moment." Quintus stood taller and his chest expanded as he drew a deep breath.

"You've lost me," said Lenny, throwing up her hands. I motioned for her to stay quiet.

"The good friend saw what was going on, witnessed the attack, came in from behind, grabbed the man by the hair and yanked his head back. The man wrenched free, turned on him and slashed him in the face, splitting his nose and laying open his cheek. Then he bit part of his nose off. The wounded rescuer hit the attacker so hard the knife flew out of his hand and when he got him on the ground, he pummeled him so hard, punching him in the nose and the temples, that the attacker died right then and there, on the very spot where he'd drawn his knife."

There was a long pause. The creature in the attic still scuttled around above us and something else could be heard scratching within the walls of the old house. Lenny's hands gripped the arms of her chair. I remained very still in my corner until Quintus continued his story.

"While the dead man lay on the ground, the man who had been attacked in the first place tended to his friend's face, stopping the bleeding, wrapping his head in so many bandages, he looked like the mummy. Then the two men carried the dead man's body back to the truck he'd arrived in, and the rescuer drove off to dump the body where it would never be found and to seek help for the slashes and grotesque damage to his face."

Lenny started to rise from the chair. I motioned her to stay put. "And then what?" I asked.

"Then nothing. The man who came to the rescue and saved a life never returned."

"Quintus!" Lenny broke in. "What are you saying?" She started crying. "Are you talking about Renard? It was *you* that stranger wanted to find and kill? And Renard saved your life that night? When he heard some noise and left the house to see what was going on out there, that's what happened? He found somebody trying to kill you? And Renny's alive somewhere?" She wiped her face with the hem of her tee shirt. "Tell me! For God's sake, quit talking in all these bullshit riddles."

"That's all of the story I *can* tell you." Quintus didn't look at her, just kept staring out the window.

She ran to him and grabbed his shoulder turning him from the window. "Quintus, you have to tell me! Is Renny alive somewhere? Damn it, tell me!" Her eyes were wild and glinted in the moonlight. She started shaking him by the shoulders.

Quintus placed his hands firmly on her arms and stopped the shaking. "Don't you think I would tell you if I could? How long have you known me?" His eyes were tortured and his face twisted in pain.

"What? He made you promise to keep your mouth shut? What for?"

"I told you a story. The only way I could. Have I ever lied to you? That's all I *can* tell you. You'll just have to believe me and let it go at that." His voice was gruff, making it clear he was determined and she could not change his mind.

"But, why? This makes no sense. Renard wouldn't just take off and leave me like that. And with no word for all these months!" She raked her fingers through her hair in frustration.

"Not without a really good reason," Quintus said. "And that's *all* I'm going to say. I'm going back to my trailer now. Said all I'm going to."

"Why did you say anything at all then? This is worse!" she yelled.

"Leave it alone, Lenny...for now. Trust me for a little longer," he said as he started walking toward the open front door.

"You know where he is!" she cried, following him.

"Good night, Harris. Good night, Lenny." Quintus stepped over the threshold, crossed the porch, descended the steps, and within a minute had disappeared into the shadows of the bordering trees.

"Damn you, Quintus!" she yelled after him from the doorway.

"Come on back in here," I said, rising from my seat on the floor. "You heard the man. That's all you're going to get out of him. We're lucky we got this much. Let's go back up to the house, have a drink and go to bed."

"Horseshit!" she called into the night, still fuming, still at the doorway. "Your story sucks, Quintus, and so do you!" Her shoulders were shaking as she continued the abuse.

"Calm down. I have a feeling you're going to find out what's been going on very soon. Come on." I went to her, took her hand and led her out of the house. Then I locked the door back up and walked her toward the main house, the shadows shifting in the moonlight as we slowly made our way back through the woods.

"Quintus has always been my friend. Why would he keep all this from me for so long?" she asked in a lower voice. "How could he do this to me? He knows how much I suffered. How depressed I was." She sniffed and wiped her nose with the back of her hand.

"If somebody saved your life, wouldn't you do whatever he told you to do?" I asked her, squeezing her hand. Fireflies flickered in the trees and bushes along the path.

"Oh, God! Why does life have to be so fucking hard?" she whimpered, then started to cry as we continued on our way toward the spotlights lighting up the back patio of the house.

57

SHOWDOWN

Despite my trying to convince Lenny that she would not change Quintus' mind, she was determined to go to work on him. She decided to remain in Wallace another few days so she could convince him to tell her whatever he knew about Renard. Her father kept a Jeep in the garage for camp use, so she sent me home in her Charger, with instructions to bring it back in three days.

"All I need is a little alone time with Quintus and I'll be able to browbeat him or shame him into telling me what's going on," she promised.

"My money says you won't turn him," I said.

"I know Quintus a whole lot better than you do," she said. She had followed me to the car and was standing at the window to see me off.

"That may be true, but you should leave it alone. It's obvious the man is keeping a secret and has no intention of giving it up."

"He'll give it up all right. I know how to handle him." She slapped a hand on the roof of the car. "Been knowing him since I was six years old. Been twisting him around my finger since I was eight."

"How much money you want to put on it?" I smiled.

"Whatever you want. Make it something you can afford to lose," she cautioned.

"I got a hundred dollars says he won't give up any secrets." I stuck my hand out the window.

"Nope. Won't take your money," she answered, shaking her head and refusing to shake on it.

"I'll see you in three days." She leaned over and gave me a brief kiss goodbye. Not her usual kiss, but a light friendly sort of kiss. The night before she'd kept to her side of the bed, rather than close by my side as she usually did. I figured it was because she was so upset, but as the car crunched over the shell driveway on my way out, I had a sinking feeling that if Renard was still alive, our affair was permanently over. I told myself not to jump to conclusions. We didn't know he was alive. We didn't know if he'd ever return, or even wanted to come back. We didn't know squat.

On the other hand, I realized I wanted him to be alive. I wanted him to come back from wherever he'd been hiding...if he'd been hiding. If Quintus' disguised story was to be believed, and Renard had saved him from getting murdered, and had his face ruined besides, then the man deserved the prize.... and Lenny *was* the prize. I certainly wanted her, but what I wanted didn't count after all that he had been through and done. I would have to concede, give up, and bow out. Not that I would have any choice about it. (I continued to coach myself along these lines as I drove through the tiny town of Wallace and headed home.) Lenny had never made any secret of the fact that she was in love with the man, and was torn up about his disappearance. No, if Renard was alive, I would become irrelevant overnight. And I had to accept that, and I believed I could without flipping out. But not without missing her. There would be a whole lot of that.

During the drive home, my cell phone rang. It was Detective Lanclos checking up on me.

"You all right? Where you been?" he asked. "I stopped by a couple of times to check on you, but they said you're not around."

"I've been up here in North Louisiana. Something came up and I had to help a friend."

"We've been keeping an eye on the motel. Seems quiet. Nothing going on."

"Thanks for checking. I'm on the way home right now."

"Then you'll be back at the motel tonight?"

"Yes."

"We'll be keeping an eye out."

"Thanks, Detective."

"Call me if you get suspicious of anything," he said and clicked off.

It felt good to hear from Lanclos and knowing he and others were looking out for me made me feel easier about going back to the motel where I could be tracked down by whoever had it in for me. When

I arrived back in Ida, I parked the Charger in front of my new room next door to the old room where my pickup was still parked.

I played with Merle and Willie for a while, thanked the Mexicans for looking after the dogs and the motel while I was gone, and had a beer with them while I explained why I had changed rooms. They were lounging around on the beds in Jorge's room with the television tuned to a Mexican game show.

"Somebody is after me," I confessed, "and things could get nasty around here. Just in case something happens, you all stay inside. I don't want anybody getting hurt. *Cuidado! Hombre peligroso! Comprenden?*"

Jorge fanned his hand rapidly like his fingers were on fire, "¡*Aiii!* ¡*Aiii!*" and shook his head as the others watched me with big brown worried eyes. When I'd finished the beer, I returned to my room to shower and get ready for bed. It had been a long, hot drive and I was tired. Lenny called to make sure the Charger and I had made it back from Wallace all right.

"No problems," I told her.

"Just wanted you to know that so far you're so right," she said.

"About what?"

"Can't get anything out of Quintus, just like you predicted. He's clammed up. But I'm not giving up so easily. Tomorrow I'll start working on him all over again until I wear him down."

"I'm telling you, you're wasting your time. He's not going to tell you anything, and you won't wear him down."

"We'll see."

After we said good night, I didn't even bother turning on the TV to catch a movie, just clicked off the lights and crashed, bone weary from that long hot drive.

I slept like a rock for six hours, then Merle and Willie started barking a short time after midnight. I recognize different kinds of barking. Sometimes they bark at possums, raccoons, or even stray cats or dogs that are passing through the property, but this was an outrage bark. Louder and more demanding for attention than the alarms they send up just for night prowling varmints. This was radical emergency barking. Two legged varmints.

As soon as I came aware of this insistent howling, I threw off the sheet, grabbed my pistol from the night table and crossed to the window, adrenaline pouring through my veins. Peering out from the side of the blinds, I could see nothing but the walkway and the grass edging the parking lot. I stepped sideways to the door and opened it a few inches to look out. A short stocky man was standing in front of the window of my old room. He cupped his hand to the side of his face as he tried to see through the closed blinds.

Startled, I pulled my head back a few inches, then as I watched he raised his other arm and aimed his pistol toward the room, taking a blind shot toward the center of the room where the bed would be. As he shot, I jerked backward just as something flashed by my door. I raised my own pistol and peered outside again through the few inches of opening I had at the doorway. Another shot blasted, and I figured he'd shot again, but then the man crashed forward into the shattered glass of the window, and drooped halfway bent over through the shards of glass.

"What the...." I said aloud, opening the door further. Jorge stepped outside of his room at the same time and came toward me.

"You okay, *hermano?*" he asked.

"Get back in your rooms!" ordered Lanclos, running forward from the parking lot, pistol still pointed toward the intruder.

We gave him no argument, both instantly retreating to the shadows of our doorways.

"He alive?" asked Jorge in a low voice from his room.

"Don't think so," I said.

"He dead?"

"Think so. Nice throw, Jorge," I said.

"I'm good, huh?"

"You're good all right."

Lanclos, still holding a gun on the man, turned the beam of his MagLite through the wreckage of the window. Then he clicked it off and pulled out his cell phone. He spoke into it briefly then turned toward our rooms.

"Both of you stay in your rooms and get cleaned up. Soon as we do what we need to do here, I'm going to have to take you two over to the office as witnesses."

"Witnesses? We still don't even know what happened!" I said.

"What happened? I shot the guy trying to kill you, that's what happened!"

"What about the knife throw?"

"What? That?" Lanclos pointed to the knife lying on the walkway a few feet past the dead man. "Somebody lose a knife around here? Looks like you missed." He kicked the knife so that it scooted towards us along the cement walkway. "Better pick it up and get it out of here before the Crime Scene boys arrive. They'll put you through the wringer over throwing a knife at the guy if you don't keep your mouth shut."

Jorge didn't waste a second running toward the knife and retrieving it. He ran back to the shelter of his doorway. "Thanks, Detective."

"No problem. Let's keep it simple. Man tried to kill Harris. Got shot in the back of the head. How am I supposed to know you weren't even in your own room fast asleep in the bed? End of story! You all got that?" He glowered at one and then the other of us in turn.

"We got it! We got it!" I said for both of us. Jorge kept nodding so fast, I figured he was going to throw his neck out of joint.

"Good." Lanclos' expression changed to weariness, and he wiped his forehead with the back of his hand. Willie and Merle finally stopped barking, and the scene became totally quiet. No traffic, no night birds; even the crickets had hushed. It was eerie. If you've ever had someone shooting at you, then you'll understand why my insides were shaken up and I felt like I'd just been hit in the head. I looked at Lanclos with what was most likely the dumbest of expressions on my face.

He pointed a finger at us. "It's a damn good thing I have two witnesses to what went down here tonight. Anytime a cop has to shoot somebody, he'd better have a witness to what happened or else all hell breaks loose, and they want to eat him for breakfast." He kept watching the dead man as though he might start moving around again, then looked over at us once more. Headlights and flashing blue lights cast a glow from down the road, then two patrol cars and a State Trooper turned into the parking lot, all sirens off. Lanclos held an arm up, while casting me one last look.

"Harris, long as you're just standing around, how about making us a pot of coffee? We're going to need it. This is going to be a long night."

"I'm on it, Detective." I took a deep breath, grateful to be still one of the living. I shook my head to get rid of the gory image of me lying on the bed of my old room all blood splattered and pale as the sheets. "Thanks for saving my life if I didn't already tell you."

He didn't answer, just waved a hand in dismissal, and stood, shoulders slumped, staring at the body as he waited on the rest of the men to arrive.

58

LOCAL HERO

By dawn the circus at the motel was still going on, but Lanclos and Jorge and I were able to get away and then meet at the Sheriff's Office in Eustis, so we could make our statements on tape. Lanclos also made a hand written statement of what we reported and we put our signatures to it. Jorge's broken English was good enough to say what he had to say without an Interpreter being called in.

When we were finished there, I took Jorge to breakfast at my favorite truck stop, and then I drove him to his roofing job. He was only a few hours late and the supervisor gave him some light work on the ground and didn't send him up on the roof with the rest of the workers when I explained how he'd had his sleep interrupted with the emergency.

They were putting a hip roof on a two thousand square foot brick house. The garage was angled off one side of the house and had a separate fancy roof job on it also.

"Looks like you'll be working on this job for the rest of the week," I said to the supervisor.

"Yeah. Huge house for two people. Kids all raised and gone. I'd hate to have to pay the electric bill on this monster."

"Thanks for looking after Jorge. He's a good man," I said.

"I know it. Him and his buddies…all of them. Good people," he said.

Ismael waved from the roof and then Cornelio saw me and waved also…both as sure footed as mountain goats as they trotted around up there. It was already as hot as you would expect it to be at high noon, yet they were working on that reflective roof as comfortably as if they were cruising aboard a raft on a breezy lake.

I said goodbye to the supervisor and to Jorge, thanking him again for helping me and losing sleep over it besides, then made my way back to the pick-up and headed back to the motel. I intended to lie down with a beer and watch a Western until maybe I could fall asleep. After I was able to catch a little R&R, I'd call Celeste and report what happened, and then I'd call Lenny.

But it was not to be. By the time I returned to the motel, the team of techs and cops were gone, but the neon yellow Crime Scene tape was in place all around the scene, there was a chalk outline on the walkway, and Celeste's car was parked in front of her house. She hurried out of the front door and down the walk as soon as she saw me pull up.

"It's been all over the news," she cried. "Thank God you're all right! Come on in and sit down and tell me what happened. I want to hear it from the horse's mouth. Acey will be here in a few minutes. Do you want some coffee or would a beer be more like it?" She slung an arm around my shoulders and led me into her house. "They're making you out like a hero cause you busted up a drug ring. My motel is famous! They even got the sign into a couple of the shots."

"All I know is I'm beat. I'm good for about ten minutes worth of playing catch up, and then I'm going to crash," I told her.

"Well, save it for Acey so he can hear all about it too. Go sit down on the couch and I'll be right in with your beer in a frosted glass." She patted me on the back and left me in the living room as she passed on through toward the kitchen. I sank onto the couch, and it was so comfortable, I wondered if I'd ever be able to get up and go to my room after the interrogation was over.

Then as though she read my mind she called from the kitchen, "Don't fall asleep in there. I want to hear every detail of what happened last night! You hearing me, *cher?*"

59

VINDICATION

My picture was all over the local news standing next to Jorge while the Crime Unit was going over everything. We were in the background of photos in the Eustis newspaper as well. And just as Celeste had predicted the first night I met her, Regina did call me within twenty-four hours and make noises about us getting together for dinner.

"Now why would I want to do that?" I asked her.

"What do you mean, why?" Her voice sounded surprised at my attitude.

"Regina! You left me at the worst time of my life!" I couldn't believe I had to explain it to her.

"I'm sorry, okay? I'll treat for our dinner. We can go some place really nice. Anywhere you want."

"You gotta be kidding me! There's not going to be any dinner." I spoke slowly since she wasn't getting it.

"You find the wife who would have put up with losing everything because of her husband doing such an idiotic thing as letting a prisoner loose to go screw his girl friend when he was supposed to be taking him to jail!" She spoke fast and her voice was tight. "Wait!" she said and her tone got all friendly again. "I don't mean to bring all that up....just wanted to get together cause now you've proven what a good lawman you are and that's all in the past. Ancient history. It's behind us, and it will stay behind us. I'll never bring it up again."

I took a deep breath. "Look, I know I put you through a lot. But to me marriage means you stick it through the rough times and the good times both. I could never trust you again, Regina. Sorry. And I don't want to have dinner with you. Even if I did, I wouldn't on principle."

"So, you have a girl friend, is that it?" Her voice was softer and lower.

I paused. It was none of her business what I was doing. "Your silence tells me you do have a girl friend," she said.

"That's true, I do. But that's not why I'm not going to dinner with you. Thank you for asking, but no thanks. And now, if you'll excuse me, I'm very tired and going to bed. Good night." I clicked off and couldn't help but smile and shake my head. It felt good, I'll admit. I turned off the TV with the remote, clicked off the lamp by the bed, and slept like a stone.

60

LOOSE ENDS

The next day I spent ordering the glass installation for the smashed window of my old room and cleaning up the residue, broken glass, and assorted litter left over from the shooting and the subsequent tracking in and out of the Crime Team. After picking up all the litter, I shampooed the carpet and tore the sheets off the bed. The techs had already retrieved the lone bullet that had lodged in the mattress and there was not enough visible damage to it to warrant throwing it out, so I flipped it over and made it up with new sheets.

Celeste had already returned to Acey's house with him the night before leaving me in charge again. Other than waiting on the glass installation, there was really not that much to do to bring order back to the room. I was due to drive the car back to Wallace by the next day, so I hoped nothing happened to delay the glass installer.

By the time I had things under control, and could call up there to Wallace and report all that had happened to Lenny, it was early afternoon. I picked up my cell phone from the nightstand and was just about ready to call her, but just then the glass men showed up early and I put off calling her until that big job was completed. They asked me a few questions about the shooting because they'd seen something about it on the news.

"Must be freaky having somebody shooting at you, huh?" one of them asked.

"You could say that," I answered.

"I just did," he said, poker faced. A comedian.

"Don't mind him. He's always like that," said his partner.

"Don't mind a bit," I said.

After they drove off, I locked my old room back up and went to the new room to relax a bit and call Lenny. I pulled a beer from the cooler in the room, slid my boots off, propped up some pillows against the headboard, and kicked back.

I pulled the cell phone out of my pocket and called her to report.

"You're not going to believe this," I said.

"What?" she asked.

So I began the saga of the Magnolia Motel True Crime scene. Lenny gasped a few times, and whispered, "*Oh, my God!*" once or twice, but other than that didn't interrupt until I'd caught her up on the whole story and the aftermath.

"And now they've identified the shooter. His name is Cozy Nasworthy and he's out of Little Rock.

Little guy. Only five foot six. Has plenty of attitude though to make up for it. I hope they can nail him for Amber's murder also, but that hasn't come up yet."

"We're so lucky you're still alive. If it wasn't for that detective…"

"Yeah. I'm running on borrowed time from now on."

"I don't look at it that way. More like your guardian angels are looking out for you." She paused. "So, what next?"

"Since I've cleaned up everything around here, I thought I'd deliver the Charger back to you tomorrow like we planned."

"Sounds good. If you leave soon as you get up, I can have a special lunch ready for you by the time you get here. How would you like some Natchitoches meat pies? Got some in the freezer. I get a craving for them from time to time. How about you? Ever had any?"

"Yes, because my parents live near Natchitoches. Love them."

"It's a date then."

"Before you go….did you find out anything from Quintus yet?"

"No. But I tried something new on him."

I was almost afraid to ask. "What did you do?"

"Tell you tomorrow when you get here."

"Anybody ever tell you you're hard to get along with?" I asked.

"Oh, many, many times," she laughed and ended the call.

61

DESTINY

By seven o'clock the next day, I had done all my chores and everything else I needed to do for the trip to Wallace. Just as I was checking the oil and the radiator on the Charger before taking off, the cell phone rang and it was Lenny again.

"Change of plans," she said. "Had to drive the Jeep back down here from the camp. You can bring the car back to my apartment whenever you're ready. We'll have that lunch I promised you over here."

"How come?" I asked.

"Something came up," she said. "See you whenever you get here," and she was gone.

I scratched my head over that one, but thought of some more things I could do before running over there. While I was doing some weeding around the bushes out front, my cell phone rang again and it was Ira.

"How're you doing over there? You doing all right?" he asked.

"Oh, yeah, and you, Chief?"

"Good, good. Look, Harris. Since you had such a big part in the Sheriff's Office busting up that gang of losers, I was hoping you might come back to St. Beatrice and go on patrol for us again."

"Thanks, Chief. Don't know what I'm going to do yet. But appreciate the offer."

"Think about it and let me know what you decide. Job's yours again if you want it."

"I will, Chief. Thanks again. It means a lot coming from you," I said and slipped the phone back into my pocket.

That felt good. I'd always liked working for Chief Ira, and it was also true I really didn't know what kind of job I wanted next. But I knew I'd figure it out, so I put the whole thing on the back burner and finished the weeding before it got too hot. After that I dragged out the hose and soaked the bushes surrounding the motel sign, picked up the litter that had accumulated along the front of the property from the night before: two fast food bags, a round tobacco tin, a paper cup, a dented hubcap and one red tennis shoe. After tossing the litter into one of the garbage cans set to the back, I returned to my room to shower again before driving to Lenny's.

On the way over to her place, I stopped at a car wash and cleaned off the road dirt from the drive from Wallace. The car was by far the shiniest car around by the time I drove into the parking lot of her apartment building. Realizing I was getting hungry, I hurried up the stairs looking forward to that lunch she had promised. I rang the doorbell and while I waited surveyed the Walt Disney blue cloudless sky. It was already hot enough for my tee shirt to be sticking to my skin in patches. I pulled it away from my skin and slapped a mosquito on my arm. Louisiana summer.

Lenny opened the door smiling. "Crime busters!" she cried and gave me a hug. "Come on in." She took my hand and led me down the hall. She had company.

"Hey, Jo-Jo," I said, "*Comment ça va?*" He was standing by the window looking out at the balcony.

"That's not Jo-Jo," Lenny said.

He turned and the man at the window *was* Jo-Jo.

"Say what?" I asked, stopping in the middle of the room.

"That's not Jo-Jo," she repeated, "Harris Viator, I'd like for you to meet Renard Bergeron."

He stepped forward, putting out his hand. "Pleased to meet you, man. Heard how you've been helping Lenny out through all this mess. I owe you."

Renard wore a plastic cover on his nose and there was a deep raised scar like a fat worm starting from his upper lip and angling up his left cheek all the way to the wide cheekbone. His skin was dark as boot leather and he wore his black straight hair long so that it fell past his shoulders. He wore a plain tan tee shirt, camo pants and black boots.

I stood there like a dummy trying to let my brain catch up with what I was seeing. Lenny let go of my hand and walked over to the window to stand beside Renard. I finally came to my senses and stepped forward to shake his hand. His palm was dry, hard and callused and he shook mine with a strong grip.

"You look like you've seen a ghost," she said to me. "Don't worry about that nose guard. I made him show me what's under it. One look and I screamed! Much better if he leaves it on, trust me." She smiled and put her arm around Renard's shoulders. "He's been through hell and back and we can talk about it some other time. Meanwhile I want to serve you all some lunch, so why don't you two sit down and have a beer while I'm putting the salad together?"

The two of us moved away from the window and toward the couch and upholstered chairs. Renard sank into the chair nearest the window and stretched out his long legs. I sat on the couch and Lenny brought us each a freezing cold bottle of beer and a handful of napkins on a tray. "Drink up, you all," she said. "Plenty more where that came from." She returned to the kitchen as we eyed one another.

"I'm sorry I had to break up whatever you had going on with Lenny by coming back, brother," he said. "But I sure do thank you for all you did helping her out. If it wasn't for you doing some digging into it, I'd still be up there in the mountains, putting off coming back down here."

"I'm not sorry," I broke in. "I'm glad you made it back. I never knew you but I heard a lot about you. But what I can't figure out….what took you so long?"

"I didn't want to spook Lenny. I look like your worst nightmare under this thing," he said, pointing to the nose shield. "I was afraid she would run the other way from me or stay with me out of guilt, so I kept putting off coming back. 'One more week,' I kept telling myself, week after week." He hooked a finger under the neckline of his shirt and pulled the gold chain and dangling St. Christopher medal out to show me. "Lenny gave me this a while back. I never took it off. Kept me safe through this whole mess."

"She told me about that. But look, you've got nothing to worry about with Lenny. She told me how she felt about you from the git go."

He nodded. "One thing about Lenny. She tells it like it is. Every time."

By the time Lenny had lunch ready to serve, the doorbell rang and Jo-Jo arrived. He hurried into the living room and Renard rose from his chair, his dark eyes gleaming. The two of them embraced and Jo-Jo's eyes teared up.

"God*damn!* God*damn!*" Jo-Jo held Renard by the shoulders and leaned back to get a good look at him. "What did they do to you, bro?"

"I'm good, I'm good," assured Renard. "Doing a helluva lot better than I look."

Jo-Jo sat on the couch next to the chair where Renard sat. I stayed on the other end of the couch watching the reunion. Jo-Jo took the hem of his shirt and wiped his eyes, shaking his head. "I can't get over this. It's like you came back from the dead."

"I almost died, let me tell you," Renard said. "Son of a bitch bit half my nose off. You got any idea how filthy the human mouth is? Infection liked to kill me."

"Yeah. Remember when I broke that guy's tooth off years ago and it took weeks to get rid of the blood poisoning that ran up my arm?"

"I remember. But this took months to heal up. And it hurt like hell, let me tell you."

"I'm serving our food," Lenny called from the kitchen. "You all come eat now while this is hot."

We filed into the kitchen and sat at the round glass table. There was a platter of at least a dozen individual meat pies and a bowl of chopped tomatoes, cucumbers and sliced red onions, and Lenny had poured each of us a stemmed glass of wine. Renard pulled out a chair for Lenny and took the chair next to her. Jo-Jo sat across from him and I sat on the other side of the table, feeling like a fifth wheel.

I wanted to leave the party and let them have their reunion, but there was no way to leave without being rude. Let me tell you it's strange sitting across from the woman you thought you were falling in love with and seeing her look at another man like she never looked at you….a man everybody thought was dead. I definitely had mixed feelings. But I wasn't lying when I told him I was glad he was safely back. Anybody who got his face ruined by saving another man's life deserves all the good will he's got coming to him. It was too bad I'd never get to hold Lenny in my arms again, but as they say, sometimes you win, and sometimes you lose. So what the hell. The way it went down was all okay by me.

She passed the platter and the salad bowl around so we could each help ourselves, and when everyone was served, she asked to say the blessing, and we bowed our heads as she gave thanks for Renard's safe return. Then Jo-Jo said *Amen,* and raised his glass to gave a toast.

"Here's to you," he said tapping his glass against Renard's. "We missed you every day since you've been gone. We didn't know what to think, but thank God you're home again." His voice caught in his throat but he managed to finish his speech.

Then we all clinked glasses and began to eat without further conversation. It wasn't until Lenny cleared the table and began to serve the ice cream that the story of what had happened started to come out. Jo-Jo asked Renard to tell us, and after hesitating a minute, he spoke.

"I don't want to go into too much about it," he said. "But I'll tell you this much. The son of a bitch who did this to me," he said as he pointed to his face, "won't be cutting on anybody else. Enough said?"

"I got you, brother. But where you been? How come you didn't call me?"

"I was bad off for a long time. A human bite can put you in your grave. I didn't want to see anybody and most of all didn't want anybody to see me." He looked at Lenny. "Didn't want to freak Lenny out either."

"Yeah, but where were you all this time?" Jo-Jo asked.

"Quintus has an older sister. She took care of me. She's a retired nurse and lives up in the Ouachitas, on the Oklahoma side."

"But, why didn't you....." Jo-Jo started to say, but Lenny put a finger to her lips as she brought him his dessert.

"Let's eat some ice cream," Lenny said as she put a bowl in front of each of us and sat down again. She put a hand over Renard's. "You don't have to talk about it anymore if you don't want to." She shot a look at Jo-Jo and then at me. "Maybe some other time. That's enough for now. We're so glad you're back where you belong. That's enough for me. How about you?" She looked over at Jo-Jo, eyebrows raised.

"Best thing ever happened in my life was seeing you today...come back to us, Renny." His voice broke again, so he picked up his spoon and started in on the ice cream.

When we finished eating, they remained at the table drinking wine, and I excused myself, standing. "I have to get on down the road. Really good meeting you, Renard. Good to see you again, Jo-Jo. Thank you for the delicious food, Lenny." I slipped the keys to the Charger out of my pocket and laid them on the table mat.

"No, wait. I'll drive you," said Lenny. "Give me a minute."

"No!" I said, "Really. Stay here. It's not that far. I'll hike it."

"Are you kidding? It's miles back to the motel and in this heat!" she said.

"We used to run twice that far with backpacks on in the Army," I laughed. "It's nothing. Stay here. I mean that!" I pointed my forefinger at her for emphasis and didn't give her a chance to argue, just passed on through the archway and quickly through the living room.

"Wait up, man. I'll drive you," Jo-Jo called from the kitchen.

"Stay and catch up with your brother, Jo-Jo. You all stay together now, hear?"

I hurried down the hallway to the front door and outside. Once down the steps, I crossed the parking lot and got out of there as fast as I could.

62

FAST FORWARD

Halfway back to the motel, I stopped for a cold glass of anything liquid at Hebert's Truck Stop. While I was sitting at the counter watching a fishing show on the overhead television, Celeste rang me on my cell phone.

"You doing okay?" she asked.

"Oh sure. What's going on?"

"Acey wants to know if you want a part time job bartending at his place?" she asked. "He had to fire somebody with sticky fingers. They were playing little games with the cash register."

"A bartending job, huh? I never did that," I said.

"Oh, it's easy around here. None of those fancy blender drinks. And the customers are really good people. Easy job. You want it?"

"Sounds good all right. Thank you. I'll have to think about it though, Celeste. Tell Acey I can't decide yet what I'm going to do. My old boss, the Chief, called today to tell me I can have my old job back.

And just like you predicted when I first met you, my ex-wife called and wanted to make a date with me for dinner. And just like I told you I would, I said I'd have to pass on that."

"Ha! Told you. Oh, well, she messed up and now she regrets dumping you in your time of need. That's what happens!" She paused. "I also wanted to tell you that after that shooting over there, Acey wants to hurry up and us get married before anything else happens. He also wants me to think about selling the motel. I don't know who would want to buy an old motel like that. But we'll see. Anyhow, the wedding is pushed up to next Sunday. We'll be married in the church in the morning, and then we'll all come back to the restaurant for the reception about eleven-thirty. Okay? See you there?"

"Of course I'll be there."

"And you can bring that nice girl friend of yours too."

"She won't be around any more. Her old boy friend came back to town."

"Oh, no! Well, there's always something, isn't there? Sorry, Harris. I know you really liked her."

"Yeah, well. It's better this way. I'll tell you about it sometime. Quite a story. You won't believe it."

"I'll bet it's quite a story if she left you for him. Well, take care and let Acey know what you decide about the bartending job."

"I will. See you Sunday."

"Bye, *cher*. Stay safe." She clicked off and I flicked my eyes back up to the bass fishing show. Two job offers, an invite to dinner from Regina, and breaking up with the most luscious woman I'd ever known… all in one day. I took another drink of the soda and some ice chips came with it. I sucked on a chip as I watched the men in the bass boat motor to a new spot on the river, anchor and then cast their lines so they whirred out over the water. Then, out of nowhere, like one of those light bulbs coming on over somebody's head in the cartoons, I knew what I wanted to do. I laughed so loud that two of the truckers at the counter looked over at me like I was either crazy or drunk.

I gave them the thumbs up, and they turned their attention back to their food, one of them shaking his head. Just then one of the bass fishermen got a bite and started reeling it in. I laughed out loud again, put a couple of bucks down on the counter and left the truck stop, feeling lighter and with more energy than I'd felt all day.

Lenny caught up with me before I'd traveled more than fifty feet from the truck stop parking lot. She pulled the Charger over to the side of the road and waited for me to get in. I opened the passenger door and slid onto the seat. There was the faint smell of roses in the car, a perfume she sometimes wore.

"I really didn't want you to have to get up and leave Renard after all you two have been through," I said.

"I know you didn't. But I couldn't stand the thought of you going off like that and it's so hot out. Besides, I wanted to tell you a couple of things. Surely you still have a few questions," she said, as she looked over her left shoulder to get back onto the road.

"Not really. Renard pretty much explained what I wanted to know."

"That's it? That's all you wanted to know?" She took her eyes off the road to throw me a look of surprise.

"He saved Quintus' life from someone trying to murder him. During the fight he got sliced up badly himself and had to kill the attacker. He got rid of the body somewhere and hauled ass cause he didn't want any of this to come out. And Quintus didn't want any of this to come out because he doesn't want anybody from his hometown..wherever that is...to find out where he is. Quintus' sister took care of him best she could cause she was protecting Quintus, and meanwhile, Renard was so afraid you'd be so horrified by his chewed up, mangled face that you wouldn't want him anymore, so he stays away much longer than he should have. What else would I want to know?"

"You're way ahead of me. I didn't get any of this until he spelled it out," she said. "So you won't say anything to anybody about what happened? Please?" She took her eyes off the road again to look at me. "I don't want anybody coming around and bothering Quintus...or Renard...not ever again."

"Lenny," I said slowly, "Did you really think you had to ask me that?"

"No. Sorry. I know better," she said as she slowed for the motel. She pulled into the parking lot and pulled up alongside the back of my pickup. "Thanks for everything you've done for me...for us." She wiped her eyes, then reached into her purse and retrieved a folded piece of paper. "It's been so great knowing you. I don't know what I would have done without you. For starters, Renny would still be in Oklahoma, and me still not knowing anything."

"You were the one who somehow wrangled Quintus into getting Renard back here."

"Well, I didn't put a gun to his head or give him a lap dance, in case you're wondering."

"So what did you do?"

"I worked on his conscience. I pleaded with him to get word to Renny that he had to come back to me. I was going crazy worrying about him. I told Quintus I knew damn well he could get a message to him and I demanded he do it."

"And it worked. Good for you. Glad you didn't take my hundred dollar bet."

"Told you," she smiled. "And this is for you. Don't look at it until I'm gone, okay?" She put the folded paper in my hand and closed my fingers around it. "Don't bitch about it. Just take it." She started to lean over to give me a kiss but thought better of it and straightened up again.

"Let me know if you need anything," I said. "But I have a feeling everything's going to be all right now."

"Goodbye, Harris. Stay safe," she said. And then I got out of the car, closed the door, and she drove off. I watched until her car was out of sight, headed back up the highway as images of our time together ran through my mind like a fast forward movie.

The picture that stood out for me the most was the one of her picking me up for our first trip to North Louisiana. No makeup, Wallace Feed Store cap, tee shirt and jeans, hair in a ponytail.

After her car was out of sight, I opened the envelope. In it was a check for five thousand dollars with a sticky note attached to it. "Don't argue about it. Just cash it. Helping me find Renny was worth every penny." A little stunned, I opened the door to my room and set the check on the bedside table, then headed to the back yard so I could tend to Willy and Merle.

After spending some time playing with them and brushing them, I went back to my room and called Celeste. I told her what I wanted to do and we worked out a plan so I could get on with it. What we worked out felt right, and I made a couple of phone calls and by the time Jorge and crew returned, I went over to have a talk with them.

63

RECEPTION

By Sunday, while Celeste and Acey were at the church getting married, I was helping set up the tables for the food back at the Lounge. The staff and I covered the tables with white sheets and set up a pirogue on one table filled with ice covering the beers and soft drinks. We had the banquet well organized by the time they were all due to return from the church.

As soon as the guests and Celeste and Acey started arriving, we put out foil covered trays of crawfish fettucine, rice dressing, potato salad, broccoli salad, jambalaya, plain rice, slices of turkey and chicken, green bean casserole, tomato and cucumber salad, shrimp with sauce piquant, red and white *boudin*, glazed yeast rolls and squares of cornbread. Crawfish pots on stands held chicken and sausage gumbo and guinea and turkey neck gumbo. For those who wanted cooked down okra in their gumbo there was a bowl of it next to the crawfish pots.

It was a royal feast, and the guests immediately filed in and started lining up to fill their plates as a tape of traditional Cajun songs played through the sound system. There were close to a hundred people eating at the booths and individual tables within a half hour. All regular customers of Acey's Lounge, and all dressed in their best.

Celeste and Acey sat at a large round table with his son and daughter and their families as they ate together. When it didn't look like the staff needed any more help, I took a heaping plate of food over to the bar and sat at the end, as I didn't know anyone else there. I wished Lenny could have been there with me because she would have loved the party, but dismissed the thought right away. *That was then, this is now,* I quickly told myself.

One of the regulars had a bakery and she had made the wedding cake with a toy piano and fiddle on top. The bride and groom cut the cake, and by the time the guests were all eating their dessert, Acey and Celeste went over to the piano and began to play. They played *I Don't Hurt Anymore, Just Call Lonesome 77203, The Waltz That Will Carry Me to My Grave, Be Careful, Come Get Me, Belizaire Waltz, The Life I Thought I Wanted,* and *Eunice 2-Step.* By the time they started in on *La Bague Qui Brille,* I ducked on out of there and drove back to the motel.

64

TIME OUT

My suitcase was already packed and standing by the door. I collected my guns and a few other things and stowed all of it in the truck. Then I went to the back, put leashes on Merle and Willie, and loaded them up into the back of the pickup with a fifty pound sack of dog food and their bowls.

I knocked on Jorge's door and when he came out, gave him two room keys in case anyone wanted to stop off for the night. Celeste had given me the okay on this as Jorge had already butted in and tried to save my life twice. So until I returned, he was in charge of the place. We shook hands and then I headed for the truck, the dogs watching my every move as they wagged their tails, impatient to hit the road.

It was late afternoon by the time I got on the Interstate and I drove on through the night, stopping a few times at truck stops for gas, food, coffee

hermos refills, and a few times at rest stops so the
dogs could exercise, drink, and sniff around. By the
time I hit the foothills, the sweet clean mountain air
was so energizing, it kept me alert whereas otherwise
I would have been road weary and fighting to keep
my eyes open after hours on those winding rock-
lined roads.

It was predawn by the time I pulled up at Dr.
Taylor's house in Stoneyville. The porch lights were
on, and there was a light in the front room. I parked
the truck, patted the dogs and told them to sit, and
went on up the porch steps to knock lightly at the
front door.

There was a sheer white curtain behind the glass
panes of the door and I could make out the silhouette of someone coming to answer my knock. The
door opened and it was Dr. Taylor. "Harris! You
made it. Good. Come on back to the kitchen. We've
got the coffee on for you. Bet you could use some."

I followed him on through the foyer and on
down the long hall beside the staircase to the swinging door of the kitchen. Irena was at the stove, long
hair tied back, stirring a steaming pot, and when she
saw me, she put down the long spoon, turned the
fire down and smiled as she wiped her hands on her
apron.

"Well, look who's here all the way up from Cajun
country," she said. "Welcome back, Harris. We left
the light on for you."

28593240R00236

Made in the USA
Charleston, SC
15 April 2014